JUNKWORLD
The Ballad of Leroy Brown

MK Stangeland, Jr.

Quantity sales and special discounts are available on quantity purchases by corporations, associations, and others. For details, contact the publisher at the address above.

Orders by U.S. trade bookstores and wholesalers. Email info@BeyondPublishing. net

The Beyond Publishing Speakers Bureau can bring authors to your live event. For more information or to book an event contact the Beyond Publishing Speakers Bureau speak@BeyondPublishing.net

The Author can be reached directly at BeyondPublishing.net

Manufactured and printed in the United States of America distributed globally by BeyondPublishing.net

BEYOND
PUBLISHING

New York | Los Angeles | London | Sydney

Library of Congress Control Number: 2023900579

ISBN Softcover: 978-1-63792-559-1

ISBN Hardcover: 978-1-63792-429-7

ACKNOWLEDGEMENTS & SPECIAL THANKS

The many men and women responsible for *Real Steel* and *Battlebots*, for providing the essential sparks of inspiration that allowed Leroy Brown and his combat cohorts to exist in the first place;

David Hilderbrand (*May he Rest In Peace*), Lilli Lea, Dalton Tindall, and anyone I've had the misfortune of forgetting who provided invaluable feedback to help mold this book into what it is;

My Grandma Lois, for her essential role getting this book off my computer and into reader's hands;

Kathryn Feather, for her editing work;

The people at Beyond Publishing for making this book a reality, and all those who led me to them;

You who are about to read this book, as well as anyone else who has, is, or will possess and read a copy of this book – you're the ones that make it all worth it;

And of course, GOD – for everything.

THE ARENA LIFE

00001.

Above the planet of New Chicago, a pair of moons hung high in the sky. There they floated against a backdrop of stars as the last red shine of daylight vanished on the horizon. It was a sight few in the city of Darby noticed, as the same city lights that allowed the people to function through the night also hid the natural beauty of the scene above. Most couldn't be bothered to care, as nearly everyone was far too occupied with other concerns. Whether relaxing after a hard day's work, or engaging in an evening of entertainment, the bustle and activity of the city continued long after the day came to an end. In some corners, it even brought about the exact opposite.

This held especially true for more illicit regions of the city, where those with illegal business to conduct did so away from the law's watchful eyes. The dark shadows and back alleyways were a haven for activities that were not taken to kindly by those in charge. While much of it was dark and underhanded, the likes of which no sensible individual could support, others participated in activities that were illegal based on mere technicalities.

Such was the case in one corner of the city, hidden beneath the old industrial districts. There lay the Battledome, a large, sturdy, circular arena more than fifty yards across and topped by a durable, transparent cover. On one such night, the seating that ringed the central combat pit was filled with hundreds of cheering fans of more than half a dozen species. They roared with excitement at the brightly lit scene below, a battle between two machines of death, built and rebuilt to maximize their destructive potential.

On one end of the pit stood the seven-foot tall Razorflame. The robot stood tall despite of missing half of his four buzzsaw-tipped arms. Two different kinds of fuel leaked from where the limbs had been ripped off, leaving puddles of liquid to form in his wake across the arena floor. His treaded feet shuffled back and forth as he assessed his situation, his mind running calculations on how to overcome the damage and pull through to defeat his foe.

Across the arena was a six-legged beast of a robot named Crunchtime. The hulking robot chewed on one of Razorflame's arms as he slowly approached along an orbital path. Each step from the six-foot tall robot was planted in a deliberate fashion as he walked, the chewing and footsteps synchronized to invoke an ominous atmosphere of doom. Then, Crunchtime came to a stop and closed his mouth entirely, crushing the arm with enough force to break it two.

Preempting an expected charge, Razorflame sped towards his opponent. Crunchtime took a step back in surprise, but soon crouched and prepared himself. The beast-like robot then rushed forward in a countercharge that ended in a lunge through the air. Razorflame stopped and pivoted in a single smooth motion as Crunchtime closed in, spinning around to slice at his opponent's legs as he flew by. Crunchtime touched down with a hard landing, and two of his legs nearly buckled on impact. The robot looked at his damaged limbs in surprise, then turned quickly back to Razorflame just in time to see the robot charging forward. With a swipe of his blades, Razorflame sliced through the Crunchtime's optical sensors and blinded the machine.

The crowd cheered and screamed for blood. Crunchtime fell back in a chaotic manner, with little on his mind other than not letting Razorflame finish him off. The beastbot took a defensive position, going low to the ground and listening for the sound of Razorflame's movements. With a growl and tilt of the head in his opponent's direction, Cruchtime made clear he was fully aware of where his foe was and that he would not be so easily slain.

In a turn of fortunes, Razorflame circled Crunchtime, maneuvering around the robot like a shark preparing to strike its prey. Razorflame started in once before quickly pulling back. He circled in the opposite direction, started in, and then pulled back again. The cycle continued as Razorflame tested his prey and dared Crunchtime to make a move. Crunchtime countered with a roar when Razorflame slowed down.

When it became clear that Crunchtime wouldn't take the bait, Razorflame charged in. Just before the two made contact, he came to a sudden stop and fired off two massive bursts of flame that nearly caught Crunchtime head on. Crunchtime stepped back, and while he was still back on his hind legs, Razorflame moved in. He shoved his sawblades up into Crunchtime's front leg joints, pushing through to cleave the limbs clean off. Razorflame quickly pulled back again, letting Crunchtime fall to the floor in a heap.

Crunchtime struggled to pick himself up, but Razorflame ensured he didn't succeed. Planting a tread on Crunchtime's head, he dug his sawblades into the robot's neck and cut through the outer plating. As soon as Razorflame penetrated the robot's exterior, he ignited his flamethrowers to roast Crunchtime from the inside out. Crunchtime put up a token struggle at first, but soon gave up and shut down. Once Razorflame was certain his foe was defeated, he stepped off and rolled back, lifting his arms into the air triumphantly and turning to the crowds.

"The WINNER – RAAAAAAAAZORFLAME!" shouted the announcer, eliciting a new round of cheers from the crowd.

The cheers continued until Razorflame was out of sight, at which point the crowds turned their attention to the next fight. Meanwhile, cleanup crews entered the arena and went about their work. In a process they all but had down to a science, the crews hauled out broken pieces and otherwise tended to the Battledome in a swift and efficient manner, ensuring the crowds wouldn't be kept waiting any longer than necessary.

Finally, Ferris Hannoy entered the area, eliciting another round of cheers that echoed through the Battledome. A dark-furred Jebbitz, his role as announcer and Master of Ceremonies ensured that the crowd knew him at least as well as any one robot to have ever stepped into the arena. The man rode toward the center of the arena atop a robotic hover-scooter that came to a halt when he reached the middle.

"LADIIIEEES AAAAAND GENTLE-MENnnnnn!" Ferris shouted, his voice carried by an earpiece microphone and intensified by the arena's sound system. "It's the moment you've allllllllll been waiting for! It's tonight's MAAAAAIN EVENT!"

The crowd gave another cheer as Ferris let the words hang in the air, allowing them to wet their own appetites for the destruction about to unfold before them.

"Tonight, the Underground Robot Combat League has an extra-special showdown for you, a matchup between two of our most fearsome competitors. Both are undefeated, but only because they've never fought each other. Tonight, we rectify that problem."

The crowd cheered again, with some chanting the names of

the two robots in question.

"Tonight, one of these robots will see their winning streak come to an end. The other...will lay claim to being the uncontested KINNNNNNG of the RINNNNNG!"

The crowd's cheers continued. An air of impatience began to seep its way in as they grew ever eager for the fight to begin.

"Without further ado, here are TONIGHT'S COMPETI-TORS!"

On one end of the Battledome, a large metal door labeled with a "1" opened. The ongoing cheers of the crowd drowned out all other noise as the two halves of the doorway slid apart.

"From Door Number One! Standing at eight feet tall! He has a taste for destruction, and he's always starving! Mother Earth hates him, and he hates Mother Earth right back! Stand up to this robot, and he'll cut you down to size. It's the Lethal Lumberjack, CHAINSAAAAAAW FREDDY!"

Chants of "Chainsaw" echoed through the Battledome as a repurposed logging robot rolled into the arena on four legs that ended in heavy treads. A head with a single eye stood atop a barrel-shaped body divided into three sections. The top and bottom sections each featured a single arm that ended in a heavy gripping claw, while the middle featured a large, high-powered, laser-tipped chainsaw. The green and brown paint job that covered his body was broken up by the occasional yellow and black warning stripes and splatter of red designed to invoke an impression of blood.

Chainsaw Freddy turned to the crowds as they cheered him on, lifting his arms up in a pre-battle celebration. Once he'd turned in a full circle, he looked to the door on the opposite side of the arena and prepared himself.

"His opponent!" Ferris shouted. The cheers slowly dimmed to a low rumble in anticipation. "Emerging from Door Number Five! Standing at six foot four! He's a former warbot with a kill count larger than you can shake an atomic warhead at! He'll follow any order, so long as that order is "*Destroy!*". In the arena, there's no bot badder – it's LEROOOOOOOOOY BROWN!"

The crowd chanted "Leroy Brown" as a large metal door with a "5" on it opened, making way for the titular robot. He was a remodeled *Centurion*-class warbot, with a body designed for equal parts form and function. His frame bore an intimidating aesthetic, including a face that consisted of little more than a shallow, glowing red "v" shape that hid his visual sensors. He was colored in a mix of blacks and gunmetal grays, save for a deep, chilling red accenting his features and highlighting his joints. Leroy glanced at crowds as he walked into the arena, showing only a bare minimum of acknowledgement.

With the two combatants in position, Ferris rushed off the field to escape the danger they posed and get to his own position. The two robots were left to size each other up as they waited for the fight to begin.

"I hope you're ready for a rebuild," Freddy said, holding up his chainsaw. "Because after I've finished with you, they're going to have to rebuild you from the ground up. You may not even be the same robot anymore."

The former lumberjack revved up his primary weapon in a handful of short, loud bursts. Leroy glanced to the saw, then to Freddy's face.

"Big talk from a big robot," Leroy replied.

"If you think I talk big, just wait till you see how hard I swing," Freddy said.

"I'm sure I'll see it. Feel it, that's another story."

"There's going to be a lot of stories about tonight," Freddy said. He leaned over and slammed his fists into the ground. "Want to know how they end? With me winning."

"ROBOTS AT THE READY!" Ferris Hannoy declared over the sound system.

Freddy went to a battle-ready position, though Leroy hardly moved at all. A loud buzzer beeped as it counted down the seconds, until a final loud beep signaled the start of the fight.

Both Leroy Brown and Chainsaw Freddy advanced. Their movements were slow at first but picked up after a few feet. Freddy revved up his chainsaw and began to spin it around his body to create a bright red glowing ring of death orbiting his midsection. He held his other two arms at high and low angles away from the ring, intent on ensuring the only direction Leroy could go if he didn't want to be sliced to pieces was away from Freddy. Leroy continued his charge anyway, coming to a sudden stop when the robots were only a few short feet apart. As he did, he steadied his feet against the ground and deployed his barrier shield, creating a curved, glowing wall of cyan energy. A split second later, Freddy's chainsaw struck the energy barrier with high speed and force.

A powerful shockwave cut between the two robots, bursting away from an explosion of energy colored in hues of light purple and green. The eruption echoed across the arena with a noise that sounded like a twang mixed with the shattering of glass. Both robots were knocked back from the blow – Leroy slid several feet back across the ground, while Freddy was tossed several feet across the air.

"WOAH!" Ferris declared. "HUGE hit there!"

The audience cheered with excitement. In the arena, the two robots took stock of the situation. Freddy discovered his chainsaw was completely inactive, giving nothing but sparks and brief bursts of energy as he tried to restart the weapon. Leroy likewise discovered his shield had shorted out and needed time to reboot. Each took a moment to recalculate and reassess their strategy before returning their attention to the enemy.

Freddy moved in first, his arms up and at the ready while his chainsaw arm hung behind him. While slower, Leroy soon charged back into the fight as well. He came to a sudden stop when Freddy's remaining arms showed themselves to be more of a challenge than first anticipated. Each one moved with dangerous speed as they tried to grab or bash Leroy. Leroy danced around the larger robot as he looked for an opening, countering each strike with a blow from his own arms and dodging whenever Freddy threatened to grab him. By all appearances, the two were as evenly matched as could be.

Then, Freddy's middle arm snuck through, and his inactive chainsaw struck Leroy across the head like a club. The blow knocked Leroy off-balance, a stance Leroy fell into to escape a grab from another arm. Leroy rolled out of the way to escape another grab attempt, and then flipped back to his feet. Freddy kept up pursuit and rushed after Leroy. He grabbed at his opponent again, but this time Leroy reached out and grabbed Freddy's arm first. Still holding on, Leroy sidestepped another attempt to grab him with the other arm, then maneuvered the first limb so that it took the full brunt of a strike from the chainsaw arm.

With Freddy momentarily distracted by the sudden turn of events, Leroy exploited the opening to reach around and grab one of Freddy's legs. Throwing the weight of his body against it, Leroy broke the leg and stepped away before Freddy even realized what was happening. Caught off-balance, Freddy fell over with a yell. While he tried to catch himself, he landed on his already damaged arm, crippling the limb. Surprised by losing his balance not just once, but twice, the robot landed on the ground in a heap. Leroy leapt atop Freddy, but the former lumberjack rolled his body segments around and swung at Leroy to force him away. Leroy immediately charged in again, but in his aggression left an opening that Freddy exploited to knock Leroy back off his feet.

Freddy used the gap to get upright once more, and found Leroy was already up and on the attack again. Freddy swung an arm at Leroy, which the warbot caught hold of, only for Freddy to swing his arm back the other way. Suddenly, Leroy found himself lifted off the ground and flying across the arena. Even before he hit the ground, Freddy was in pursuit, dragging his broken leg behind him as he rushed after his foe. Freddy reached Leroy just as the robot was back on his feet. Freddy swung his arms down at Leroy, only to be surprised when they collided with a curved, glowing wall of cyan energy.

Taking advantage of Freddy's surprise, Leroy slipped underneath and slammed into a second leg. The strike set Freddy off balance long enough for Leroy to grab hold of the leg and break it. Down two legs, Freddy was unable to keep his balance and toppled to the ground like a tree. Leroy leapt into the air and came down elbow first directly at Freddy's head, but Freddy held his arms up above him. Leroy reached out, grabbed the arms, and then swung around to slam his feet into Freddy's head. The blow knocked Freddy's head loose, leaving it hanging by a series of wires. As Leroy landed on the ground, Chainsaw Freddy shut down and his body went limp.

"The WINNER and CHAMP-ION!" Ferris declared. "LEROOOOOOOOOY BROWN!"

The crowd erupted into cheers in celebration of Leroy's victory. Leroy didn't acknowledge them at first, instead turning to observe the fallen form of his defeated foe. After a few moments, he stepped back and turned to the audience. He raised a single victorious fist into the air, held it there for a few seconds, then turned for the exit and began a slow walk out of the arena. Chants of "Leroy Brown" echoed through the Battledome as he walked out. By the time he reached the open doorway, cleanup crews were already on their way in, though Leroy paid them no mind.

"There's my bot!"

When he stepped into the rounded corridor surrounding the arena, Leroy heard the familiar voice of his owner, Mr. Garry Hannz. He came to a stop and turned toward the man, an early middle-aged character with a sleek persona, and hair he intentionally dyed to a premature gray. Close behind him were League reporter Jannah Kirrif and a two-man camera crew.

"Come here, come here," Garry said, beckoning Leroy toward him. They took a position near the wall alongside Jannah, while the two cameramen set up their equipment.

"Are we ready?" the Zelophean asked as she made a last-second adjustment to her hair. The lead cameraman gave her a thumbs-up, then silently counted down from three with his fingers.

"I'm here now with Leroy Brown, who just emerged as the

undefeated champion of the U-R-C-L, and his owner, Mr. Garry Hannz," Jannah said once the countdown ended, and the camera light turned green. "Mr. Hannz, that was without a doubt a thrilling fight we just witnessed. How are you feeling now that it's over?"

"It feels amazing, Jannah," Garry replied. "It always feels great to win, but this win, knowing it puts us over the top, that just takes the winning to the next level."

"Was there any point during the fight that you were worried?" she asked.

"No, not really," Garry answered. "We were confident from the word "Go" that Leroy had this victory in him. Honestly, Chainsaw Freddy may look intimidating, but I think he's overrated as a fighter."

"Even with his undefeated record?" Jannah asked, surprised.

"He's not undefeated anymore," Garry said with a chuckle, eliciting a similar laugh from Jannah.

"So where do you go from here?" she asked. "What comes next?"

"For now, we're just going to enjoy this victory," Garry answered. "We've got some ideas in mind. The team and I are going to talk it over, and we'll be putting some plans in place soon."

"I'm sure we'll all be eagerly waiting to hear what those plans are," Jannah said. "Any final comments?"

Garry casually pointed up at Leroy, and Jannah held her audio recorder up toward Leroy's head. The camera crew likewise aimed up to focus on the robot.

"I look forward to the next fight," Leroy said. Garry smiled and gave the robot a couple of lighthearted knocks against his body.

"That's my bot," he said with a grin.

"And there you have it," Jannah said once the camera was focused on her. "This is Jannah Kirrif. Back to you, Ferris."

A couple seconds later, the camera light went out. Jannah shook Garry's hand and offered her thanks while the camera crew broke down their gear. Then, even faster than they'd arrived and set up, they were off. With the reporting crew on their way, Garry turned and led Leroy down to the pits. There was no shortage of people all too happy to congratulate both Garry and Leroy as they went along, and Garry stopped to thank each as he was able. As they walked through the pits, even the rival teams took time to grant the two their cheers and congratulations. Then, at last, the largest and most excited celebration came from their pit berth when it came in sight. A few cheers of "Leroy!" found their way into the mix as well.

"Thank you, thank you," Garry said as the two rounded the corner.

"Undefeated!" shouted one of the half-dozen individuals present who made up Leroy Brown's pit crew.

"Again, thank you!" Garry said. "And yes! Yes we are!"

Garry raised his fist into the air in celebration, though Leroy kept walking toward his repair dock. Halfway there, Hali'Vax and two others met him and guided him into position.

"And I do say 'we,'" Garry said. "Because neither I nor Leroy would be here if it wasn't for the best team in robot combat!"

Garry started another round of applause, which the crew quickly joined.

"So where to from here, Mr. Hannz?" asked one of the crew as the clapping died down.

"Well, I think that after tonight's victory, the sky is pretty much the limit," Garry answered. "But we're not going to worry about that tonight. Tonight, is about reveling in our victory. Specifically, Leroy's *undefeated* track record. So, for now, we're just going to enjoy the moment, then we can wait till tomorrow to worry about what comes next."

"Mind if I get started on diagnostics?" Hali'Vax asked.

"Should be unnecessary," Leroy said. "My damage should be minimal."

"Don't get cocky on me, Leroy," Hali'Vax replied. "Last thing we need is for you to go undefeated and then lose your next fight because we skimped on the details."

"Yes, fine," Garry said. "You can start running diagnostics. But please, save the real work till tomorrow."

"Yeah, sure," Hali'Vax said. "Goodnight, Leroy."

With that, Hali'Vax deactivated Leroy, leaving the robot to go limp and lifeless as the world turned black around him.

1st VERSE

WELCOME TO JUNKWORLD

00010.

[Initiating Startup Sequence]

[Systems Loading...]

[Systems Loading...]

[Systems Loading...]

[ERROR: Systems Not Responding]

[Loading Available Systems]

[Systems Loading...]

[Systems Loading...]

[Activating Available Systems In 3...]

[2...]

[1...]

Aside from the initial error message, there were three signs that immediately told Leroy Brown that something was wrong. The first sign was the low rumbling all around him, indicating that wherever he was, it was moving. The second was that the world was sideways. The third, once he looked past the askew position of his head to the world beyond, was the decrepit scene before him. Spare parts, scrap metal, and other miscellaneous junk colored in a motley array of reds, browns, and grays sat nearby in organized piles. None of it bore a resemblance to any location he recognized; let alone anywhere he was supposed to be.

Leroy found a fourth sign when he tried to move his body, only to discover he couldn't. Only a single arm provided any real feedback. A follow-up search for signs of the rest of his body likewise came back negative. Leroy focused on what little success he had and turned his attention to his arm, testing it by opening and closing his fist.

"He lives after all," came a voice that had a notably mechanical sound to it. Leroy tried to look toward the voice but was promptly reminded he was physically incapable of doing so.

"Hali'Vax?" Leroy asked, expecting that if the Toz wasn't nearby, someone who knew him would be.

"Excuse me?" the voice asked.

"Where is Hali'Vax?" Leroy asked. "Or Mr. Hannz."

"What is what now?"

"Hali'Vax?"

"What's a Hali'Vax?" the voice asked.

"You don't know Hali'Vax?" Leroy asked, confused.

"Why should I?"

Leroy processed the question and what it meant, then checked both his GPS and chronometer. All he got from the former was an error message, while the latter was zeroed out.

"Who are you and where am I?" Leroy asked.

"You don't know where you are?" the voice replied.

"I know I'm supposed to be on New Chicago, but something tells me that's not where I am."

Leroy heard the shuffling and clanking of metal footsteps against an uneven, aged metal floor. Suddenly, the room shifted around him. When his head came to a stop, it was held up in the air and most of his view was occupied by a humanoid robot who looked like he had been rebuilt at least half a dozen times from whatever spare parts were lying around. The robot had a "mechanic" aesthetic to him, though Leroy wondered if he'd been designed that way or if it was the result of years of rebuilding either by himself or someone else.

The mechanic then held Leroy out at arm's length, granting him a better if still limited view of the room, though most of what he saw was more of the same - assorted machines that sported an oddly familiar design, an intermixing of tools arranged in a pattern Leroy presumed only the mechanic understood, and distressingly, various robots in various states of deconstruction. Mixed among them was Leroy's body, hanging from the ceiling with his missing arm right next to it. Off to one corner, he spotted a small cage hanging from the ceiling, where a smaller robot was being held. Out of the opposite corner, Leroy spotted the arm he still had control of, lying on the table below him.

"That's my body," Leroy said, pointing his fingers in its direction. The mechanic turned to look where Leroy was pointing, then looked back to Leroy.

"That it is," the robot said.

"Why is it over there instead of over here with my arm and head attached?" Leroy asked.

A second time, the mechanic looked over to Leroy's body, then back to Leroy.

"Because," the mechanic said.

"That's not an answer."

"You're a talking head. Why should I care?"

"Let me put it a different way," Leroy said. "Why am I not in one piece?"

"Because I'm figuring out which of your parts are worth anything," the mechanic answered.

"They're all worth something," Leroy said.

"I'm the mechanic here, so I'll be the judge of that."

"I don't need a mechanic to tell me that I can't function properly if I'm missing some of my parts."

"There's your mistake," the mechanic replied. "You're assuming I care whether you function properly."

"Do you have any idea who I am?" Leroy asked.

"I peg your base design as Valorous War Industries, probably part of the *Centurion*-warbot class," the mechanic answered. "Your official ID and serial number have been scrubbed, so I'm guessing your last owner wasn't supposed to have you and used you to do something illegal. But other than that? Nope, I've got no idea."

If Leroy had been able to nod his head, he would have done so in a slow, acknowledging manner. Instead, he was forced to continue to stare in whatever direction the mechanic pointed him.

"Back to my earlier question," Leroy said. "Who are you and where am I?"

"Most people call me Doctor Clank," the hodgepodge of a robot answered. "And you are aboard the *Eternal Horizon*."

"What's the *Eternal Horizon*?" Leroy asked.

"It's a scraptrawler," Clank answered.

"A what?"

"You really are out of the loop, aren't you?" Clank said. "It's a big land ship, basically. Rolls around looking for parts we can use or trade."

There was a pause as Leroy considered what he was hearing and his next question.

"What planet am I on?" he asked.

"If you want the official designation, I haven't a clue," Clank answered. "Most the robots here just call it Junkworld."

While Leroy had suspected he wouldn't like the answer, Clank's words hit him hard all the same. Only now was it truly clear to him just how wrong things were. If what he had been told was the truth, Leroy was in pieces on a vehicle of questionable quality, on a planet he'd never heard of, with nary a hint of anyone or anything he recognized in the slightest.

"I'll give your old owners this much," Clank said as he put Leroy's head down on the table again, forcing him out of his inner contemplation. Leroy's view of the world went askew again, and the doctor stepped back to his body to rummage it over. "There's definitely some wear and tear here, but someone went to a lot of trouble to keep you operating in top shape."

"Put me back together," Leroy ordered. "Now."

Slowly, Doctor Clank turned back toward Leroy's head. He stopped part way there to look at Leroy's arm, which Leroy had tried to point at the mechanic in an intimidating fashion. Not surprisingly, the effort had come up exceedingly short and came off as humorous more than anything instead.

"Why?" Clank asked.

"Because I told you to," Leroy answered.

Clank stood there and stared at Leroy's head for a few moments, his body language telling the story of a robot deep in thought.

"No," Clank finally answered. He then turned back to Leroy's body to resume his examination.

"I told you to put me back together," Leroy said.

"And I said 'no," Clank replied, this time not even bothering to glance away from his work.

"Do you have any idea who I am?" Leroy said. Clank lifted his head up and turned back to Leroy.

"I am *Leroy Brown*," Leroy said. "I have killed countless hostiles across countless battlefields on countless worlds. I am the undisputed, undefeated champion of the Underground Robot Combat League. You will put me back together, or else I will find a way to put myself back together. And when I do—"

"Put yourself together?" Clank interrupted. "Now there's a sight I'd love to see."

Doctor Clank stepped to the side and held his arm out towards Leroy's body in an inviting manner.

"Please. Go ahead. Be my guest."

Leroy laid there, his efforts to shift his focus hindered by his inability to move his head.

"Please, I insist," Clank said, motioning to Leroy's body.

Leroy flexed the joints on his active arm, testing them with an emphasis on range of motion. Once he was confident about what they could do, he made his arm drag itself across the table to the edge. There, he forced the arm to stand up, at which point it became clear there was a problem he hadn't accounted for. In addition to the distance between his arm and body, he also had to contend with the wires that connected his arm to his head.

"Problem?" Clank asked as he observed Leroy's new delay.

"Just keep taunting," Leroy replied. "I'll enjoy hearing what you have to say when I'm finished."

Turning and flexing his arm, Leroy tried to pull his head across the table. It was a slow, grueling, meticulous process. After dragging his head a few inches across the table, he found one problem replaced with others. First among them was the pull on his head which had shifted his vision so he could no longer see his body. He continued to work at it all the same, with Doctor Clank watching on all the while. For all the difficulties he faced, there was a moment of hope that with enough time and determination, he would succeed in reaching his body and putting himself back together.

The next moment, Leroy found his arm off-balance and threatening to slip off the table. When he was unable to fix the imbalance, he went for broke and lunged his arm toward where his body was supposed to be. To his disappointment, his arm failed to connect, and the next thing he knew his head was being pulled across the table again. With a metallic thud, both limb and head came to a rest, with the arm lying on the floor. Leroy tried to recover but stopped when he heard clapping.

"Bravo," Clank said with a deadpan delivery. "Bravo."

"Minor setback," Leroy replied. "Nothing more."

He flexed his hand again as he prepared to continue his efforts. Before he made any further progress, however, Clank picked up both the head and the arm, then tossed them toward the middle of the table.

"Are you trying to help me or hinder me?" Leroy asked.

"Whichever is easier for you to compute," Clank answered.

Leroy watched Clank for as long as he was able, seeing what

he would do next. Ultimately, it proved to be very little, at least so far as Leroy and his parts were concerned. Once he realized Clank was all but leaving him to his own devices, Leroy tried again to reach his body with his one active arm. The second attempt played out much the same as the first, ending with arm on the floor before Clank threw it back onto the table.

Undeterred, Leroy tried a third time, only to meet with similar failure. The scene likewise repeated the fourth time, the fifth time, and beyond. With his chronometer nonfunctional, it was difficult for Leroy to tell how long he spent trying to reach his body. He had only the audio and visual clues around him to go on, including when he was able to observe Doctor Clank, when he felt the *Horizon* make a stop and then start moving again, and the occasional arrival of other robots.

"What's with the arm?" Leroy heard one robot ask from somewhere behind him during one of the numerous conversations he overheard. Leroy couldn't tell much about him, only that his voice sounded far more mechanized than Clank's.

"He told me he was going to put himself back together," Clank answered. "I'm waiting for him to prove it."

"How long has he been at it?" the other robot asked.

"Far longer than I expected. He's determined, I'll give him that much. Though I'm not sure if it's out of willpower, stubbornness, or good old fashion stupidity."

"Is the Captain alright with it?"

"With what?" Clank asked. "Letting him try to put himself back together? Doesn't matter. It may be the Captain's scraptrawler, but down here is *my* domain."

"Yeah, for now."

"He hasn't stepped in yet; I see no reason why that should change."

"Nobody expected the Captain to start answering to anyone either, yet here we are."

"Don't you have something better to do?" Clank asked. "You brought me what I need; I don't need an interrogation to go with it."

"Fine, alright, I'm going," Leroy heard, which was joined by the sound of metal shuffling.

"Your domain?" Leroy asked when he heard Clank return to the room.

"I give the Captain what he wants, I keep everyone running, I make sure we have the parts we need to make it happen," Clank answered from out of view. "I even help keep the *Horizon* running from time to time. In exchange, the Captain gives me all the leeway I could ask for."

"Including giving me free reign of your domain?"

"Ha," Clank said with a mixture of clanks and grinding simulating a kind of laughter. "Sure, if crawling around with one arm is what you want to call 'free reign.'"

"You should be thanking me, really," Clank continued, briefly crossing Leroy's view as he walked across the room. "If it were up to the Captain, I probably would have shut you down permanently long ago."

"Without even asking if I wanted to join his crew?" Leroy asked.

"It's all complicated, especially for someone who doesn't know anything about Junkworld. But I think that's kind of irrelevant at this point anyhow."

"But hey!" Clank said, momentarily crouching to get in Leroy's face. "If you actually do put yourself back together again and don't run off or try to smash us all, maybe we can put that topic on the table."

Undeterred, Leroy continued his efforts to reassemble his body. As those efforts went on, further problems that made the task far more difficult than he anticipated continued to reveal themselves. First and foremost was Doctor Clank himself. Each time Leroy was certain he had made genuine progress, Clank was there to step in and put Leroy back to step one. Despite any talk the doctor may have had about giving Leroy the opportunity to try to reassemble himself, it was impossible for him to not suspect Clank was merely using Leroy's efforts as entertainment.

His second major problem laid in the connection between his arm and head. While it allowed Leroy the means to try to put his body back together, the only way he was able to do so was by dragging his head behind his arm. As result, it was near impossible for Leroy to determine what direction he was looking at any one point in time and see what he was actually doing. It was a problem that so slowed down his efforts he found himself unable to get past the first problem.

In time, Leroy all but gave up on achieving his goal of putting himself back together by himself. While he continued the appearance of doing so, these efforts were mostly for show. It was an act intended to keep Clank from suspecting anything had changed, giving Leroy time to consider his other options. Waiting until Clank was out of the room, Leroy turned his attention toward the small robot in the cage.

"Hey, cagebot," Leroy said. He received no response, not even so much as a hint the robot even heard him.

"Hey you, in the cage," Leroy tried again. He clapped his hand against the table a couple times to emphasize his presence. Again, the robot showed no reaction.

"I know you're alive up there, cagebot," Leroy said. "I saw you peeking a glance at me earlier. Don't you dare play dead on me!"

Finally, the robot responded, if only to glance in Leroy's direction. It was small and subtle, but enough to confirm he was listening.

"Yeah, you," Leroy said. He pointed his finger in the robot's direction. "You have a name, or should I just keep calling you cagebot?"

The robot looked toward where Clank had last left the room, then back to Leroy. He stared at Leroy for a few moments, then turned around to put his back toward Leroy again.

"Something wrong, cagebot?" Leroy asked. The robot gave no response.

"You just going to keep ignoring me, cagebot?" Leroy asked. This time, the robot turned around again, shifted to the edge of the cage, and looked directly at him.

"My name is not 'cagebot'," the robot finally said with a simple, stilted voice pattern that spoke of a basic vocalizer.

"Then what is your name?" Leroy asked.

Once again, the cagebot looked out the doorway before turning back to Leroy.

"My name is Walter," he finally answered.

"Hello, Walter," Leroy said. "Do I need to tell you who I am, or do you know already?"

"Your name is Leroy Brown," Walter answered.

"You have been paying attention. Good."

Leroy held back his next words when he heard approaching footsteps. Clank soon entered the room, and Leroy returned to his attempts to reach his body until Clank left again.

"So, what are you doing up there, Walter?" Leroy asked once he was confident the mechanic was out of earshot.

"I am a prisoner," Walter answered.

"Same as me, then."

"No, it is not the same. I am a prisoner. You he intends to scrap."

"If that's what he's planning, he's doing a terrible job of it so far," Leroy said.

"He is merely amusing himself right now," Walter replied. "Once you have bored him, he will finish disassembling you for spare parts."

"Then I better escape before I wear out my welcome."

"I regretfully doubt your ability to do so," Walter said. Despite the simplistic tone of the words, a hint of sadness found its way through.

"Is that why you're just doing nothing up there?" Leroy asked. "Because you think it would be futile to do otherwise?"

"It would be a waste of energy to attempt what I can not do," Walter answered. "It would also jeopardize my current safety."

"Safety? In a cage?"

"I am currently a prisoner," Walter explained. "He has no plans to scrap me. He thinks of me as a pet. To attempt an escape would put that status at risk, and then I would be in jeopardy of being shut down and scrapped."

"I guess that makes sense," Leroy said. "If you're content to just sit on your butt for the rest of your sad existence."

"It may be a sad existence, but it is an existence all the same."

If Leroy had been capable of sighing, he would have done so at that moment.

"So what is your plan, then?" Leroy asked. "Just sit around and wait until something happens?"

"Affirmative."

"Good news," Leroy said. "I'm here, I'm happening. You want to escape? Help me escape so I can help you escape."

Walter looked to Leroy, then turned out toward an approaching noise. Clank and a handful of other robots arrived soon after, forcing Leroy back to throwing his arm around while the crewmembers worked around him. He continued the act until he was left alone with Walter again.

"As I was saying," Leroy continued. "Do you want to work together, or do you just want to wait there for divine intervention?"

"How am I supposed to help you?" Walter asked. "I am stuck in a cage. You are stuck on the table."

"I'll break you out," Leroy answered. "You're closer than my body, I think I should be able to reach you. Then you help me get to my body, we work together to put me back together, and then we escape together."

Walter glanced between Leroy's head, Leroy's body, and the doorway. Leroy waited for him to respond, but Walter said nothing.

"I'm going to aim for your cage," Leroy said. "If you want to stay trapped forever, tell me now."

While Walter sent him multiple looks, he said nothing.

"Let's escape, then."

Leroy carefully looked over the space between the table and the cage, committing both their respective locations and his own position to memory. He then pulled himself to the edge of the table and pulled his head toward his arm as far as he could to maximize the space he had to work with. Using his combined data, including what he'd acquired from his multitude of attempts to reach his own body, Leroy lined up and aimed at the cage. He mentally counted down from three, then threw his arm out when he reached zero. The limb flew through the air, but failed to hit the cage. The result was little more than an all too familiar thud.

"That did not appear to be helpful," Walter said.

"How close was I?" Leroy asked.

"Not close enough."

"But how close did I come?" Leroy repeated.

"Didn't you hear him?" said the familiar voice of Doctor Clank. "Not close enough."

"That doesn't mean anything," Leroy said. "It's only helpful if I know how much I missed it by."

"That's where you're wrong," Clank said. Leroy heard footsteps approaching, then the world twisted around him as he was lifted into the air and brought face to face with the mechanic once more. "What it means is that you've given up."

"Hardly," Leroy said.

"What do you call it when you say you can put yourself back together but then start trying to get help?" Clank asked. "Because I call it giving up."

"I'm not giving up," Leroy said. "I'm adapting. Trying new solutions."

"You said you were going to put yourself back together," Clank said as he picked up Leroy's arm and put it on the table. "Getting help does not qualify as putting *yourself* back together. Which is a shame. I was almost rooting for you to succeed. Almost."

Clank reached around Leroy's head with both hands and prepared to shut Leroy down.

"Nice knowing you, Leroy Brown," Clank said. "You were entertaining while it lasted."

Leroy braced himself for shutdown, but the moment didn't come. Instead, it was interrupted by a blaring alarm which immediately caught Clank's attention. A moment later, the room shook with a heavy jolt signaling a rapid acceleration by the *Horizon*. Clank put Leroy's head down on the table and stepped away.

"What's going on?" Leroy heard Clank ask.

"*It's a Scrapwyrm!*" came another voice. "*A big one! We think it's picked up our trail and hunting us!*"

A series of cursing noises followed from Clank's direction. They were followed by a quick series of footsteps, the sound of a machine being activated, and then another series of footsteps rushing out of the room to signal Clank's exit. Turning his attention to Walter, Leroy couldn't help but notice the robot was absolutely terrified.

"What's a Scrapwyrm?" Leroy asked.

Walter looked to Leroy's head, and then spoke with a voice of terror.

"It is how we are all going to die."

00011.

"Can you give me a less fatalistic answer?" Leroy asked as the *Eternal Horizon* tore forward, the entire vessel shaking at dangerous levels. From somewhere outside, he heard a terrible explosion that echoed through the scraptrawler.

"Does that tell you enough?" Walter asked. "It is a scrapping robot. Not very intelligent, but large. It exists entirely to eat scrap for harvesting. If it catches us, we are all dead."

"So how about we put me back together before that happens so I can go out there and kill it?" Leroy asked. He promptly went back to work moving his arm toward Walter's cage.

"Kill it?" Walter asked with shock. "You are planning to kill it?"

"Yes. But first we need to put me back together," Leroy replied

"How are you going to kill it?"

"I'm the undisputed URCL champion," Leroy answered. "I will *find* a way."

He stood his arm up on the edge of the table and aimed for Walter's cage.

"How do you plan to do that?" Walter asked.

"Help put me back together before we die, and you'll find out."

With that, Leroy launched his arm through the air once more. For the first time since he'd found himself aboard the *Eternal Horizon*, he finally connected with his target. His fingers latched on to the bottom of the cage, but nearly slipped when the tilt and swing of the cage pulled his head off the table. After several tense moments, Leroy stabilized his grip, and then immediately began moving his fingers around the cage bars. In one moment, a violent shake of the vessel threatened to knock him loose again, but Leroy held on tight. With a careful balance of speed and care, he finally reached a door hinge.

"If you don't want to fall all the way to the floor, I recommend grabbing hold of something when the door opens," Leroy suggested.

Leroy tightly gripped the cage and squeezed. He then opened and closed his fist in a rapid, repeat motion that first bent, then broke the connection point. While it didn't open the door on its own, it allowed Walter an opportunity to finish what he started. Soon, Walter fell toward the floor and grabbed hold of Leroy's arm. There, Walter gave a brief countdown, and then leapt across and caught hold of Leroy's body. He climbed up and released Walter's body, then his arm, letting both fall to the floor. Dropping down after them, the robot quickly went to work attaching the two.

"You appear to know what you're doing," Leroy commented.

"I have some experience and retrofitting for these matters," Walter answered.

"Even better," Leroy said. He then let go of the cage and dropped his head and other arm to the floor as well.

With the *Horizon* still moving at high speed and the sounds of danger echoing from outside, Walter reassembled Leroy's body as quickly as he could. In seemingly no time at all, Leroy Brown was finally back together and fully operational once more.

"Now that's more like it," Leroy said after he stood up.

He started to look over his body, flexing each limb to confirm it was functioning properly. The process was interrupted by the sound of an explosion and a rumble that shook the room. It was a clear reminder they had wasted more than enough time already. Leroy picked up Walter and rushed out through the nearest doorway.

"You know where to go?" Leroy asked.

"Why should I?" Walter replied.

"Just asking."

Leroy plowed through the hallways. With no idea where he was going, he took any path he thought might lead him outside, including up every stairwell he found. As he rushed across the vessel, he passed multiple robots running one way or another. Not a one of them paid him much attention, however, the outside threat clearly at the forefront of their minds. Continuing to rush through the twists and turns of the scraptrawler's interior, and with Walter riding on his shoulder, Leroy felt the vessel shake and briefly threaten to tip over entirely when something hit it. Another alarm siren blared, with shouts coming from every direction. Leroy picked up his pace, plowing through anything and everything in his way with little concern for what damage he might do in the meantime. At last, he finally emerged at the top of a stairwell and through a door leading to the outside.

What he found was best described as organized chaos. Orders were being shouted in every direction, with robots running about likewise. There was a pattern to be found amongst the madness, just enough to convince Leroy they had some idea what they were doing, but there was panic and fear to their movements, too.

Looking out and around, Leroy found himself on what was best described as a short container ship mounted on massive tracks. Despite the countless signs of wear, tear, and age covering the *Eternal Horizon* from bow to stern and port to starboard, the vessel showed no indication it was ready to stop working or fall apart on its own any time soon. On either side of the vessel, Leroy noted an array of large weaponry mounted at irregular intervals consisting of multiple designs.

Beyond the *Horizon* was a world bearing all the hallmarks of an utterly desolate wasteland. Nothing about the landscape so much as hinted at the possibility it could support even the hardiest and strong willed of biological life. As far as the eye could see, there was nothing but vast mountains and piles of junk lying strewn about a rocky surface, broken up by the occasional mound or pillar of stone. Even the colors spoke of lifelessness through an array of foreboding shades and hues, including a dead sky bearing a smattering of clouds that looked like they had been sprayed with a light coating of liquid garbage.

At first, Leroy had difficulty finding signs of the Scrapwyrm itself. There was the noise and the rumbling to be sure, and the behavior of the crew confirmed something was happening. It wasn't until the ground shook up ahead that he finally had his first glimpse of the creature that had everyone terrified. Then, the robotic monster burst forth from the ground directly ahead of the *Horizon*.

It was several yards across and had a dirty metallic sheen. Its head was shaped like a rounded drill but opened into four pieces as it curved toward the vessel. Its thick-beaked mouth gave way to a throat guarded by a three-gear drilling saw, with the tip of each blade sporting a deadly red glow. A mix of plating, curved spines, and tank tread formations covered its body in a carefully arranged pattern.

To the credit of whoever was steering the *Horizon*, the vessel turned just enough to avoid crashing into the Scrapwyrm entirely, merely scraping its bow across the monster's hide as it curved away from the large pillar of a robot towering into the sky. The robotic beast tilted and leaned over the *Horizon* as it continued out of the ground. From deep within its throat, a high-intensity flame burst forth and continued to burn until the robot closed its mouth again, just before it finished arching over the vessel and began burrowing into the ground once more. By the time its tail end finally emerged, Leroy judged the Scrapwyrm to be well over a hundred yards long.

As the monstrous robot passed overhead, weapons fired from both sides of the vessel. Explosions and bursts of destructive energy hitting their target erupted from the metallic monster's hide, though there were no signs any of it was causing worthwhile damage of any kind. By the time it finally disappeared beneath the ground again, it was clear that unless the Scrapwyrm was dealt with, the *Horizon*'s time was very much limited.

"You said you were going to kill it?" Walter asked.

"I do recall saying that, yes," Leroy replied.

"How?"

Leroy didn't answer, his mind preoccupied with that exact problem. He searched the deck for signs of anything that looked explosive, paying particular attention to any signs of fuel containers or ammunition with extra 'oomph' to them.

"Stay here," Leroy said, shuffling Walter off his shoulder.

"What if 'here' isn't safe?" Walter asked.

"Then run if you feel like it!" Leroy shouted back.

Leroy first ran for an arrangement of power batteries, then to a batch of ammunition shells held in a safety container. As he reached them, he picked up one of each and carried them under his arms.

While some of the crew noticed him stealing their stuff, their protests and efforts to stop him were cut short when the Scrapwyrm emerged again and began scraping along the side of the *Horizon*. The vessel rumbled and shook with violent ferocity as hunter and prey slid against each other in opposite directions.

"It's going to break the treads!" someone shouted.

The recurring chaos distracted from Leroy, giving him the opening he needed to continue his mission. He ran for the edge of the vessel, then leapt off and landed on the Scrapwyrm's back. He nearly lost both his footing and his cargo, but a careful series of footsteps kept him steady. Once he was secure, he ran toward the front end of the robot. He quickly stopped and reversed course when he discovered it was burrowing again on the far side of the *Horizon*.

Leroy ran swiftly along the back of the mechanical monster, leaping over treads and sidestepping around the towering spines. He leapt off when he reached the tail, landing in a roll that brought him right back to his feet. Turning around, he saw only a pile of rocks where the Scrapwyrm had burrowed into the ground. Looking back to the *Horizon*, he got a full view of the damage it had caused. While the vessel still moved, it was all but limping along, with extensive damage to the undercarriage and a series of massive gashes along the lower hull.

Unsure of the Scrapwyrm's next angle of attack, Leroy chased after the *Horizon*. With the vessel's reduced speed, he had no trouble at all matching it. There was exhilaration from the run – by all recollection, it was the first time since his days as a genuine warbot that he'd had a real opportunity to stretch his legs. It didn't last long, however, before he was forced to refocus on the danger at hand. From up ahead, another explosion erupted from the ground.

As Leroy ran toward the noise, the *Horizon* slowed down. A grinding of rocks sounded beneath the vessel while groans and screams of metal emerged from around the treads, the cries of a vessel that was fighting physics in a desperate effort to stop far quicker than was safe. From beyond the corner of the bow opposite of where it had struck last, the Scrapwyrm towered into the sky once more.

The Scrapwyrm came crashing down on top of the *Horizon*'s deck and slid across, leaving a deep scar in its wake that threw all manner of metal in all directions. Some of the robots on deck were likewise tossed about, with some even thrown overboard. One unfortunate individual the Scrapwyrm caught in its mouth as it plowed off the opposite side. With a turn of its head, it pulled the screaming robot into its maw entirely, then burrowed its way back underground.

A pair of deck guns followed the Scrapwyrm to the ground. On impact, one of the guns fired in Leroy's direction. Leroy immediately dropped what he was carrying and threw up his shield. While the shield blocked the shot, the impact still threw Leroy several yards back through the air. He quickly climbed to his feet, then rushed back to where he'd dropped his cargo. Halfway there, the ground rumbled beneath him. Shortly after, the Scrapwyrm burst forth once more. It nearly drilled straight through Leroy in the process, but a narrow miss broke up the ground in such a way that he was merely tossed aside instead. He hit the ground in a heap amid a rain and pile of rubble before the Scrapwyrm nearly landed on him the same way, but Leroy was on his feet and out of the way just barely in time.

The mechanical monster continued to flow past him as it

emerged from the ground, turning up ahead and digging through a pile of scrap as it turned. Leroy again ran for the shell and battery, but once more was nearly run over when the Scrapwyrm reemerged and drove right through where Leroy had been mere seconds earlier. Assorted scrap rained down during his continued run, while the Scrapwyrm scraped across the back end of the *Horizon* as it continued onward.

Leroy stopped at the shell and battery, but then turned and looked back at the cannon that had fired on him. Hedging a bet, he picked up the items and then continued toward the cannon. A quick investigation of the weapon confirmed it was still operational, if barely. He looked up when he heard the Scrapwyrm again and saw that it was coming right at him.

Leroy aimed the cannon at the Scrapwyrm, while the Scrapwyrm continued to plow straight at him. It opened its mouth as it closed in, and Leroy fired the weapon. The shot impacted off the corner of the massive robot's mouth, leaving nothing to show for itself but smoke and black scarring. Leroy lunged aside, narrowly avoiding getting run over when the Scrapwyrm drove through and consumed the weapon.

Once the Scrapwyrm had passed through and driven out of sight again, Leroy rushed back to where he'd dropped the battery and shell. The battery was smashed, leaving Leroy doubtful it still possessed any explosive potential. The shell, however, still looked functional. Leroy picked it up and ran to find the Scrapwyrm again. Leroy found the beast tunneling through a pile of wreckage, throwing pieces of metal refuse around as it burrowed through. Leroy continued running and watching as he waited for the Scrapwyrm to present another opportunity to attack.

An eruption of metallic rubble signaled the Scrapwyrm's reappearance. It let out a roar and turned in Leroy's direction, its mouth open in preparation to swallow up the robot. Leroy steadied his feet and aimed the shell he was carrying at the Scrapwyrm. He threw his fist back, and then slammed it forward at high speed to strike the back end of the shell. The warhead launched forward and into the Scrapwyrm's mouth, where it exploded in a fiery display. The robot continued forward all the same, lifting and coming down on Leroy from above, its mouth closing around him when it reached the ground.

****

The crew of the *Eternal Horizon* watched in stunned silence as the Scrapwyrm burrowed back underground with Leroy inside. For a brief period, the robot's fight against the metal beast had generated a fleeting hope that perhaps he might actually succeed in killing the thing. When Leroy disappeared, the crew's hope vanished with him. Fear swiftly returned to take its place. Panic spread, dissolving what little organization the crew had left.

The Captain tried to give orders and keep the ship together, but it was clear he was fighting a losing battle. Chaos quickly spread, with some crew even readying to abandon ship and take their chances on foot. Amidst it all, Walter retreated from view, returning to a strategy of going unnoticed and hoping he'd survive the fallout long enough to make an escape of his own. By all signs, it was working – against the threat the Scrapwyrm posed to everyone's survival, nobody cared about a small robot that wasn't bothering anyone.

Another rumble and eruption soon followed, and the Scrapwyrm burst forth from the ground once more. However, it didn't take long for Walter to notice the Scrapwyrm sounded different. There was slowness to the noises it made, including a metallic groan inconsistent with its usual terror. After scuttling out of his hiding place, Walter rolled to the edge of the *Horizon* to see what was happening. Several other crewmen took notice something was off and soon joined him along the railing.

The Scrapwyrm fell to the ground in a heavy, uncontrolled manner, then rolled and drove around in an erratic pattern. A handful of times, it thrashed around like a beast amidst its death throes, tossing the scrap around it in every direction. With one final groan, the creature lifted into the sky once more as black smoke seeped out of its mouth. Then, it collapsed in a heap, crashing against the surface in a loud and mighty impact. There it lay, dead.

A great deal of hesitancy surrounded the *Horizon* and everyone on it as they looked down at the fallen Scrapwyrm. All of them had difficulty believing what they were seeing was real. Despite the massive robot lying there in a motionless heap, with large quantities of smoke slowly escaping from its mouth, nobody dared to climb down and approach the terrifying monster.

"So…what do we do?" someone asked.

"Should we shoot it some more?" asked another crewman.

Panic threatened to return when movement was spotted from the Scrapwyrm's body, but it died just as quickly when they realized it was caused by something inside the Scrapwyrm rather than the Scrapwyrm itself. Everyone watched intently as the metal corpse shuffled with a subtle motion. At last, a segment of the robot's drill beak tilted up with a creak, and then an arm flew out a short distance. Soon after, the segment lifted higher and gave way to a one-armed Leroy Brown.

The crew murmured amongst themselves, still in disbelief at what they were seeing. Leroy stepped over to his disconnected arm, picked it up, and then turned toward the crew.

"You're welcome!" he shouted.

"Get him up here!" shouted the Captain. The crew quickly went to work, with a mobile lift moved into place and lowered to the ground. Before long, Leroy Brown stepped onto the deck to a series of applause, though far more out of relief than celebration.

"Make way, make way!" the Captain ordered as he stepped through the crowd, until finally standing face to face with Leroy. The two looked at each other a moment, Leroy sizing up the robot before him, while the Captain just took Leroy in.

"You killed it," the Captain finally said.

"Yeah," Leroy replied in a plain and simple manner.

"You killed the Scrapwyrm."

Leroy looked at the Captain a moment, then turned to look back down at the fallen monster. A moment later, he looked back to the Captain.

"That's what I said I'd do," Leroy answered.

"You killed it with one arm," the Captain said. Leroy looked down at his broken arm, then back to the Captain.

"I wanted to make it a fair fight," Leroy answered.

The Captain looked Leroy over a bit more, then placed a hand on the bot's shoulder and began to laugh. The others around him soon joined in. The Captain turned to them and raised his fist.

"Give a cheer for…" he started, but stopped and turned in Leroy's direction.

"Actually, I don't recall getting your designation," the Captain said.

"His name is Leroy Brown!" declared Walter, emerging from the crowd and rolling up next to Leroy's feet.

"Give a cheer for Leroy Brown!" the Captain said. The crew threw their arms into the air and gave a cheer of celebration. Leroy looked down to Walter, then held his broken arm down to Walter's level, letting the smaller robot climb his way up to Leroy's shoulder.

"I don't think we've met, Leroy," the Captain said as he led Leroy through the crowd away from the edge of the ship. With the Scrapwyrm confirmed dead beyond all doubt, several crewmembers made their way toward the creature to take a closer look. "Just who are you, where did you come from, and to what do I owe you saving my ship and my crew?"

"You owe me answers, too," Leroy replied. "Starting with who you are."

"A fair enough question," the Captain replied. "I'm Captain Danger, commander of the *Eternal Horizon*."

"Where is Doctor Clank?" Leroy asked.

"You know Doctor Clank?" Captain Danger asked.

"He's the one who's been keeping my head down in his laboratory since I last activated."

Danger looked about for signs of Clank and was pointed below deck. Both Captain Danger and Leroy Brown made their way inside and along a path leading to Clank's domain.

"Doctor Clank!" Danger called out. "Where are you?"

They found him standing off in a corner of the room in front of a pile of unusually arranged metal that sported an odd assortment of glowing lights. Clank turned around suddenly when they entered the room, looking like he was trying to elicit as little suspicion as possible. Ironically, all it did was make him look more suspicious.

"Hello, Captain," Clank replied. He slowly turned to look at Leroy. "I see you brought the big hero of the day down here with you."

"Doctor Clank," Leroy said. Both he and Walter stared at the mechanic intently. Clank slowly glanced back and forth between them and the Captain.

"Leroy Brown," Clank said. "Hello."

Captain Danger likewise looked between Leroy and Clank.

"So, you two *are* acquainted already." Danger said.

"That we are," Leroy answered with a nod.

Danger glanced between the two again, then took a step inward away from Leroy.

"You were one of his projects," Danger said, looking around the room. "Before you killed the Scrapwyrm. He was working on you."

"He was planning to take me apart," Leroy said.

"Then we should all thank the makers he didn't carry through on that," Danger said.

"That's my robot," Clank said, pointing in Walter's direction. Walter tilted and leaned back on Leroy's shoulder, hanging off the edge to put the warbot between him and his former captor.

"Not anymore, he's not," Leroy said.

"You claiming him as yours?" Clank asked.

"I'm not claiming ownership of anyone," Leroy answered, "But

I am placing him under my protection. You want him back; you're going to have to fight me for him."

"With one arm?"

"I just killed your oh-so-terrifying Scrapwyrm with one arm. You, I'd need to lose the other arm too before it would even come close to being a fair fight."

"Neither of you are killing each other," Danger said. "Doctor, this robot is the hero of the day. Fix his arm, and then anything else on him that's broken."

Clank looked to the Captain, then to Leroy, then back to the Captain.

"Yes, Sir," he said.

"Good," Danger said, then he turned to Leroy. "I'm sure we both have questions for each other. After the Doctor fixes you up, come find me. I'll be seeing to your kill and if my trawler is still salvageable."

00100.

"How bad is it?"

Standing on the ground outside the *Eternal Horizon*, Captain Danger glanced from the vessel to where Otra 24 was standing nearby. The *Horizon*'s chief engineer, Otra was a former deep-space repair unit with a trashcan body atop four spidery legs.

"We haven't had an opportunity to go in-depth yet, but if the preliminary damage reports hold true, we got lucky," Otra answered.

"You mean other than the fact that the Scrapwyrm caught us, but we survived?" Danger asked.

"Yes, other than the obvious," Otra replied. "As far as the *Horizon* is concerned, the deck is an absolute mess, most the guns are gone, and there's an absurd number of hull breaches. Not to mention an endless checklist of minor problems we'll need to address."

"But we still got lucky?" Danger asked.

"The good news is the major systems are effectively unscathed. I don't expect there to be any concerns about the *Horizon* threatening to blow up or fall apart on us, if we get it moving again."

"If," Danger said, the word sitting somewhere between a statement and a question. "The treads?"

"The treads," Otra confirmed with a nod. "Everything else we have the means to patch up, at least until we reach a port with dedicated repair facilities. The tracks, they're another problem entirely."

Danger nodded and looked at the vessel for several moments as he took in the weight of the problem.

"What options do we have?" Danger finally asked.

"I note four," Otra answered. "We could try to secure a new vessel."

"You're going to give up that easy?"

"No. It's a bad option, but an option all the same."

Danger nodded with a grumble, then waved for Otra to continue.

"We could try limping along to a settlement that can help us with basic repairs," Otra said. "At least enough to patch up the tracks so we don't have to worry about them falling apart on us. But that would require they don't fall apart on us first, and I can't say how long until that happens."

"And that would just make things worse," Danger said. Both he and Otra nodded in unison, then Danger gave the engineer another signal to continue.

"We could try fixing them out here ourselves," Otra said. "But that would take parts that are going to be difficult to get out here."

"So what's option four?" Danger asked, though he suspected he already knew the answer and wouldn't like it.

"You ask the Top Dog for help."

"There's an unpleasant thought," Danger said as his eyes glanced over his vessel.

"You've already sworn fealty to him," Otra said. "What's the point if you can't request his help when you really need it?"

"I didn't think there'd be much of an option otherwise. Yet somehow, I still think I made the wrong choice."

"Nonetheless, it's the choice you made, Sir. You can't unmake the choice, but you can make the best of it."

"Understood," Danger said with a slow, casual nod. "I'll make a decision soon."

"Don't take too long, Captain," Otra said. "The *Horizon's* mobility is its greatest defense, and that's currently not an option. I don't think we can afford another attack right now."

"At least we should be able to cross Scrapwyrm off the threat list for the time being."

"I wouldn't take that risk."

"Why not?" Danger asked. "They don't gather together, and Leroy Brown killed this one."

"As far as we know," Otra countered. "But they aren't supposed to die, either. We don't know what happens if they do."

"If you're worried about more of them showing up, I'll just kill them too."

Danger and Otra turned to see Leroy approaching with his small friend rolling right behind. It was a credit to Doctor Clank's work that Danger wouldn't have guessed that Leroy's arm had ever been torn off in the first place.

"How many can you fight off at once?" Otra asked.

"As many as I need to," Leroy answered.

"I can't tell if you're joking, or just suicidally overconfident."

"Let's hope we don't have to find out, shall we?" Danger said. "Otra, fix what you can for now, I'll let you know my decision on the tracks soon."

Otra acknowledged the order, then made his way back to the *Horizon*.

"You're looking good," Danger said. "Especially for someone who just faced a Scrapwyrm head on."

"Winning is what I do," Leroy replied.

"Is that so?"

"You familiar with the Underground Robot Combat League?"

"Never heard of it."

"Undefeated champ," Leroy said, tapping his fist against his chest.

"How long ago was that?" Captain Danger asked as he began his own walk back to the *Horizon*.

"As far as I'm concerned, it might as well have been yesterday," Leroy answered as he started after Danger. "I can't make an accurate assessment since my chronometer was out of sync and I have no idea how long I was down in Dr. Clank's dungeon."

"Did he fix that?"

"He got it running again, but it's set to local time. That doesn't help me with the time I'm missing."

"So why did they get rid of you?" Danger asked.

"What do you mean?" Leroy replied.

"You are on Junkworld," the smaller robot said. "You would not be here unless you were discarded."

"Clearly, there was a mistake," Leroy said, glancing back to the robot.

"You don't come to Junkworld by mistake," Danger replied. "If you're here, someone wanted you here."

"Is that why they call it Junkworld?" Leroy asked.

Danger stopped next to a lift, then looked to Leroy and held his arm out toward the horizon.

"Have you looked around you?" Danger asked, turning to look in the direction of his arm. "Junk is the only thing this blasted planet has. It's basically a giant garbage dump."

He then stepped onto the lift and waited for the other two robots to join him.

"It's a dead planet, then," Leroy said as the smaller robot rolled right past him onto the lift.

"By biological standards, yes," Danger answered. "If there was ever a point when the planet could support fleshy things, I've never met anyone who's aware of it."

The Captain looked at Leroy a moment.

"You waiting for something?" he asked. Leroy looked back, and Danger motioned to the lift. Leroy gave a nod, stepped on, and then Danger activated it.

"How long have you been here?" Leroy asked as the lift carried them up.

"Roughly fifty years," Danger answered. "Doctor Clank's been here for at least twice that. I've been Captain of the *Horizon* for over two decades."

"I have been on Junkworld for an approximate time span of forty rotations," the small robot said. The three continued to ride the lift a bit before Leroy spoke again.

"So what were you before you came here?" he asked.

"Doesn't matter," Danger answered. "That was another existence. All that matters is who I am now."

"I used to work with garbage," the smaller robot said.

"Junkworld must not have been much of a change for you, then," Danger said, while Leroy glanced down at the small robot.

"That would be an inaccurate statement," the robot replied. "It took a great deal of adjustment to–"

"Nobody cares," Danger interrupted, right about the time the lift came to a halt. Danger stepped off onto the deck, and Leroy followed. The small robot hesitated a moment, but soon continued after them.

"Where are we, then?" Leroy asked.

"The Stone Graveyards," Danger answered. "We were trying to take a shortcut to the Bridge of Steven."

"Neither of those names mean anything to me," Leroy said.

"Right, you just got here," Danger said with a muted nod.

"And that wasn't what I meant, either. I want to know where Junkworld is."

Danger slowed down a moment and shot Leroy a glance.

"Why does it matter where it is?" he asked.

"Do you know where it is or don't you?"

Danger rolled his head and turned to keep walking.

"As far as I know, we're on the tail end of the galaxy," he said, and soon after started up a set of stairs. "Might as well be a different universe, as far as I'm concerned."

"Not much traffic, then?" Leroy asked.

"Couldn't say. There aren't any starports on Junkworld, and the closest thing that might exist is beyond where any robot has ever gone."

"So how do they bring in the junk?"

"It's flown in," Danger answered. "Ships visit, but they don't land. They just dump it wherever it's convenient at the time."

"So how does anyone leave?"

Danger stopped next to a doorway, then looked at Leroy with a confused motion.

"They use the ships they arrive in," he answered.

"How would I leave?" Leroy asked.

"You don't," Danger answered with a matter-of-fact tone. He turned back to the door, opened it, then stepped through to his personal command room. It was a square room of a cozy size, built around a square desk that sat in the middle. Various trinkets and monitors lined the walls, and a recharging station sat off to one corner next to a small assortment of weapons.

"Why not?" Leroy asked as he and his small friend followed the Captain into the room.

"Where are you going to go?" Danger asked.

"Back where I came from," Leroy answered with a defiant point outward.

"Why?"

"Because it's where I belong."

"Leroy, you're here because someone threw you out," Danger said. "You can't just go back to someone who threw you out."

"Not without a spaceship I can't."

"Your old life is over, Leroy," Danger said. "You need to accept that and be thankful you have an opportunity at a new one."

"I'm here by mistake," Leroy said. "I don't want a new opportunity here; I need to get back to the life I had."

"No one is here by mistake, Leroy," Danger replied. "Let's say you find a way to leave. All you'll be doing is going back to people who don't want you anymore, and all that will bring is disappointment and probably a quick dismantling. You know how many machines are sent here and are never reactivated at all? You have an opportunity they'll never get, and you made a big splash in the process. You want a place in my crew? I would be more than happy to make a place for you in my crew."

"I am here by mistake," Leroy said, emphasizing his words with a verbal punch. He then pointed down and firmly pressed his finger against Danger's desk. "As far as I know, last night I won the fight that made me the undefeated champion of the URCL. I had a team that loved me, an owner that believed in me, and a pit crew that poured their heart, sweat, soul, and tears into making me the best fighting robot I could be. I had fans. I was a favorite with the crowds. I was at the top of the world. There were plans. Then the next thing I know, I'm reactivated in pieces on a dead planet of refuse and rejects."

Leroy let his words hand in the air a moment, then lifted his finger and planted it back on the desk.

"I am here by mistake."

Leroy Brown and Captain Danger stared at each other, with the small one looking back and forth between the two.

"I recognize that your story doesn't make sense," Danger said. "I'm sure that to you, it must seem like a mistake. But I can guarantee there is a piece of your story missing that makes clear that whatever the reason may be, you are not here by mistake."

The two robots stared off again.

"One way or another, I am finding a way off this planet," Leroy said. "Somehow, I will find a ship, and then I will find a way back to New Chicago."

For the third time in a row, the two robots engaged in a stare-off. Minutes passed, with no outward hint as to what was going through either one's processors. Then, at last, Danger slowly lowered his head before straightening up.

"There may be a way to leave," Danger said, his words slow and reluctant. "There's a robot, he's known as the Top Dog. I've heard rumors and reports that suggest he's actually trying to build some ships. I'm going to contact him and ask for help fixing the *Eternal Horizon*. I'll see if I can bring up the topic while I'm at it, and maybe ask if there might be an opportunity for you to get what you want."

"Could I ask him myself?" Leroy asked.

"The Top Dog, he's a very particular individual," Danger answered. "It's probably for the best if you leave the talking to me."

Leroy looked at Danger, his head turning and tilting in a subtle manner as he considered the Captain's words.

"Understood," Leroy finally said. "Thank you."

"You're welcome," Danger said. "Now if you'll excuse me, I have a call to make."

After escorting Leroy and his small friend out of the room, Danger traveled down to the *Horizon's* bridge. Much like the rest of the ship, the room was a mess. To their credit, the command crew was already hard at work putting everything back in order, and most stations already appeared functional. There was only a minimal acknowledgment of Danger's presence as he entered.

"Xerox, where's Commander Echo?" he asked once he noticed that his first officer was absent.

"The Commander is overseeing cleanup efforts and assisting Chief Otra with full damage assessment," the command and control robot replied with a voice that was equal parts digitized and feminine.

Captain Danger nodded.

"Speaking of which, see to it that Otra is informed we will be requesting assistance from the Top Dog," he ordered, then he turned to another station.

"Frigjar," Danger said. "Contact the Top Dog, inform him the *Horizon* is facing an emergency situation and that we request his assistance."

Frigjar-Zeta nodded, then she proceeded to send the message. Five minutes later, she turned back to Danger.

"Response negative," she reported. "We have been informed that the Top Dog is currently out tending to an important matter and we should try again later."

"Were you told how long we'd have to wait?" Danger asked.

"Negative."

Captain Danger stared out the main bridge windshield a moment, then turned back to Frigjar.

"Try again," Danger said. "Emphasize the urgency of our situation and ask if there's anyone else we can talk to if the Top Dog is unavailable indefinitely."

Five minutes later, Frigjar turned to Danger again.

"They sent a set of coordinates," she reported. "They said if it's so urgent that it can't possibly wait, we should pay him a visit in person."

Danger nodded. While it wasn't the response he was hoping for, it was better than nothing.

"Have Commander Echo and Leroy Brown meet me in docking," Danger said, turning for the door.

****

The flight to visit the Top Dog was not a pleasant one. While nothing of note happened during the trip, it was overshadowed by an air of silent tension. Neither Captain Danger nor his pilot, Iggy, said much as they went. This further confirmed and built upon the lingering tension, which only served to make the trip all that more awkward. Briefly, Danger wondered if he should have left Iggy behind. It wasn't as though he needed the robot with him, not in the strictest sense. While ostensibly Danger's pilot, the fact was their small shuttle practically flew itself. More than anything Iggy's presence was to provide Danger with backup in case of an emergency.

And, ironically, peace of mind.

"Our destination should be in view shortly," Iggy reported.

Looking ahead, Danger was surprised to see smoke towering into the sky.

"Those coordinates," Danger said, "They matched up with Gearport, didn't they?"

"They did," Iggy confirmed.

"Then the smoke, does that mean…"

It wasn't long until Danger's fears were confirmed. When the small city came in view, the two robots saw it was half-ruined and burning. The source of the devastation was equally apparent, with heavily armed land vessels surrounding the city on all sides. Among them was a super-cruiser Danger recognized as the Top Dog's command vessel, the *Ultimatum*.

"He laid siege to Gearport," Danger said. Before he could think any further on the subject, the shuttle received an incoming transmission.

"*Approaching shuttle. Identify yourself.*"

Danger hesitated, and Iggy prepared to change their flight path as he waited for the Captain to say something.

"*I repeat, identify yourself,*" the voice continued. "*If you refuse to do so, we will open fire.*"

"This is Captain Danger, from the *Eternal Horizon*," he finally answered. "I've come to speak with the Top Dog about an important matter concerning my scraptrawler."

"*Please hold,*" the voice responded. "*You may circle overhead until further notice.*"

Danger and Iggy shared a slow look, then the pilot took the shuttle into a holding pattern lasting for several minutes.

"*Captain Danger, your request has been noted,*" the voice finally said. "*We will be setting up a landing marker, please prepare to set down near it.*"

"Thank you," Danger replied.

Before long, a landing zone was established. It was small and very much spur-of-the-moment in appearance and included a dozen armed robots of various shapes and sizes standing nearby. Despite the clear variety in design among the machines, each one wore exterior plating that gave them a uniform look all the same.

Iggy set the shuttle down nearby, and both he and Captain Danger stepped out. Four of the robots approached them, weapons positioned as threateningly as possible without aiming at the two.

"Captain Danger," one of the robots said. Danger raised his hand in a half-hearted motion.

"Come with us," the robot said.

Danger and Iggy began to walk forward, but only made it a few steps before they were stopped again.

"You," the robot said, pointing to Iggy. "Stay here."

Iggy turned to his captain, looking for confirmation.

"Stay with the shuttle," Danger said.

Iggy nodded, then stepped back again. Danger continued and was escorted to the *Ultimatum* by the four-robot team. After being led up into the massive vessel, the robots marched Danger through a winding path leading through an array of corridors and multiple doors of various shapes and sizes. Finally, after an extended ride up a lift that Danger suspected was moving far slower than it was capable of, a door opened to reveal a small room.

Danger took a couple steps forward but stopped when he noticed the other four weren't moving. He took a few more steps, and when nothing happened, he stepped the rest of the way into the room. The lift door closed behind him, and once it sealed shut, another door opened on the other side of the room. Danger looked around, and then slowly stepped toward the second door. There was a faint buzzing noise as he neared it, and a close inspection revealed a small membrane of energy covering the open doorway. The buzzing intensified when he waved his arm through it, though Danger didn't notice any other result. With a shrug, he stepped through to the other side.

The room Captain Danger entered was dimly lit, though his visual receptors adjusted in short order to reveal he was in a command room. It was neither overly large nor elaborate, designed for practicality more than theatrics, reminding Danger of his own quarters. Monitors and displays took up much of the room, though any real controls were limited to a circular formation in the center of the room. While constructed from an array of recycled parts, its assembly bore a notably professional appearance.

Noticing he was alone, Danger stepped toward the windows located on the far side of the room. On the other side, he saw the still-burning ruins of Gearport. While the smoke and flames had died down, a glance to the area outside the city revealed that ground troops were assembling to prepare for an attack. Captain Danger turned away from the window when he heard a door opening.

Looking behind him, he saw the Top Dog emerging from the floor in a slow, intimidating fashion. When he finally came to a stop, the two looked at each other for several moments. Staring at Danger with a large central eye flanked by two secondary receptors attached in a firm but crude fashion, the Top Dog towered over the Captain in both size and presence.

"Captain Danger," the Top Dog finally said. His four arms, attached to a pair of barrel-shaped body segments, were crossed behind him. "I was informed that you had an important request to make about your scraptrawler."

Behind the Top Dog, attached to a bottom third segment, a tail-like limb subtly swayed back and forth. A chainsaw-tipped appendage hung at its end in an ever-threatening fashion. Danger glanced at the chainsaw, up at the Top Dog, and then briefly out at Gearport before composing himself and turning to the Top Dog in full.

"The *Eternal Horizon* was attacked by a Scrapwyrm out at the Stone Graveyards," Captain Danger explained. "We survived, but the *Horizon* took serious damage, especially to the tracks. I came to request the assistance of your resources to help with the repairs."

"You were attacked by a Scrapwyrm?" the Top Dog asked.

"Yes," Danger answered. "It was a very harrowing experience

for my crew."

"But you survived."

"Yes," Danger confirmed. "And in surprisingly good shape for a Scrapwyrm attack, despite our current needs."

"You and your vessel survived a Scrapwyrm attack?"

"Mostly, but yes. That is exactly what I'm saying."

The Top Dog's body language shifted from disbelief and confusion to intrigue and surprise.

"I presume you have proof?" he asked.

"We have its corpse," Danger said, letting a hint of pride slip through.

"How did you kill it?"

"It's the strangest thing," Danger explained. "You know of Doctor Clank, correct?"

"I am well aware of him, yes."

"He had a robot he was working on in his laboratory. Name of Leroy Brown. When the Scrapwyrm–"

"Leroy Brown?" the Top Dog asked.

"Yes," Danger answered, surprised. "You know him?"

"The Scrapwyrm was killed by Leroy Brown?" the Top Dog asked, ignoring his question.

"Yes," Danger answered. "When the Scrapwyrm showed up, he pulled together and killed the thing practically on his own."

"On his own."

"He used a cannon and some explosives, but yes, he fought the Scrapwyrm one-on-one and killed it."

The Top Dog looked at Danger for a moment, then quietly looked up and past the Captain to an unseen point. Danger waited a few moments to see if the other robot would say anything else, then spoke again when the Top Dog remained silent.

"If I'm not out of place in doing so, I hoped to bring a request on his behalf."

"How long have you had him?" the Top Dog asked, looking back at Danger.

"It's difficult to say," Danger answered. While having his questions ignored twice left him annoyed, he took care to avoid letting it slip into his words. "I wasn't aware he even existed until he fought the Scrapwyrm."

"Then guess."

"I'd estimate a few days," Danger said. "Probably no more than a few weeks. But that's only how long I'd guess he's been active. As to when we picked up his body, it's impossible to say."

The Top Dog retreated inward and looked up past Danger one more.

"If I might ask, how do you know him?" Danger asked again. The Top Dog looked back down at Danger and once again ignored his question.

"Good news," the Top Dog said. "I'm granting your request. Let me know what you need, and I'll have my people restore your scraptrawler. They'll make it better than it was before the attack, even. I need two things in exchange."

Danger hesitated, one portion of his processors questioning if he should press the Top Dog on his own question, another portion taken aback at the nature of the Top Dog's answer to his request. Ultimately, the better part of his programming held back the former.

"I'll take your silence as preliminary acceptance of my terms," the Top Dog continued. "First, I will be laying claim to the Scrapwyrm's corpse."

Danger hesitated again, but quickly pushed through.

"Understood," he answered. "And the second?"

"I want Leroy Brown," the Top Dog answered. "I want him alive, but disabled. If you can find whatever container he was stored in, all the better. But when my people return from repairing your scraptrawler, I want them to bring Leroy Brown's inactive body back with them."

Again, Danger hesitated, lost deep in thought as to what the Top Dog was requesting.

"I shall take your silence as acceptance of my terms," the Top Dog said.

"You want Leroy Brown?" Danger asked.

"Or perhaps not," the Top Dog said with a subtle roll of his eye. "Yes, that is what I just said. I thought I made myself clear."

"You want Leroy Brown, alive but inactive?"

"Yes."

Once again, Danger hesitated as he considered what the Top Dog was asking and what the specifics of the request implied.

"I'm detecting an irritating level of hesitation on your part, Captain," the Top Dog said.

"Leroy had a request he hoped to make," Danger said. "I could tell him you want to see him; he'd probably be happy to come meet you."

"Alive, but disabled. Inactive. Turned off."

"He saved my vessel," Danger said. "And my crew."

This time, it was the Top Dog who hesitated. After a moment, he turned to the window and looked at the burning sight of Gearport.

"Captain Danger, are you familiar with Gearport?" the Top Dog asked. Danger looked at the robot and noticed the inactive chainsaw hanging precariously close.

"Yes," Danger finally answered after a few moments.

"We had a disagreement, Gearport and I," the Top Dog said. "I said they were in my territory and belonged to me. They vehemently disagreed. As you can see, I won the argument."

Danger glanced at the Top Dog again and noticed that the chainsaw hung even closer. Danger tried to shuffle away from the weapon a few inches, but it followed his movements closely.

"Personally, I would have preferred to raze the entire city to the ground," the Top Dog continued. "Much more enjoyable that way. But I learned long ago that's a rookie mistake. Sometimes, you really do need to build upon what's already there."

Turning to a tap on his shoulder, Danger noticed the chainsaw resting dangerously close to his neck.

"But you don't have to worry about that happening to you or your crew. Certainly not from me. After all, we are both on the same side, aren't we? You did swear loyalty to me, didn't you?"

The Top Dog lifted the chainsaw off Danger's shoulder, and the Captain turned to see the larger robot towering over him. The chainsaw still hung dangerously close, and for a moment the Top Dog revved it up, the sound blaring through the room as the blade glowed red.

"Or are you loyal to Leroy Brown?" the Top Dog asked, a menacing tone slowly creeping into his voice.

"I...am loyal to you," Captain Danger answered after a moment.

"That's what I thought," the Top Dog said. He rolled back away from the Captain a few feet on his treads. "It's because of that loyalty you were able to come to me when your precious, beloved scraptrawler was in need of significant help. It's because of that loyalty I'm willing to lend you my aid, my people, and my resources. That loyalty is why I'm certain that, since I have told you I want you to have an alive but inactive Leroy Brown ready for my people to bring back with them when they return from repairing your precious, beloved scraptrawler, I can expect you will successfully carry through with that request."

"Of course," Danger said.

"Sounds like a good answer," the Top Dog replied. He rolled over to the command circle at the center of the room and stepped inside it. "As I said before, send a full list detailing the full extent of the repairs your vessel needs. I'll send my people over as soon as possible."

"Thank you," Danger said.

"You're welcome," the Top Dog replied.

A bulkhead door opened on the far side of the room, and Danger saw the four-robot team that had escorted him in waiting for him.

"I'll be appreciating your swift departure, Captain," the Top Dog said. "I'm a very busy robot. I'm sure you are as well."

Captain Danger gave a slow nod bordering on a bow, then turned and left the room. He was quickly escorted along a path leading out of the *Ultimatum*, and then left to make his own way back to his shuttle. With each step he took away from the vessel and along the flight back to the *Horizon*, Danger found himself questioning if having sworn loyalty to the Top Dog had been the right decision after all.

00101.

After Captain Danger informed Leroy Brown and Commander Echo of his intent to visit the Top Dog, Leroy went to work finding ways to assist the *Eternal Horizon*'s crew. Once word spread of the Captain's intent to request help with repairs, work focused on preparing the vessel for when help arrived. Teams went across the ship from top to bottom, bow to stern, and port to starboard taking stock of the damage left behind from the Scrapwyrm attack. After the teams finished surveying and taking stock of the damage, work began in tearing out the layers of damaged parts. Twisted metal was cut, wrecked machinery was removed, and loose scrap was rounded up. All of it was gathered and carried to the top deck, where it was laid out in piles organized as good as could be expected.

Leroy mostly contributed to hauling broken pieces to the top deck. Despite not being a member of the crew, he had no trouble working alongside them toward a common goal. On more than one occasion, he even found himself practically drafted into taking lead thanks in no small part to the reputation he'd earned from his fight against the Scrapwyrm. His base warbot programming helped him settle into the role with ease. Walter, meanwhile, primarily helped with cataloging the damage, though occasionally he was drafted to climb into smaller spaces thanks to his size.

Everyone aboard the vessel worked hard and diligently at their tasks, with an ongoing effort that ran all but nonstop. The only interruptions to the work were the brief occasions when movement was spotted out on the horizon. Most passed without incident. A few changed direction to approach the *Horizon*, but with no effort made to signal intent, each was assumed to be hostile by a crew very much on edge and unwilling to take any unnecessary chances. Fortunately for the vessel, each was easily driven off when the crew showed they weren't quite as helpless as they first appeared and more than willing to fight if necessary.

Good news finally came with word that Captain Danger's shuttle was on its way back, complete with encouraging news he promised to expand upon when he returned. From that moment, at least one set of eyes was always kept looking to the distance. The news was well received when the shuttle was finally spotted.

"*All crews are to continue with their work,*" Commander Echo ordered across the ship. "*Everyone will be informed of the Captain's news in due time.*"

Not being an official member of the crew, Leroy ignored the order anyway. The moment he was able to do so without leaving anyone hanging, he left for docking. Leroy arrived just as the shuttle was doing the same, slowly backing up to slide into its very limited parking space. Danger's pilot exited the ship first, followed closely by the Captain himself.

"Captain Danger," Leroy said as soon as the robot was in view. Danger seemed strangely taken aback by Leroy's presence, which caught him by surprise.

"Leroy Brown," Danger said.

"Did you learn anything about those spaceships?" Leroy asked.

Danger looked at Leroy, but resumed walking.

"Danger?" Leroy asked as he watched the Captain walk past

him.

"We'll talk later," Danger answered. "I have a lot I need to deal with right now."

While Leroy couldn't help but suspect something was wrong, he refrained from pushing the matter further. Instead, he kept it in the back of his mind and returned to assisting with cleanup.

Within the next few hours, Captain Danger confirmed the Top Dog would be sending a repair team as soon as he was able, as well as laying claim to the Scrapwyrm corpse. While there was a small degree of grumbling that the crew wouldn't be allowed to salvage it for themselves, confirmation that repairs for the *Horizon* would be taken care of was enough to dissuade any serious complaints.

Over the next few days, work to prepare both the *Horizon* and the Scrapwyrm for the Top Dog's repair team continued. Leroy tried on several occasions per day to talk with Captain Danger during this time, but each effort was met with the claim the Captain was too busy to speak with him and he should try again later. With each new rebuff, Leroy's suspicions that something was wrong increased. After three days of Danger excusing himself, Leroy decided he'd had enough. Tracking the Captain across the ship, Leroy finally caught up with Danger on the bridge.

"Captain Danger!" Leroy said. He stood in the doorway, looking none too friendly. At least three robots moved to intercept him, including the bulky form of Commander Echo. They only took a few steps before Captain Danger waved them down.

"Leroy Brown," Captain Danger said. "I do believe that this is quite inappropriate."

"I don't care," Leroy replied. "You've been making a point

of avoiding a conversation you said we'd discuss later. I'd call that inappropriate, especially when you previously made such a big deal about how thankful you were for me saving your vessel that you offered me a place in your crew."

"Then as Captain of the *Horizon*, I shouldn't have to explain myself to my crew."

"I'm not part of your crew," Leroy said. "If I'm no longer welcome here, just tell me so I can leave and go find a spaceship elsewhere."

Captain Danger and Leroy Brown stared at each other, the rest of the bridge crew looking on. Then, Danger lowered his head.

"You're right," Danger said. "You're absolutely right."

"Then let's talk," Leroy said.

Danger nodded.

"If you'll step outside, I'll be right with you," he said, his arm pointed toward the other side of the door.

"Is this another trick to get out of talking?" Leroy asked.

"No," Danger replied. "This…this is not a trick. Step outside, give me one moment, and I'll be right with you."

Leroy looked at Danger, then turned back to the door and stepped through. With one foot on the other side, he looked over his shoulder before slowly turning back and continuing through. There, Leroy waited, and out of suspicion began counting how long it took Danger to follow. It proved unnecessary when Danger kept his word and joined him less than half a minute later.

"Leroy," Danger said.

"Cut to the chase, Captain," Leroy said. "There's clearly something wrong. If all you had for me was good news, you wouldn't be going out of your way to not tell me."

"An acute observation," Danger replied. "You're right. I've been avoiding this conversation because it's not all good news."

"I said cut to the chase," Leroy said.

"I owe you an apology, Leroy," Danger said. He started walking away from the bridge.

"Where are you going?"

"I owe you multiple apologies," Danger said as he continued walking.

"I hope one of them is for walking away from me right now," Leroy said. Despite his frustration with the situation, he followed Danger all the same.

"Yes, I'm sorry about that as well."

"Then stop it."

"I tried to ask the Top Dog about the spaceships," Danger continued. All the same, he refused to stop walking.

"Did he say no?" Leroy asked. "Or do they just not exist."

"I don't know," Danger answered as he stepped onto the *Horizon*'s main deck. "He didn't give me a chance to actually discuss the topic."

"You said you tried to ask him about them."

"I did. But he didn't let me actually get there because he was focused on you."

Leroy thought a moment as he considered Danger's words.

"So, he was impressed that I killed the Scrapwyrm but didn't let you ask about his spaceships for me?" Leroy asked. "I don't think that computes."

"No, Leroy. He knows you," Danger explained. "He recognized

you. He'd heard of you."

"He knows me? How?"

"I asked, but he didn't tell me."

"So what was he focused on?" Leroy asked.

"That's…the good news," Danger said. He stopped to open a door, then stepped inside and made his way below deck. Leroy considered the tone of Danger's words before following.

"What interpretation of 'good news' are you using?" Leroy asked.

"It's the other thing he wanted," Danger said. "When I asked for his help to fix the *Eternal Horizon*, he required two things in exchange. The first was the dead Scrapwyrm. The second was that when his people were finished fixing the *Horizon*, you'd go back with them."

"He wants to see me?"

"That's the most optimistic possibility."

"What did he request?" Leroy asked. "Don't spin the answer, tell me exactly what he wanted."

Danger stopped, turned to look at Leroy, then turned back and kept walking.

"Captain Danger!" Leroy said. "I want a direct answer – what did he want?"

"Leroy, I said I'm sorry for several things," Danger said. "I mean it. I also want you to understand that I personally bare you no ill will. I'm still grateful to you for saving my vessel and my crew."

"I don't think I like the direction this conversation is going, Danger," Leroy said. He came to a halt and planted his feet firmly against the floor.

"Doctor Clank told me you're a *Centurion*-class warbot almost all the way through," Danger continued. He stopped when he realized that Leroy was no longer following him, then turned and slowly stepped back towards the robot.

"A military unit through-and-through," Danger continued. "So I hope you'll understand when I say that as someone who's both commander of this vessel and as someone who answers to a higher power, there are a lot of calculations I have to consider for every major decision I make."

"What did he want?" Leroy asked again.

"He wanted his people to take you back with them when they returned," Danger answered.

"In what condition?"

Danger looked at Leroy, but said nothing. When Leroy grew tired of waiting, he leaned in toward the Captain.

"What condition did he want me in?"

"Alive," Danger finally answered. "But disabled."

"Disabled?"

"Inactive. Turned off."

Leroy stood his ground and glared at Captain Danger. They stood there, looking at each other for several moments, but said nothing.

"My apologies," Leroy finally said. "But I'm sure you'll understand if I refuse to let you live up to your obligation."

Leroy then turned and walked away from Danger, slowly at first.

"Leroy–" Danger started.

"Thank you for your hospitality, but I'll be taking my leave now," Leroy interrupted.

Leroy then turned his walk into a run. Danger called after him, but Leroy ignored the Captain, and soon left the robot behind. He ran through the decks of the *Horizon*, using what familiarity he had with the vessel to make a path for where he'd last known Walter to be. Fortunately, the little robot hadn't gone anywhere, allowing Leroy to find him with ease. When he did, Walter was in the middle of a holographic game against another robot, with half a dozen others watching them closely.

"Walter," Leroy said as he approached.

"Hello, Leroy," Walter said. "Is something needed?"

"We're leaving," Leroy answered. All the other robots in the room quickly turned their attention toward him.

"That does not compute," Walter said.

"I'll explain later," Leroy said. He stepped in and picked Walter up, eliciting no shortage of protests from the others.

"But I am winning!" Walter said.

"Then consider this affirmation of your victory."

"What's the idea?!" one of the robots said. Leroy didn't answer and continued moving until a message blared over the ships intercom, just as he reached the doorway.

"*All available hands! Apprehend Leroy Brown!*" Commander Echo's voice boomed over the intercom. "*I repeat, all available hands are to apprehend Leroy Brown, and he is to be taken alive!*"

Before the message had finished, Leroy was already on the run again with as much speed as the halls around him allowed.

"What did you do?" Walter asked.

"I'll explain later," Leroy said.

"Explain now!"

"Now is a bad time," Leroy said. He came to a sudden stop when a pair of robots came around the corner and charged at him. Retreating a few steps, Leroy changed course and turned down a hallway.

"Why can you not tell me?" Walter asked.

"I said it's a bad time. I'll explain later," Leroy answered. He came to a stop when three more crewmembers appeared and approached him from the other direction.

"I want an explanation now," Walter repeated.

Realizing he'd have to fight his way through regardless, Leroy backtracked again and charged at the first pair of robots. When he neared them, he lunged forward and activated his barrier shield. When Leroy's shield connected, it combined with his momentum to toss the two robots aside. Hitting the wall on the other side, he landed, centered himself again, and then resumed running along his original path.

"Trust me, I didn't do anything," Leroy answered as he continued running.

"Then why are they trying to catch you?" Walter asked.

Leroy started up a flight of stairs and refrained from answering Walter right away. He stopped when he came to the top of the first flight, waiting as an oncoming robot charged the short distance toward him. Leroy ducked as the other robot reached him, then he threw himself at the robot's lower body and tossed the robot over his shoulder to send him down the stairwell. To Leroy's surprise, the robot caught himself on the railings and swung back in a full vertical circle, striking Leroy with an upward blow to the visor when he came around.

Leroy stepped back with the blow, then stepped forward again to deliver a counterpunch to the robot's face, which he followed up with a spinning strike that sent his foe down the stairwell for real. He wasted no time seeing if the robot would stay down but continued up the stairs.

"Leroy Brown!" Walter shouted. "Why are they trying to catch you?!"

"The Top Dog wants me turned off and handed over to him," Leroy finally answered. "Captain Danger agreed to it."

"Oh."

Leroy continued up the stairs till they ran out. He was presented with two directions to choose from, and robots approaching from both. He picked the path of least resistance and charged forward. Once again, he used his shield to plow straight through the oncoming foes. Without missing a step, Leroy continued down the halls until he reached another flight of stairs. Running to the top and through a door finally brought him to the *Horizon*'s top deck.

Leroy looked around just long enough to find the ships nearest edge, then ran straight for it. A volley of blue, electric ion shots flew at him from across the ship. Half missed him entirely, but the half that hit quickly began to put a significant strain on his systems when Leroy blocked them with his shield. Only a single physical obstacle stood between Leroy and his destination, an orbicular, five-eyed robot standing on five thin pointed legs and sporting just as many tentacular arms.

The multi-armed robot reached for Leroy as he got close, trying to entangle their limbs together. Leroy smacked the first arm away, though the second and third wrapped their way around an arm and leg. Leroy tried to break one of the arms by slamming his free arm down on it, but the orbicular grappler took advantage of the leverage he already had to keep a safe distance between his body and Leroy's strikes.

While Leroy tried to figure out an angle of attack, Walter leaped off Leroy at the other unit. He landed on the robot's head and immediately attacked the eyes. The robot leaned backwards away from Leroy as he tried to get Walter off his head, and together the three fell toward the edge of the ship in an uncoordinated, chaotic motion. The other robot finally caught hold of Walter and pulled him off but had no opportunity to return his focus to Leroy – seconds later, Leroy threw himself forward and launched all three over the edge of the vessel. The tentacle-armed robot grabbed the *Horizon's* railing, and all three swung back toward the vessel's hull. The robot's grip quickly began to fail, and he let go of Leroy to keep from falling. Leroy grabbed hold of the robot long enough to retrieve Walter. Then Leroy let go and fell to the ground, tilting and twisting his body as gravity pulled him down.

Leroy pulled his legs in as he neared the vessel's tracks, and then threw them out again to leap out and away from the junktrawler. Several yards out, Leroy hit the ground in a roll that carried him several yards more, his shield cushioning the worst of the collision. When he finally came to a stop, he laid there for a split second before he picked himself up, grabbed Walter, and continued to run away from the *Horizon*. He pushed his legs as fast as they could go, and in a few short seconds his body was moving with as much speed as it could sustain for any reasonable length of time. A few shots flew at him from the ship, but most came up short or went wide. The handful that came close to hitting him were once again blocked by his shield. Both the dust and the *Eternal Horizon* were soon left in his wake, with the land ship swiftly shrinking in size behind him as he ran off into the distance beyond.

****

Captain Danger stepped onto the deck of the *Eternal Horizon* with a gait bearing little connection to the situation he walked into. If anything, his walk was of a man who had no concerns at all, which was at direct odds with everyone around him. Looking around, he took notice of where attention was focused, and then walked in that direction. There were a handful of robots gathered at the *Horizon's* edge, including one named Pentabot who was being pulled up from the side.

"What's the situation?" Danger asked. The crewmembers turned and stepped aside for their Captain, giving him a clear path to the vessel's railing.

"Apologies, Sir. He escaped," Pentabot said. He and every other robot around him pointed out away from the vessel. There, Danger spotted Leroy Brown running into the distance like a maniac.

"Captain Danger!" Commander Echo shouted from the bridge. "I have two teams prepping the shuttles for immediate departure! We should be able to catch him if they leave now!"

Danger turned to his First Officer and gave a wave of his hand.

"Negative!" Danger said. "Let him go!"

"Sir?" Echo asked, a sentiment mirrored by the other robots

around him. Danger waved them off and walked toward Echo and the bridge.

"As far as I'm concerned, he's already escaped," Danger continued. "No sense wasting further resources on him. He'd probably just wreck our shuttles."

"Confirm that, Sir?"

"Yes, order confirmed – He's out of our hands now. We tried our best to catch him, but clearly it was a task beyond our means. If the Top Dog wants him, we can tell him where he went last, but otherwise, that's his problem now."

Danger turned back to the crew and gave them another nod and wave.

"Good job, everyone. Your efforts are much appreciated. As you were."

00110.

With Walter riding on his back, Leroy continued running for several hours. The winds rushed past them as he ran as fast as his legs would carry him. Mile after mile, both terrain and piles of refuse flowed in size and makeup as he pressed onward. The sun refused to show itself in the sky, but the daylight waned all the same and gave way to the darkness of night. Even so, Leroy continued running straight ahead, not stopping until the terrain made it impossible to keep going. He slowed down when he spotted a drop off ahead, and finally came to a halt when his feet reached the ledge.

Looking across the moonlit horizon, Leroy and Walter found a wretched excuse for a lake. It was a shiny expanse stretching out for miles. The occasional rock or stone pillar pointed into the air, but not nearly close together or frequent enough that anyone could expect to use them as steppingstones. Further peppering the fluid surface were piles of still more garbage, collections of scrap metal and wrecked machines of countless shapes, sizes, makes, and models. From over Leroy's shoulder, Walter shone a light on the water, painting an even more unflattering appearance on an already ugly scene. While the surface was covered in a fluid, it resembled water only in that it was a liquid. A mixture of greens and shades of rust blended in swirls and patterns almost artistic in their own right. Leroy could only guess at what the liquid was, but one thing that was clear was he didn't want to even try to walk through it. While subtle and easy to miss, a closer look at the junk standing up from the lake revealed that the liquid had a mild corrosive element to it.

Leroy stood up, stepped back, and looked around him as he calculated the best direction to go next.

"Do you know where you are going?" Walter asked.

"No," Leroy answered.

"Do you have a target destination?"

"No," Leroy said. "I know nothing about this lousy excuse for a planet. All I can do is keep them from catching us again and make calculated guesses about where I'm going."

"Then I will take lead," Walter said.

"Take lead at what?"

"As I said, I have been on Junkworld for a period of approximately forty rotations," Walter said.

"Forty years or forty days?" Leroy asked.

"Forty solar rotations."

"Forty years, then."

"That is likely an accurate phrasing, yes," Walter said. "I estimate my own knowledge of Junkworld, while not all encompassing, still far exceeds your own. Therefore, it would be a prudent course of action to utilize that knowledge to determine our next course of action."

"I can't argue with that logic," Leroy said. "Where to, then?"

"Before I was captured, I was the member of a settlement. It is known as Rustbucket," Walter explained.

"Sounds like a terrible name." Leroy said.

"I can not argue with that assessment." Walter said. "Even so, it is both home and a safe location. I was captured while assisting with a search for useable parts. Since then, I have made a point of tracking my position relative to Rustbucket so if I were ever freed, I could find my way home again."

"Sounds like a plan," Leroy said. "Point the way."

Leroy held his arm out, and Walter climbed off his shoulder and to the end of the arm. Looking about, Walter scanned the horizon, and then pointed in a direction approximately 45 degrees to the left of where they'd just come from.

"How far out is it?" Leroy asked.

"Calculated based on a straight run, using your previous top speed, and at a continuous travel, I estimate a travel time in the general vicinity of seven planetary rotations."

"A week," Leroy said. "Rustbucket is a week away."

"Before accounting for unknown variables," Walter said. "Travel time could last up to ten planetary rotations. Outer estimates place travel time at fourteen."

"That's not going to cut it," Leroy said. "It may be a safe place, but I'm not in favor of a trip that could last up to two weeks."

"It is the best I have to offer."

Leroy looked back at the toxic lake, and then scanned the horizon opposite it.

"How much do you know about the area between here and there?" Leroy asked.

"My direct knowledge about this region of Junkworld is limited," Walter answered. "I may be able to provide more assistance when we get closer."

Leroy nodded.

"I suppose that's a start," Leroy said. "I'll want to navigate around the *Horizon* so I don't run into them again, and we're definitely going to want to find faster transportation sooner rather than later."

"Those are both reasonable assessments," Walter said.

Leroy nodded, and Walter climbed onto his back again. Leroy then started running in a rounded path that led mostly toward Rustbucket. Within a dozen steps, Leroy Brown was running at top speed again. He charged forward in a relentless motion, running up and over whatever obstacles he could and around those he couldn't. For over two days and nights he continued running, speeding along an invisible perimeter that circled the *Eternal Horizon* and kept him at more than a safe distance from the vessel he'd escaped in the first place. As the miles passed them by, the terrain shifted from a flat expanse littered with scrap to a rocky terrain of uneven hills that in turn shifted to broken mountains. Signs of metal became scarce, and Leroy's speed slowed considerably as his high-speed run turned into a slow, careful climb. Relentlessly, he trudged over and across the massive border of rock in his ongoing journey. Throughout all of it, neither Leroy nor Walter saw any sign of anyone else, save for a brief period when Walter spotted a pair of small drones floating about in a casual fashion off in the distance.

It was past midday when Leroy finally reached even terrain again. He entered a thick forest of rock, with pillars of stone pointing high into the sky around a thin web of pathways. Both above and behind him, the mountains still towered over the horizon, making their presence known wherever the sky was allowed to peek through the looming terrain. While still slight, there was also the occasional sign of scrap metal and other wreckage. Without a clear sight of where he was going, Leroy's speed was still significantly diminished, but not nearly as much as during the climb.

"You know anything about this area?" Leroy asked.

"Negative," Walter answered. "We are still outside my realm of knowledge."

Looking up, Leroy noticed the stone pillars growing progressively shorter, leading toward a point somewhere up ahead. Soon after he turned his focus forward again, he heard the sound of crashing metal. It was slow and singular at first, then increased in rate and number. Leroy sped up to a brisk pace and weaved in and out between the rocks till he spotted the source of the noise. There, he and Walter found a large clearing littered in piles of junk laying about in a disorganized mess.

Turning toward the noise, Leroy spotted a wide pillar of light descending from the sky. Descending through it was all manner of discarded metal miscellanea. Curiously, each piece landed with an impact far softer than it logically should have, especially since the source was high enough in the sky that Leroy had to magnify his vision to see it. It was a spaceship of a model he couldn't make heads or tails of, unloading its supply of refuse through a glowing hatch near its back end. Before long, the light went out. Soon after, the ship moved on and disappeared entirely. The glowing pillar of light descended alongside the last of its cargo and hit the ground about the same time as the final piece, a large rusty shipping container.

"*So that's how it happens,*" Leroy thought.

He looked around for signs that anyone else was in the area. When he determined the coast was clear, he walked out into the clearing and looked around, hoping that perhaps there just might be some kind of transportation waiting to be found.

"Remain careful," Walter said.

"Then stay alert," Leroy replied.

Walking around the hills of broken machinery, nothing stood out as having any potential. Anything that looked like it had once been capable of transportation was broken beyond Leroy or Walter's ability to fix, either by missing one or more critical pieces or by being so worn out and rusted that even if they got one running, they expected it would fall apart before they even made it out of the clearing. Despite his far greater experience in the art of "scraphunting", Walter likewise failed to find anything to suit their needs. With neither suspecting they'd have any more luck digging into the piles of junk beyond the surface, attention turned to the handful of unopened shipping containers that lay scattered about.

Climbing up one of the piles of junk, Leroy pushed on a container till gravity took hold and pulled it to the ground. It came to a halt with a muted metallic "thud" when it impacted with the planets rocky surface. With Walter's help, Leroy easily broke the container's seal, allowing the doors to swing partway open. What they soon found within were smaller containers far newer and cleaner than the shipping container they occupied, with writing neither one recognized. Forcing one of the smaller containers out, Leroy opened it up to find it held several likewise tightly packed robots. The units resembled metal humanoid skeletons, with an aesthetic intended to invoke terror.

"What are they?" Walter asked. "Who are they?"

"I think they're wardrones," Leroy answered. "They look like they're part of some *Terminator*-class. I broke dozens like them before I was retired, but this model is unfamiliar to me."

"Should we turn one on?"

"I don't think we can," Leroy replied. "I think they're drones, not genuine robots. They would have been operated remotely by a central intelligence."

Undeterred, Walter promptly went to work looking for a way to turn the machine on anyway.

"Even if it works, I don't think it's a good idea," Leroy said. "We don't know if it's hostile or not."

"If it is hostile, I calculate you should be able to break it," Walter said. "If it is not hostile, it and its fellow units should be an invaluable asset."

"It also complicates our efforts to find transportation,"

"You would abandon these robots to an unknown fate?" Walter asked, looking up at Leroy.

"Under the circumstances, yes."

Walter gave Leroy a hurt look, and then continued his work with a renewed passion. That work soon gave way to disappointment when he discovered that not only was he unable to turn the unit on, but it was also missing several critical internal components. As disappointing as the discovery was for Walter, Leroy had little difficulty getting the smaller robot to move on and turn his focus to the next container.

While the two gained access to a second container with ease, they didn't have a chance to open it before they heard an approaching noise. It sounded like a vehicle, though Leroy didn't wait to see what it was before he picked up Walter and ran for cover. He stopped behind the first shipping container, where he waited and listened to the approaching noise. As it grew closer, the sounds of the vehicle gave away more about it.

It sounded small, like a van or a truck, with multiple sets of wheels covered with metal rather than tires. Leroy guessed it was heavy set, but not overly heavy or sporting an exceptional level of power. It came to a halt near the next junk pile over, well within sight if he were to step around the cargo container. He then heard three sets of footsteps climb out, belonging to robots that spoke to each other in a binary-style language neither Leroy nor Walter understood.

"What do we do?" Walter whispered.

"You're going to stay out of sight," Leroy whispered back.

He put Walter on the ground, then peered around the corner. He spotted a vaguely humanoid form covered in a strange cloak of equal parts cloth and metal, bound together by an odd, irregular assortment of connectors. The robot also wielded a large rifle that he fired nearly as soon as he laid eyes on Leroy. A ray beam pierced though the air with an electric hum. Most of the beam dispersed when it hit Leroy's shield, but just enough penetrated to leave black scarring on Leroy's shoulder. Not interested in testing the weapon further, Leroy quickly pulled back behind cover.

"We're not hostile!" Leroy shouted. One of the other robots said something in response, but it was more of the same binary beeps that might as well have been static as far as Leroy and Walter were concerned. Leroy tried a non-verbal approach by holding his arm out around the corner and waving it up and down. He did this for several seconds in search of a response, which unfortunately came in the form of another ray beam that missed his arm by inches.

"I think they are hostile," Walter said after Leroy pulled his arm back.

"I'm assuming as much," Leroy said.

"So what do we do?"

"I'm going to try to beat them without killing them and see if that convinces them we can communicate," Leroy said. Listening to the trio of robots, he heard them speaking to one another and moving about in what he suspected to be a flanking maneuver.

"What if that doesn't work?" Walter asked.

"Then I break them and we steal their transport," Leroy answered.

Leroy turned around to see one of the robots emerge at the top of the scrap pile. Running forward, Leroy dodged a ray beam, picked up a broken piece of machinery, and threw it directly at the attacker. The projectile clocked the robot upside the head and knocked him off balance long enough for Leroy to bound up the junk pile. He grabbed the robot's weapon by the barrel when he arrived, then held tight while he drove the bottom of his foot into the robot's midsection. The machine went flying backward off the junk pile, losing hold of his weapon and landing in a heap on the ground below.

A ray beam hit Leroy's shield from the side, leaving a scorch mark along his head. Leroy ran down the junkpile after the robot he'd kicked off it, evading two more shots in the process. The unarmed robot stood up and tried to strike back against Leroy, but Leroy threw himself at the machine as he neared the bottom. The impact knocked the other robot to the ground again, and Leroy took position directly over the robot's body and planted a foot on his chest. Leroy aimed his rifle out and gave it a quick scan for signs of alternate functions but found nothing. His focus back outward, he swept the rifle across the scene looking for the two other robots. While he saw no sign of them, he could hear them talking to each other.

The scene was interrupted by another approaching noise that

quickly caught the attention of the robot Leroy was standing over, and silenced the conversation of the other two. It shook the ground with an increasingly heavy clanking sound bearing the hallmarks of multiple legs. As the noise came closer, there was a constant loud metallic buzz that further heralded its approach. The closer the noise got, the more the robot Leroy stood over slammed a fist against his leg.

Leroy lifted his foot up, and the robot quickly climbed to his feet and ran to join his cohorts. Leroy followed close behind to keep tabs on him, then stopped when he spotted the robots vehicle and the two others that had come with it. The three of them climbed into a six-wheeled, open-backed truck with a small crane that sat up between the cab and cargo area. The vehicle almost left the third robot behind, revving up just as the robot caught up with it. There was an air of desperation to their movement, showing a desire to escape as soon as possible.

As the truck began to make its escape, the source of the robot's terror finally showed itself. Emerging over the hilltops, it was a large machine that invoked the idea of a giant metal spider standing more than three stories tall. Like so much of what Leroy had seen on Junkworld, it was built as a mashup of an untold number of sources. Its legs alone looked like they'd been constructed out of the remains of at least a dozen different vehicles. Its head, while closed, looked like a cockpit rather than a head with a mind of its own. Underneath the head was mounted a turret with two large cannons flanking an assortment of other miscellaneous tools. Two cranes sat on its back – one near the neck and the other near its tail end – while a third utility arm was mounted to the center of its undercarriage.

The truck drove to escape through a gate-like formation in the rocks but came to a sudden stop when one of the spider-mechs' eight legs slammed into the ground directly in front of it. One of the robots in the truck fired its ray beams up at the spider-mech as they backed up, but the shots had no discernable impact. Driving backward, meanwhile, merely made it easier for the robot to shoot the truck with a massive ion burst. A wave of blue electric energy washed over the truck and its passengers, causing the entirety of it all to go dead. The spider-mech backed up further, and then the crane on its back went to work, twisting over and lowering down to retrieve its prize. Leroy didn't watch any further, choosing that moment to turn and run.

"What is it? What happened?" Walter asked when Leroy reached him.

"Something bigger showed up," Leroy answered.

"But you can kill it, right?" Walter asked as Leroy picked him up.

"That's the problem," Leroy answered as he ran for the forest of rocks. "I don't *want* to kill it."

Leroy heard the spider-mech move toward him as he ran. Glancing over his shoulder, he saw the machine look in his direction, then fire an ion blast that sped across the air straight at him. The shot impacted with his shield, shorting it out and knocking Leroy forward across the ground. He wasted no time getting back on his feet and picking both Walter and the rifle back up. A second ion shot narrowly missed, hitting the ground where he'd been only moments before. The spider-mech advanced in his direction and continued to fire, but Leroy moved with an irregular pattern to throw off the aim and escape to the safety of the forest of stone.

"Why do you not want to kill it?" Walter asked.

"I think it's a ride, not a robot," Leroy replied. He snuck around the inner edge of the stone forest. "And it already took the truck, so I think it's the only option we have right now."

A handful of ion blasts struck harmlessly against the pillars of rock, then the weapons fire ceased. Glancing out into the clearing, he saw the spider-mech had changed focus and turned its attention toward the piles of junk scattered on the ground.

"Stay hidden," Leroy said.

He set Walter down, then backtracked and snuck around the outer layer of the rock forest, looking for a clean shot at the spider-mech cockpit. The large machine went about its work, ignorant to the threat lurking about the fringes, the body lowered halfway to the ground to provide a closer look at its targeted material. Once Leroy had a clear aim at his target, he raised his rifle, aimed, and fired. The weapon let out its familiar electric hum, followed by another noise that was new but didn't sound like anything being damaged.

A moment later, the spider-mech turned its head in Leroy's direction and returned to a full standing position. Leroy pulled back behind cover again, avoiding another salvo of ion blasts that dispersed harmlessly off the rocks. They were followed closely by a salvo of laser beams that began to pepper the area, hitting both the stone pillars and the ground around them. Leroy held his position and pressed against his cover, timing the shots to anticipate an opening. As he waited, he heard the spider-mech moving, first in a circle, and then slowly advancing in his direction.

Once an opening presented itself, Leroy moved from one pillar of rock to the next, putting himself on the outside of the weapons fire. He traveled deeper into the stone forest, continuing around the perimeter to find another angle of attack. As he did, he heard the spider-mech continue its approach, though the laser blasts had died down. After Leroy traveled halfway around the stone forest, he moved back out and glanced from behind cover.

Aiming his rifle, he fired on the cockpit again. Once again, the shot did nothing other than catch the spider-mech's attention. Turning its head, it fired its lasers and changed course. Leroy retreated into the forest of rock to avoid the lasers and plan his next move. Moving through the rocks, he heard the spider-mech climbing up above. While Leroy wondered what it was trying to do at first, he soon realized that it was trying to tear down the rock pillars entirely.

Turning his attention upward, Leroy began to climb the nearest pillar of rock. Using the proximity of the next pillar over to aid his ascent, foot by foot he pushed and pulled himself toward the top. As he continued to climb, the sound of crumbling and then collapsing stone echoed through the area, signaling the first of the pillars had finally fallen.

Once he reached the top, Leroy glanced over the edge. After locating the spider-mech again, he climbed up and aimed his weapon. The spider-mech spotted him before he could fire, forcing Leroy to drop back to the ground to escape a series of laser blasts flying overhead. The spider-mech shifted backwards then moved over toward Leroy's location as it continued to hunt him down.

Taking advantage of the situation, Leroy ran out of the stone forest and toward the nearest of the mech's legs. As soon as he reached it he dropped the rifle, leapt up, and began to climb. The spider-mech quickly took notice and tried to shake Leroy off. Leroy held fast with an iron grip, prompting the spider-mech to try to scrape Leroy off on one of the stone towers. Before he was crushed between rock and metal, Leroy leapt to the next leg over.

The spider-mech tried to dislodge its unwelcome passenger, moving its legs as much as it could and stepping back away from the stone pillars. It tried to grab at Leroy with the undercarriage arm, but Leroy again lunged from one leg to the next. While the arm was busy readjusting and retargeting, Leroy climbed around to the outside of the leg. The spider-mech tried to step back toward the rocks and scrap Leroy off again, but by then Leroy was already beyond where that trick would work.

Once he reached the top, the spider-mech stepped away from the stone forest once more and attacked him with the aft crane. Leroy dodged then ran across the back of the spider-mech, evading a similar attack from the front crane. With a mighty leap, Leroy easily made it to the head. The spider-mech shook its cockpit back and forth in a continuing effort to dislodge Leroy, while the front crane swung around again, intent on knocking him off. Leroy narrowly shifted past the crane as it swung by but lost his footing and fell free before catching himself at the last moment. The head continued to shake in an effort to dislodge him, while the crane swung back around to grab him if the shaking didn't work.

Leroy held fast, but the constant movement of the head prevented him from gaining any ground. The crane lowered, approaching in an ominous fashion. As it neared ever closer, Leroy took a gamble. The moment the head tilted upward, he pushed himself up and grabbed hold of the crane. Caught off-guard by the maneuver, the spider-mech's driver failed to compensate fast enough to stop Leroy from climbing the crane and using it as leverage. Swinging around while holding tight, Leroy leapt from the crane to the cockpit hatch and grabbed hold.

Once his feet were secure, Leroy forced his strength on the hatch, slamming both fists and weight against it. Once, twice, three times he slammed against the entryway, with each blow weakening the last obstacle between him and the cockpit. The crane swung back toward him, the driver making one last effort to dislodge their much-unwelcomed passenger. At high speed, the weight of the crane grip flew straight at Leroy to smash him.

At the last moment, Leroy dropped down and grabbed hold of the cockpit just below the hatch. With Leroy out of the way, the crane hit the door with the full force of its impact, smashing it open. The crane slowly swung back away again, and Leroy climbed up and started into the cockpit. He immediately stepped back out again to avoid laser blasts fired from inside.

Leroy dodged across to the other side of the hatch, drawing further laser fire from within. Counting to three, Leroy swung around the corner and dived into the cockpit, rolling beneath further weapons fire. Leroy grabbed the robot's rifle the moment he reached it, then punched the robot in the face. He followed up by ripping the rifle from the robot's arms before tossing the robot out of the cockpit entirely.

Rifle in hand, Leroy turned to the cockpit seats to see a second robot he wasn't sure how to classify. By all accounts the robot was little more than a pole of wires with arms. He beeped and whistled, presumably at Leroy, but Leroy didn't understand a word he was saying. Rather than attempting to communicate with the robot, Leroy instead focused on the rifle in his hands. Fortunately, he found it indeed did come with an ion setting. Aiming the weapon at the robot, Leroy pulled the trigger. An electrical beam of energy struck the target, shutting him down with a wave of energy that coursed over the machine.

Pulling the robot away from the control panel, Leroy looked at the cockpit interior to see if there were any warning signs he needed to be concerned about. When he was convinced everything was alright, he returned to the hatch. Looking down, he spotted the robot he'd thrown out of the cockpit picking himself up. Leroy aimed and fired his rifle, hitting the robot with a burst of energy that disabled him.

"Walter!" Leroy called out. "It's safe to come out now!"

Looking around, Leroy watched for several moments for the robot to show himself.

"Walter?" Leroy called again. "You still there? And alive?"

More time passed, and Leroy began to worry that perhaps the little robot had run off or gotten lost. Or worse, perhaps he'd been broken somehow. Then, just as Leroy was prepared to climb down and look for Walter, he popped into view.

"Here!" Walter called back while he waved his arms above his head. "I am here!"

Walter continued rolling toward the spider-mech while Leroy waved back, but Walter stopped halfway there.

"How do I get up there?" Walter asked.

"Give me a minute," Leroy replied, stepping back into the cockpit. Not sure what to make of the tower of wires, Leroy tossed the robot out of the cockpit, then returned to the controls. He scanned them over and tried to deduce what everything did, then carefully tested them to confirm. Once he had a basic understanding, he lowered the front crane to the ground. Once it was down, Leroy stepped back to the hatch.

"Climb on!" he called down. "I'll lift you up and pull you in!"

Walter rolled over and with a little difficulty, climbed atop the crane. Leroy took to the controls again and lifted it back up until it hung just outside the hatch. With Leroy's help, Walter made his way to the cockpit.

"This is a much better ride," Walter said. He rolled over to the controls, climbed into a seat, then examined the cockpit. Leroy followed, picked Walter up, and placed him on an empty section of the control panel.

"Next stop, Rustbucket," Leroy said once he was seated.

"What about those robots?" Walter asked.

"What robots?" Leroy asked. "You mean the ones that tried to kill us?"

"Did you destroy them?"

"No, I hit them with ion shots," Leroy said. "What about them?"

"You are going to leave them?"

"I repeat – they did try to kill us."

"We are taking their vehicle," Walter said. "It would be inappropriate to leave them behind."

Leroy looked out the open hatch, then back to Walter.

"You're really pushing that 'no bot left behind thing', you know that?" Leroy noted.

Walter looked to the hatch, then turned back to Leroy. Leroy rolled his head and threw his hands up. Then, he used the spider-mech's crane to retrieve its previous owners and drop them in the storage unit.

"There, you happy?" Leroy asked. Walter replied with a nod.

"Good," he said. "Let's try this again."

Leroy turned the spider-mech outward, then drove it out of the clearing and onto the path, leading toward their original destination.

"Next stop, Rustbucket."

00111.

Two days after Leroy Brown escaped the *Eternal Horizon*, the Top Dog's promised repair team finally emerged in the distance. The massive vehicle they arrived in rolled along on a series of similarly massive wheels and was flanked by a pair of light gun platforms. The repair vehicle resembled an armed mobile dry-docks, and while it carried the same hodgepodge aesthetic of most the vehicles on Junkworld, it showed signs it had been designed and built with far more care and precision than most of its kin.

Upon arrival, the repair team wasted no time getting to work. Their leader, an unassuming robot named Commander Wrench who bore an unusually basic appearance, promptly located Otra 24 to compare notes. He then quickly turned around and used those notes to ensure his team did their job efficiently and without delay. Over the next three days, they kept hard at work fixing the vast array of damage the Scrapwyrm had left behind. On Wrench's insistence, the crew of the *Horizon* had minimal interaction with the repair team and kept their distance as much as they were able when their aid wasn't strictly necessary. When the work was finished and the *Horizon* was finally restored to full operational status, the repair vessel pulled away and parked nearby while the repair team finished with a few last details. First among them was loading up the Scrapwyrm corpse to haul it away. The second matter quickly became a far more complicated issue.

"Captain Danger."

From within the bridge, Danger and his officers turned to see

Commander Wrench standing by the door.

"Yes?" Danger replied.

"There appears to be a problem," Wrench said.

"What problem would that be?"

"I was told by the Top Dog we were to bring the disabled body of one 'Leroy Brown' back with us," Wrench explained. "He made a point of explaining the importance of it in great detail. However, I've asked your crew about the matter, and they keep telling me he's not here."

Danger looked around at his crew, then turned back to Wrench.

"Yes, about that," Danger said. "It's unfortunate, but true. He's not here. We don't have him."

Wrench looked at Danger, his head tilting with concern and confusion.

"Can you clarify that answer?" he asked.

"Yes, my apologies," Danger answered. "He was here when the Top Dog asked for him. However, the situation has changed since then. Leroy Brown learned about the agreement, and he didn't take kindly to it. We tried to capture him, but he escaped. As I'm sure you can imagine, our situation left us unable to pursue. We can point you in the direction we last saw him, but otherwise we have no idea where he is right now."

Wrench looked at Danger for several moments, then nodded.

"I see," Wrench said. With that, the robot turned and left the room.

"Captain, if I may?" asked Commander Echo. Danger turned and signaled for him to continue.

"I'm concerned this is not going to end well," Echo said.

"We'll just have to make the best of it," Danger replied.

Several hours later, Frigjar-Zeta informed the Captain the Top Dog himself was calling, and he insisted on speaking to Captain Danger personally.

"How 'personally' are we talking?" Danger asked her.

"He didn't say," she replied.

Danger thought a moment, then nodded and signaled for everyone to go quiet.

"Put him on," he said. A second later, she signaled him with an affirmative.

"Top Dog," Danger said. "To what do I owe this...pleasure?"

"*Captain Danger,*" the Top Dog replied. A touch of static weaved its way through the robot's voice as he spoke over the radio. "*I've been informed that my people have finished with your vessel. I trust they did a satisfactory job?*"

"That they did," Danger answered. "Everything is in order and all systems are fully functional once more."

"*Excellent! It's always a wonderful thing when people carry through on what's expected of them, isn't it?*"

Danger looked around at the bridge crew, then back to the radio.

"I can't argue with that," he answered.

"*Glad to hear we're in agreement,*" the Top Dog said. "*So perhaps you can answer a question for me.*"

"What question would that be?"

"*Captain, if I'm not mistaken, I made it extremely clear that when my people returned, they were to bring Leroy Brown's inactive*" *body back with them,"* the Top Dog said.

"I do recall you saying that," Danger replied.

"Then given that we agree on our thoughts regarding people doing what we expect of them, I'm sure you'll understand if I'm confused to learn that you don't have Leroy Brown anymore."

"An unfortunate turn of events," Danger answered. "My crew tried to apprehend him and prepare him for delivery, but he escaped. I'm sure you can understand."

"No, I don't understand."

Captain Danger momentarily found himself at a loss for words. It was quickly apparent the situation was becoming significantly more complicated in a way nobody was going to like. A glance at his crew told him they were having similar concerns.

"My apologies," Danger said. "I'd be happy to clean up any questions you have."

"Let's start with a simple one," the Top Dog replied. *"Why did he escape? What reason did he have to leave your ship?"*

"He found out you wanted us to hand him over to you," Danger answered.

There was a moment of silence that filled the room with an underlying atmosphere of dread.

"Right," the Top Dog said. *"My next question would be 'how did he find out?', but I'm pretty sure you don't want me to know the answer to that question."*

Another moment of silence followed. Danger looked to his crew again as he debated if he should say anything.

"Captain Danger?" the Top Dog said.

"I'm still here," Danger answered.

"Ah, good. I was worried we might have a dropped call there for a moment," the Top Dog said.

"Captain, we don't know each other that well," he continued. "You haven't worked for me that long, so I think I owe you a lesson."

"As I'm sure you can imagine, I didn't get where I am overnight. It took several years of hard work. And in those years, I learned a lot of skills and tricks. You know one of my favorites? I learned the very fine art of detecting humbug and filtering through finely crafted wordplay."

The underlying atmosphere of dread in the room grew as everyone recognized what the Top Dog was saying.

"I'm going to do us both a favor by not worrying about the specifics of how you've failed me, Captain Danger," the Top Dog continued. "All I care about is that you have. It's the kind of failure I just can't overlook. So now I'm going to tell you what you're about to do. And I recommend you think very hard about what I've just told you, Captain, because when I tell you what I want you to do, I expect you to do it without trying to be clever or creative with your interpretation of my orders."

Silence hung in the air a moment before the Top Dog spoke again.

"Do you understand?"

"Yes," Danger answered. "I understand."

"Good. These are your orders: You are going to figure out who is responsible for letting Leroy Brown escape. Once you have identified that individual, you are going to bring said individual with you to come visit me at my headquarters."

"And then?" Danger asked.

"Those are the only orders you need to worry about right now," the Top Dog answered. *"The rest can wait until we meet face-to-face."*

"Do you understand what I am saying, Captain Danger?"

"Yes," Danger answered.

"Do I need to repeat myself, or can I expect you to follow those orders as intended?"

"The repeat will not be necessary," Danger answered.

"Good," the Top Dog said. *"See you soon."*

With that, the line cut out from the other end. For a moment, Captain Danger couldn't help but feel very alone in the universe.

"Orders, Captain?" Commander Echo asked.

Danger looked to his first officer, the potential answer to that very question running in circles through his processing units. Finally, he stood tall and looked across the bridge to nowhere in particular.

"We determine who was responsible for Leroy Brown's escape," Danger said, his words thick with reluctance. "And then we visit the Top Dog."

****

An air of gloom and dread hung over the flight to the Top Dog's lair. Multiple possible scenarios ran through Captain Danger's head. None of them were good. While he briefly entertained the potential of a positive outcome, he quickly dismissed the idea out of an inability to consider it in an honest manner. Several times during the trip, Danger glanced next to him, where Pentabot sat so still and silent Danger could have sworn the robot was inactive entirely if he hadn't known better. Whether the situation being otherwise would have made things better, he couldn't tell. While he found himself wishing for something to lighten the mood, he couldn't escape the thought a lighter mood would betray the reality of the situation.

As the shuttle neared its destination, dark clouds swirled over the horizon in an ominous fashion. It was a sight that Danger recognized from his one previous visit to the Top Dog's headquarters. Soon after, the base itself emerged from over the horizon, beginning with the central command tower. It was an ugly mess of a structure, built from a mishmash of dissected large-scale wrecks and various miscellanea. Along the uppermost levels was attached the remains of a starship bridge adorned with emplacements equal parts decorative and defensive. When the shuttle came closer still, the base walls came into sight. They stood tall and thick at a safe distance from the central tower and armed with numerous defenses that centered around an array of mounted guns and cannons. Danger couldn't help but notice several of the weapons aiming at the shuttle as it closed in on the outer perimeter.

Soon, they received a signal, directing them along a designated flight path. Slowly, the shuttle followed and entered a small docking bay barely twice the size of the shuttle itself. Eight robots of various designs stood against the walls, each one more than ready for a fight if need be.

"Both of you are to come with us," one of the robots said once the shuttle had come to a complete stop. Captain Danger and Pentabot complied without complaint.

The guards escorted Danger and Pentabot through the base in a manner like Danger's visit to the *Ultimatum*, but along a much quicker and direct path. With each step they took, the feeling of dread grew thicker. It was almost a relief when they finally arrived at their destination, a room much like the command chamber from the *Ultimatum*. There, standing in a circle of consoles on the far side of the room, they came face-to-face with the Top Dog himself.

"Captain Danger," the Top Dog said once Captain Danger and Pentabot stood before him. Danger merely nodded in acknowledgement.

The Top Dog slowly looked back and forth between Danger and Pentabot before focusing his attention on Danger.

"I see you've learned to follow orders," the Top Dog said. "Good."

"You said you'd have further orders once we spoke face-to face," Danger said. "I'm here, I've done as you said. Now what?"

"You're responsible for Leroy Brown's escape?" the Top Dog asked, giving Pentabot a slight glance.

"Yes." Pentabot answered with sorrowful acceptance.

"How so?"

"I had an opportunity to stop him," Pentabot answered. "He was about to escape the ship. I intercepted him. I nearly prevented him from leaving. Then he leapt off the *Horizon* while I had a hold on him. I grabbed the railing but let go of Leroy Brown when doing both became difficult. That allowed him to escape."

The Top Dog turned to face Pentabot more fully, then stared at him for a moment. He then shifted his attention back to Danger.

"I suppose that will have to do," the Top Dog said. "Captain Danger, I believe it is necessary that you discipline such failure. And there is only one discipline I can think of that will adequately set an example."

"And what discipline would that be?" Danger asked.

Slowly and deliberately, the Top Dog pressed a button. From the ceiling, a metal arm holding a very dangerous looking ray gun lowered to Danger's level. Once the arm finished moving, the Top Dog said a single word that underscored what Danger already feared.

"Execution."

The word struck deep at Captain Danger, though he refrained from letting any of the resulting thoughts show through. Pentabot's reaction was far more panicked. In a jittery fashion, his head rotated back and forth between Captain Danger, the Top Dog, and the ray gun.

"Is that really necessary?" Danger asked.

"Yes," the Top Dog answered. "Letting Leroy Brown escape, and requiring a search to find and catch him? That is a big mistake. Big mistakes require major discipline. It's the only way people are going to learn that big mistakes are not acceptable. We've already established that your crewmember here is responsible for this big mistake. Therefore, he must be punished."

"But what does he learn from it?" Danger asked, pointing to Pentabot.

"Nothing," the Top Dog said. "That's not the point. The point is to educate the survivors. Such as yourself."

Danger looked between the Top Dog, the ray gun, and Pentabot, hesitating to even lift his hand towards the weapon.

"Is there a problem, Captain Danger?" the Top Dog asked. Danger looked to the larger robot, then back to Pentabot, but said nothing.

"Captain, I believe that under the circumstances, I am being very understanding," the Top Dog continued. "But if this behavior continues, I will have to question just how loyal you truly are. And if I can't be assured of your loyalty, then perhaps we aren't on the same side after all. It would be a terrible thing, wouldn't it? Especially for your crew."

Danger's eyes shot back toward the Top Dog.

"After all, how am I supposed to know where they all stand? I'm not sure if it would be worth the effort to sort through them and find out who could be trusted to fall in line. For all I know, none of them would take well to new direct leadership."

Danger looked to Pentabot, who started taking several terrified steps backwards.

"Do not make me repeat myself, Captain," the Top Dog said.

Once more, Danger looked to the ray gun, then back to Pentabot.

"I'm sorry," Danger said.

With a swift series of motions, he grabbed the ray gun, aimed it at Pentabot, and then pulled the trigger multiple times. A manifold of energy beams flowed from the weapon and pierced through Pentabot at several points across his body. Even while the robot fell to the ground as a black, smoking pile of wreckage, Danger continued to fire until he was absolutely certain that Pentabot was dead, driven by a determination to ensure the robot's death came as quickly as possible.

Finally, once the job was done, Danger let the ray gun sit quietly, with smoke seeping out its barrel. As his central processors did all they could to suppress any thought about the implications of what he'd just done, he let his arm lower before dropping the ray gun to the floor. There he stood, looking upon the dead, broken, smoking remains of his former crewmember.

"Good," the Top Dog said. "For a moment there, I suspected you might do something illogical and ill-advised."

Danger said nothing but shifted his head just enough to glance at the Top Dog out of the corner of his optical sensors.

"Now that we've seen to that, we can tend to the remaining business at hand," the Top Dog continued. "We previously came to an understanding that you would hand an inactive Leroy Brown over to me. That hasn't happened because you and your crew let him escape. That's a mistake that needs to be fixed."

Slowly, Danger turned his head to look at the Top Dog directly.

"That is why you are going to find Leroy Brown for me," the Top Dog said. "Then, you are going to catch him and deliver his inactive body to me yourself. Understood?"

Danger continued to look at the Top Dog in silence.

"Am I correct to assume that I can interpret your silence as a full understanding and acceptance of your new orders?"

Danger continued to stare at the Top Dog in silence.

"Good!" The Top Dog said. "Now go do it."

Slowly, Captain Danger started toward Pentabot's body.

"Ah, ah, ah. No," the Top Dog said. "That piece of junk? That's mine now. Leave it."

Danger stopped, slowly looked between Pentabot's body and the Top Dog, then turned for the door and slowly made his way out of the room to begin the very long journey back to the *Eternal Horizon*.

****

Captain Danger found Commander Echo and half a dozen other crewmembers waiting for him when he returned to the *Eternal Horizon*. A solemn atmosphere hung in the air as he stepped out of the shuttle. Everyone looked at him, then turned inward and waited for Pentabot to join him. It soon became clear no one was there, and their attention shifted back to their Captain.

"Captain Danger," Echo said. "Where's Pentabot?"

Danger looked to his first officer. He glanced back to the shuttle for a moment, and then he tilted his head downward before straightening himself and standing tall.

"His failure..." Danger started. The words hung in the air as he found it in himself to force the rest of the sentence out. "...could not... go unpunished."

Danger and his crew looked at one another for several long moments as they all came to terms with the Captain's words.

"Where is Doctor Clank?" Danger finally said.

"In his lair, I think," Echo answered.

"As you were," Danger said, dismissing the crew with a nod. He turned and made his way to find the mechanic. He passed several crewmembers on his way, each of them with words or questions for their captain. Danger addressed none of them, refusing to say anything nor acknowledge anyone on his way down to Clank's domain.

"Doctor Clank," Danger said once he stepped through the door. Clank turned around and faced the Captain.

"Captain Danger," Clank said. "What can I do for you?"

"When Leroy Brown escaped, he had a small robot with him," Danger said. "You originally laid claim to that robot. Where did you get him from?"

Clank looked at Danger and gave the matter some thought.

"Ah, yes," Clank said. "The one he stole from me. Why do you need to know?"

"We need to find Leroy Brown," Danger said. "Right now, knowing where that robot came from is our best lead."

"Ah," Clank said. "I understand. I can actually do you one better, Captain."

"How so?"

"While he was still in my possession, I took the liberty of installing a tracking device in the little guy. If the two are still together, I can lead you straight to them both."

DENIZEN BROWN

01000.

The sun faded from the sky as Leroy Brown drove his newly acquired spider-mech across the horizon. While the ride was bumpy and uneven, there was no denying it made for a much faster journey. Above all else, the machine cared little for the terrain underneath them. Mountainous, flat, jagged, clear, or covered in junk, the spider-mech traveled across them all with ease. As a result, Leroy and Walter cared little about what lay between them and Rustbucket as they traveled along a straight, direct path.

"I think I may have recollection of the terrain," Walter finally said after they'd been traveling for a while. "Though I cannot say with certainty at these angles, and what I see does not properly align with where we should be."

"Are you saying we're lost?" Leroy asked.

"Not precisely," Walter replied. "I maintain we are getting closer. A minor adjustment to our course may be necessary, but we should find it if we continue onward."

Onward they continued. Leroy weaved an irregular, swerving pattern into their path, and slowly tilted the cockpit back and forth to scan the horizon. At regular intervals, Leroy again asked Walter if he could tell where Rustbucket was supposed to be. While the robot had recollections of the area, the exact positioning continued to elude them. It wasn't until the wee hours of the morning when that finally changed.

"There! Over there!" Walter exclaimed as he bounced in place.

"Where?" Leroy asked.

"There!" Walter said, pointing fervently. "Over there!"

Leroy looked to where the little robot was pointing and focused on it closely. All he saw in the horizon was a series of artificial lights.

"You're sure?" He asked.

"I am positive!" Walter said with an intensified bounce.

Leroy gave a shrug and a nod, then turned the spider-mech toward the lights and pushed full speed ahead. The lights rapidly approached, even as they faded against the ever-brightening sky above. As they came closer and more details developed, Leroy saw a massive cave entrance located at the base of a drop off, with a series of growing hills rolling into the distance behind it. There was a heavy dip to the cave opening, as if it had tried to merge with a poorly conceived and quickly abandoned attempt at a canyon. A loose collection of structures stood around the opening, including a series of platforms that resembled ship docking and several skeletal utility towers for lights, radio antenna, and similar instruments.

"Take it slow," Walter said as they neared the cave. "We do not want to send the wrong message."

Leroy nodded in recognition of what Walter was saying, then turned the spider-mech into a large loop that ended with the machine a few yards out from the exterior construction and the open hatch facing the cave. There, Leroy parked the spider-mech and put it in standby mode. Walter promptly leapt off the control panel and rolled to the exit.

"Hello!" Walter called out from the open hatch. "Hello? This is Walter! I have returned!"

At first, there was no response. Walter looked around, then

focused on the entrance, wondering if something might have gone wrong while he was away. He looked to Leroy when the warbot stepped up behind him, hoping for some insight.

"Walter?" came a voice from within. Both robots looked toward the source. "Is that you?"

"Destructo?" Walter asked. "Are you there?"

"Destructo?" Leroy asked, surprised to hear the name. "You mean Mr. Destructo?"

"You know Mr. Destructo?" Walter asked, looking back up at Leroy.

Out of the cave came half a dozen robots of as many different designs, led by a pair that looked more than ready for a fight. The first resembled the top half of a floating metal skeleton with a pair of oversized guns mounted on its back. The second was a robot Leroy recognized from the Underground Robot Combat League. He was nearly as tall as Leroy himself, with a wider girth. His body was mostly colored in shades of white, but with a wear far beyond anything Leroy had ever seen on him before. Originally built as a deep-space terrestrial explorer, he stood upon a pair of short legs that ended in twin treads designed to rotate and split into longer legs when needed. He had a pair of strong, blunt arms, with shoulders that bore the ridiculously oversized orb pauldrons that were his most noticeable combat additions.

"Mr. Destructo?" Leroy called out. The robot came to a halt when he heard Leroy.

"Leroy Brown," Destructo replied. "At long last he shows his face."

"You kidding?" Leroy said. "I just arrived on this stupid planet.

How did you ever wind up here?"

"What–" Destructo started, but Walter interrupted him.

"Can we please come down?" He asked.

"Fine, yes," Destructo answered. "Park by the docking ramps. And no funny movements, you hear me?"

"I'll try not to break anything," Leroy said.

He returned to the controls and revved up the spider-mech again. With a little coordination from the robots outside, Leroy moved the machine so the hatch lined up with one of the docking ramps. As soon as Leroy brought the mech to a stop again, Walter zoomed out of the machine, even before Leroy had an opportunity to turn it off and lock it down. Exiting at far more leisurely a pace, Leroy followed Walter out and down the docking structure to ground level. While Walter received a warm welcome from more than a dozen robots that had left the cave to greet the little guy, Leroy couldn't help but sense a chill in the air. Alongside the friendlier robots, there were two robots that were clearly military models, each one a variety of walking gun turret.

"Walter, I'm presuming you can vouch for the new arrival?" Destructo asked from the outer edge of Walter's welcoming party.

"I am only here thanks to his assistance," Walter said.

"Good to hear," Destructo said. "Alright then, let's move it inside everyone. I recognize we're all glad to see Walter back, but we've got procedures we need to go through."

While there was no shortage of disappointed expressions, the group broke up and moved into the cave all the same, taking Walter with them.

"That means you too, Leroy," Destructo said, turning to face the robot.

"What kind of 'procedures' are you talking about?" Leroy asked.

"It's standard for all new arrivals. We're not going to take you apart, if that's what you're worried about."

"Walter told me he lived here," Leroy said, pointing after the smaller robot.

"It's also been months since we last saw him, and we have no idea where he's been," Destructo replied. "For sake of procedure, he counts as a new arrival."

"Months?" Leroy asked.

Destructo looked at Leroy and stared at him for several moments.

"What of it?" Destructo asked.

"I'm surprised to see you here at all," Leroy said. "When did they get rid of you?"

"What kind of question is that?"

"How'd you wind up on Junkworld?" Leroy asked.

The two robots stared at each other for several moments more.

"We can talk about it later," Destructo said. "Assuming you stick around. Let's get you inside and we can take care of those procedures."

"I'm currently wary on procedures I know nothing about," Leroy said.

"It's either that or climbing back in the spider-mech and heading back out into the wilds," Destructo said. "But I'd very much prefer it if you were willing to stick around."

Briefly, Leroy looked to the spider-mech and then out away from the cave as he considered the possibility. Even damaged, the mech was still an impressive and dangerous machine. It would have been easy to head back out and search elsewhere for what he wanted.

It didn't take long for him to table the idea, however. Even with his suspicions about whatever "procedures" were required, Mr. Destructo was the first face he'd recognized since he'd arrived on Junkworld. He already trusted Walter, and Walter trusted Destructo, which was enough for Leroy to conclude that whatever the procedures involved, it was probably safe.

And if not, Leroy had little reason to think he couldn't fight his way back out if he needed to.

"Alright then," Leroy said. "Lead the way."

Destructo gave a nod, then led Leroy into the cave. Once inside, Leroy finally had his first proper view of Rustbucket itself. The cave interior was even larger than what the already large entrance hinted at and wove deep into the planet's surface. Along every side were a series of loosely organized buildings bearing a wide assortment of shapes, sizes, and designs. A few of the larger and more important looking buildings had signs, but most he was left to guess at. All of it was interconnected by a vast, carefully organized web of walkways, pipes, conduits, and wires. With just a brief scan of the area, Leroy saw hundreds of robots of nearly as many different designs in various states of repair or lack thereof.

From among them, one robot approached Leroy and Destructo directly. He stood at about half Leroy's own height and wore an array of rags and loose cloth practically stapled together with miscellaneous bits of scrap metal, making it hard to see much underneath. His face was about the only thing truly visible, showing Leroy a screen made up of pixilated cyan lights.

"I'll take it from here," the robot said with a heavily synthesized voice.

"I've got it, Isaac." Destructo replied.

"No, no." Isaac said. "You go attend to your part of the procedures. I've already seen that he brought Walter back to us, I don't think I should have any trouble."

Destructo glanced at Leroy, then turned back to Isaac and nodded before turning and rolling back out of the cave.

"This way, please," Isaac said, continuing into the cave with a walk that was over-emphasized and overly mechanical. Leroy followed without objection.

"So you are the robot we have to thank for Walter's return," Isaac said.

"That sounds right," Leroy replied.

"He said that your name is 'Leroy Brown," Isaac said.

"That also sounds correct," Leroy said. He then changed the subject to a matter he considered more pressing. "May I ask where we're going?"

"Maintenance hall," Isaac said. "Our mechanics will give you a full look over."

"What are they looking for?" Leroy asked.

"Anything that might be a danger to Rustbucket, mostly."

"What counts as dangerous?" Leroy asked.

"They'll know if they see it," Isaac answered.

"Might I inquire how you found yourself here?" Isaac added, similarly shifting the topic.

"Here in Rustbucket or here on Junkworld?"

"Both, I suppose."

"Mistake," Leroy answered. "I don't know how, but the only reason I'm on this planet is by mistake."

"Is that so?" Isaac mused. "Because I've never known anyone to come to Junkworld by mistake. If you're here, you're here because someone sent you here."

"So I've heard," Leroy said with a hint of annoyance.

It was then they came to an elongated building built out of several cargo containers. Stepping inside, Leroy found a segmented room far more put together and organized than most anything he'd seen since arriving in Rustbucket. Isaac led him further inward, where a pair of robots were waiting for them. One looked like a thick metal stick figure wielding an oversized rifle, while the other was tower shaped with an oversized saucer for a head and four tentacular arms positioned at ninety-degree angles.

"Right this way, sir," the tower robot said, his head slowly spinning one way and then the next as the multiple eyes positioned along the outermost ridge of his saucer looked at both Leroy and his immediate surroundings.

"And you are?" Leroy asked.

"I am Yutah," the robot answered. "I shall be conducting your inspection."

"What about him?" Leroy asked, pointing to the stick figure.

"Don't worry about Steek," Isaac said. "He is merely here as a precautionary measure for you and Walter."

Leroy nodded, then slowly followed Yutah further inward while keeping a look out for Walter.

"I can't help but notice that this place is really on edge," Leroy said.

"Rustbucket used to be nicer," Walter said. Leroy soon spotted him in a booth as he passed by, the robot sitting atop a metal table located in the middle of a ring-shaped structure on the floor. "But that was before the Top Dog began to expand his influence."

Leroy stopped to give Walter and the room a close look over, but nothing he saw looked amiss.

"In here, please," Yutah said, arms indicating to the next booth over. Stepping forward, Leroy looked in to see it was much the same as Walter's, minus the metal table.

"So, who's responsible for these 'procedures'?" Leroy asked as he stepped into the booth. Following Yutah's direction, he took position in the middle of the circle.

"They fall under Mr. Destructo's purview," Isaac answered. "He organized them when it was clear things were not likely to improve any time soon."

"So Destructo is in charge of Rustbucket, then?"

"Most in Rustbucket defer to his judgment to keep us safe," Isaac said. "An increasingly difficult task these days, unfortunately."

"And who are you supposed to be?" Leroy asked him.

"Isaac is our leader," Walter said.

"Are you now?" Leroy asked.

"Those in Rustbucket do tend to defer to my judgment, yes," Isaac answered.

Leroy heard a humming noise first from the ground, then from overhead. Looking up, he saw a circle hanging from the ceiling that matched the one on the floor. Looking back down, he noticed a series of energy beams passing over him. When he failed to detect any changes to his body, he concluded they were scanning him.

"So Junkworld was a nicer place before this Top Dog happened?" Leroy asked.

"No, Junkworld has always been a lousy place," Walter said.

"It is sad, but true," Isaac agreed with a nod. "Junkworld has never been an easy place to survive, but we found a way to make it tolerable and endure. But ever since the Top Dog rose to power, he has made things far more difficult. He has been building power, gathering followers, expanding his territory, and all but run a carefully orchestrated conquest of Junkworld itself."

"Nobody's united against him?" Leroy asked.

"Nobody has figured out how," Isaac answered. "Those who occupy Junkworld have never been much for large-scale organization. It's mostly just been individual settlements. There have been those who tried to gather power and expand it from time to time, but they've never had much success. The Top Dog is merely the first to make it work. Talk has been floated regarding an organized counterattack, but he has been quite skilled at dismantling those efforts before they gather any real strength."

"So what happens when he expands out here?" Leroy asked as the scanners ceased operation.

"By all accounts he already has," Isaac answered. "His recognized territory stretches well beyond us."

"And yet he doesn't seem to have any presence here," Leroy noted.

"That is true," Isaac answered. "As far as we can tell, he doesn't even know we exist. We're hoping to keep it that way."

"Trying to stay under the radar?" Leroy asked. Isaac nodded.

"It is a difficult balancing act," he said. "It is not easy to maintain enough strength to protect ourselves while still avoiding the Top Dog's attention."

"You are quite an impressive individual," Yutah said as he rolled around the corner. "Have you been informed that your body is very well maintained?"

"It's been mentioned," Leroy said. "I credit my team."

"You have a team?" Walter asked as he rolled around the corner, coming to a stop next to Isaac.

"Back on New Chicago."

"And how long have you been on Junkworld?" Yutah asked.

"Too long already."

"Could you phrase it in terms of a timescale?"

"One month," Leroy guessed. "Maybe a month and a half."

Yutah gave a series of acknowleding noises, then rolled back around the corner.

"Does that mean I'm done?" He asked.

"Please wait there," Yutah called back.

"So, what of you, Leroy Brown?" Isaac asked. "You said you were here by mistake. What will you do now?"

"I'm going to fix that mistake," Leroy answered. "I'm going to find a way back home."

"Where is that?"

"New Chicago," Leroy answered. "Where my team is, with the Underground Robot Combat League."

"I'm unfamiliar with those things."

"Really?" Leroy asked. "Because Mr. Destructo is part of the same League."

"Is he now?" Isaac asked. He briefly glanced outward before

turning back to Leroy. "Are you sure? He's never said anything of it."

"No mention at all?" Leroy asked.

"No. If it's ever come up, I've yet to hear about it."

"Then you're hearing about it now," Leroy said. "Where did he say he came from?"

"He didn't. He's never said anything about his existence prior to Junkworld. Nobody has ever had reason to pressure him on the matter."

"Leroy Brown, was it?"

Leroy turned to see Yutah standing alongside a bulbous robot with spider legs and an array of manipulator arms.

"Yes?" Leroy asked.

"I am Synnapses, I lead the mechanics department here in Rustbucket," he said. "You are a *Centurion*-class warbot, correct?"

"Yeah," Leroy said. "What about it?"

"Impressive," Synnapses said, while Yutah rolled past him. "Not many machines of war arrive on Junkworld intact and still functional. I hear most of them are properly dismantled first."

"Lucky me," Leroy said with a less than enthusiastic tone.

"You are also of a singular design?"

Leroy stared at Synnapses, then turned to Isaac and Walter.

"What's that supposed to mean?" Leroy asked.

"He is asking if you are a hybrid," Walter answered.

"No, I'm not a hybrid," Leroy answered, turning back to Synnapses. "Modified, but a modified *Centurion*-class."

"Pardon me," Yutah said, then he began to examine Leroy closer, including opening what hatches and panels he had access to.

"Watch it," Leroy said, looking at the robot.

"Don't worry," Yutah said. "I'm not going to break anything."

"I think I'll worry all the same."

"If I might make a request?" Synnapses asked, drawing Leroy's attention back toward him. "Or, alternatively, make an offer?"

"I hope you'll understand if I'm immediately suspicious."

"It is accurate to say you still have your shield system?"

"Yes," Leroy said. "What of it?"

"It's a fascinating design, that." Synnapses said. "Curiously, we believe that we in fact have similar parts saved in storage."

"You have a spare barrier shield system?" Leroy asked with suspicion. "How did you get one of those?"

"Parts for one," Yutah replied. "Not the whole thing, but most of the critical components."

"All manner of machines wind up on Junkworld," Isaac said.

"Indeed," Synnapses said. "The engineering department will go on to no end about all the unusual pieces sent their way. But back to the matter at hand. We were hoping we might be able to borrow your barrier shield system."

"Why?" Leroy asked.

"The engineering and mechanics departments had an experiment we hoped we might be able to run."

"I'm already inclined to say 'no,'" Leroy answered. "Experiment implies risk I'm not interested in subjecting myself or my shield to."

"Are you sure?" Yutah asked. "If we combine the parts we have with yours, we believe we might be able to super-charge the system and–"

"Definite 'no,'" Leroy interrupted. "That sounds like a plan where I lose my shield so you can use it to protect Rustbucket."

"Is that a bad thing?" Walter asked.

"For me it is," Leroy said. "My apologies, but I'm not planning on staying. That doesn't give me much reason to sacrifice my shield for the sake of your town."

"You are not staying?" Walter asked, his eyes showing a surprising level of sadness.

"No," Leroy answered. "One way or another, I'm finding a way off this planet and back to the URCL."

"And what if you can't?" Isaac asked.

Leroy ignored the question and turned back to Yutah.

"You almost done?" He asked.

"Yes, I believe so," Yutah answered, then he rolled back. "For now, at least."

"For now?" Leroy asked.

"We'll be sure to let you know if there's anything else we need," Synnapses answered.

Leroy waved the two robots off and stepped out of the ring.

"I assume you don't know where I could find a spaceship, then," Leroy said, looking down at Isaac.

"Not that would be of any use," Isaac answered.

"Because you don't have a reason to leave or because it doesn't work?"

"There are countless starship parts scattered across the planet," Isaac answered. "But none of them are intact and functional."

"Sounds like a start all the same," Leroy said. He then stepped out of the booth and made for the exit with Walter trailing close behind. After he left the building, he stopped and noticed a small caravan carrying the robots that had been dumped in the spider-mech. He stepped aside to let them continue into the maintenance hall.

"Leroy," Mr. Destructo said, approaching from the tail end of the group. "Would you care to explain those?"

"They tried to break me and Walter," Leroy explained. "Two of them were the owners of the machine you pulled them out of before I hijacked it."

"It is true," Walter said. "I do not think they were very nice."

"And yet you insisted on bringing them along all the same," Leroy said to Walter.

"Duly noted," Destructo said.

"Is rummaging through people's stuff a normal part of your procedures?" Leroy asked.

"Yes," Destructo answered. "Though you did just admit to hijacking that thing, so whether it's truly yours is debatable. Do you even know what it's carrying around?"

"Does it have any spaceship parts in it?" Leroy asked.

"Why do you care about spaceship parts?"

"If I can't find a spaceship, I'm going to build one."

Destructo looked at Leroy for a moment with a confused tilt of the head.

"What are you going to use a spaceship for?" Destructo asked.

"How else am I going to leave this dump of a planet?" Leroy answered.

"Where are you planning to go?"

"He wants to go back to New Chicago," Walter answered.

Destructo looked to Walter, then back to Leroy.

"You want to go back to the URCL." Destructo said.

"My last fight made me the undefeated champion," Leroy said. "Of course I want to go back to the URCL. I don't know what mistake brought me here, but I can only imagine how terrible my team must feel right now not knowing where I am."

Destructo stared at Leroy once more, again with a head tilt that told Leroy something was off.

"Is that the last thing you remember?" Destructo asked. "Before you came to Junkworld?"

"Close to it," Leroy answered. "There were congratulations, they talked about big plans for the future, then they shut me down for maintenance. Next thing I know, I power up to find I'm in pieces on an unknown planet."

"You were in pieces?"

"Was," Leroy answered. "Walter helped."

Leroy gave a nod of the head to the little robot, who looked up and waved his arm happily. Destructo glanced down at him, then turned back to Leroy.

"You're acting dysfunctional," Leroy said.

"Am I?" Destructo asked.

"You're acting like something's wrong; I know that much."

Destructo looked out the cave entrance, then back to Leroy.

"So your current plan is to acquire a spaceship and fly to New Chicago so you can rejoin the URCL," Destructo said.

"Yes, Destructo," Leroy said, a hint of annoyance creeping into his voice. "I think we've firmly established that. Why are you acting so weird about all this? Does it have to do with why they got rid of you?"

"Don't worry about it," Destructo said, putting a hand on Leroy's shoulder.

"Am I still free to leave if I want?" Leroy asked.

"I'd still prefer it if we could convince you to stick around, but no, we're not going to force you to stay."

"Can I have the spider-mech back when you're done with it, or are you going to requisition it for Rustbucket?"

"We'll let you have it back," Destructo said. "We're almost done with it, but if you'd give us the opportunity, we can probably repair the damage to it as well."

"That would be appreciated," Leroy answered.

"Consider it a 'thank you' for bringing back Walter," Destructo said. The tings of metal bumping against metal sounded as he gave Leroy a couple brief pats on the shoulder.

"Thank you, then." Leroy said. "How long do you expect that to take?"

"We'll let you know when we're done," Destructo said.

"In the meantime, I can show you around!" Walter said.

"Sure, why not," Leroy said. "Maybe someone around here will know something about a spaceship after all."

01001.

It was with an abundance of energy that Walter showed Leroy Brown every corner of Rustbucket he was allowed to. He started by showing Leroy around the outer regions, where he pointed out all the important locations and introduced him to everyone that would let him. By the time Walter was ready to show him deeper into the settlement, Leroy was certain he already knew half the robots living there. To his disappointment, but not his surprise, not a one of them knew a thing about any spaceships.

Deeper into the cave was the "industrial region", which included workshops, engineering bays, central power, and other such areas. For as small a community as Rustbucket was, Leroy found himself surprised at how well set up their production and repair facilities were, allowing their engineering teams to take all manner of junk and spare parts and put it back to use with impressive levels of efficiency. Rustbucket's power source left Leroy similarly impressed. As he learned, the cave was linked to a dormant volcano, likely part of an ancient magma shaft. Craftily, someone in Rustbucket had devised a means to exploit this to use the volcanic rock not just to aid with their industrial work, but also to provide them with a valuable source of geothermal power.

"I must admit, it's a nice settlement you have here," Leroy said as he and Walter stood atop a bridge overlooking both the outer areas of Rustbucket and the outermost section of the industrial region.

"Nice enough to stay?" Walter asked.

Leroy looked down to Walter, then back out.

"Is that all this was?" he asked. "You were just trying to sell me on staying?"

"No, not entirely," Walter replied. "But did it work?"

"Yes and no," Leroy answered. "I'm not planning to move in if that's what you're hoping for. But I am wondering if it might be possible to get a spaceship here after all."

"We do not have any spaceships here," Walter said.

"Not yet, you don't."

"Where are you expecting Rustbucket to get a spaceship?"

"I'm going to get them to build one."

"And how do you expect to get Rustbucket to build you a spaceship?" Mr. Destructo asked.

Leroy turned to see the robot approaching from across the bridge.

"I'm not," Leroy answered. "I'm going to convince Rustbucket to build themselves a spaceship."

"Why do you expect Rustbucket to build itself a spaceship?" Destructo asked.

"I see no reason for them not to. Your leader tells me this planet is in rotten shape as it is and getting worse. Why not build a ship and leave it all behind?"

"Where do you expect them to go?"

"It's a big galaxy," Leroy answered. "I'm sure you'll find a planet after you drop me off on New Chicago. Assuming you don't want to come with me."

"That's not an option, Leroy."

"Why not? What happened? I'm shocked I didn't hear anything.

Last I heard you were still a big deal in the League. A headline fighter and everything. Why did they get rid of you?"

Mr. Destructo looked at Leroy for a moment, then turned toward the cave opening.

"They didn't have a choice," he answered.

"What does that even mean?" Leroy asked. He glanced to Walter to see if he had anything to say, but the small robot remained silent.

"From what I was told, you haven't told anybody here where you came from, who you used to be," Leroy said. "Just what happened to you, Destructo?"

"I should ask the same thing of you," Destructo said.

"I already told you," Leroy said. "The other night, I won the fight against Chainsaw Freddy. The next thing I know, I wake up on this rotten excuse for a planet in pieces with no idea where I am or why I'm here. Then I killed a Scrapwyrm, and then I learn that this Top Dog wants me handed over to him for some reason, and the next thing I know I find myself running across the wasteland with no idea where I'm going. If I didn't have Walter with me, I'd still probably be running around aimlessly out there."

"You've met the Top Dog?" Destructo asked.

"No, not directly," Leroy answered. "But apparently he knows who I am."

"Why do you think he wanted you?"

"I have no idea. Isaac tells me he's conquering the planet, so maybe he thinks I'm a threat, or maybe he wants to recruit me. Your guess is as good as mine. But what I do know is that he might be building spaceships."

"He is?"

"Yes. And if he's building spaceships, I say that Rustbucket should do the same."

"You really think they'll agree to it?" Destructo asked, waving his hand out to the robots below.

"I think I need to try," Leroy replied. He then turned and walked off to work towards exactly that.

Over the course of the next day, Leroy attempted to recruit the inhabitants of Rustbucket to that very goal. The results were mixed at best. Few rejected or protested the idea outright. A handful of robots agreed with him and quickly joined in Leroy's enthusiasm for the project. Most either didn't care or failed to comprehend the idea. In time, it became clear that while Leroy's goal wasn't unattainable, it would be a long and difficult road to accomplish.

Yet before he could truly push forward with the plan, another matter interrupted his efforts. While he was in the middle of discussing how to proceed with those who were already on board, the group was interrupted by Steek.

"Destructo needs to see you," the robot said.

"What about?" Leroy asked.

"We have a situation."

"Am I in trouble?"

"That remains to be seen."

Without further question, Leroy relented, dismissed the group, and then let Steek show him the way. The robot led him up lifts and stairs and across pathways leading him to a circular room overlooking most of the outer region of Rustbucket. Inside, he found a small assembly of robots, including Mr. Destructo and Isaac.

"What's the problem?" Leroy asked.

"We need to know everywhere you've been since you arrived on Junkworld," Destructo said.

"I've already told you my story twice now," Leroy said. "How many times do I need to recite it?"

"You've given a brief overview a couple of time," Destructo said. "We need to hear the full version."

"Why? What's wrong?"

"Please, if you could just tell us?" Isaac asked.

"Fine," Leroy relented.

He then gave them a full summery of the events leading to his arrival at Rustbucket, starting with his activation aboard the *Eternal Horizon*. He gave them a brief overview of his initial efforts to put himself together, how he'd met Walter, and how the two had helped each other after the Scrapwyrm attack. He told them how he had killed the Scrapwyrm and originally earned the good graces of the crew and its captain as result, his discussions with Captain Danger, and his time aboard the scraptrawler. He told them what he knew of Danger's visit to the Top Dog and how afterword it had been Danger's intent to hand him over, but how he'd escaped with Walter instead. He finished with a quick summary of his time out in the wilderness after his escape from the *Horizon*, and the subsequent journey before arriving at Rustbucket.

There were several moments during his story Leroy could tell the others wanted to interject or ask questions, but Isaac kept everyone quiet and on topic. This ensured nobody said anything until Leroy was finished talking and they could tell he had nothing else to say.

"His story lines up with Walter's, at least," Destructo said.

"This was an interrogation?" Leroy asked.

"In a manner of speaking, I suppose," Isaac said.

"Why?" Leroy asked. "What's wrong? You don't trust me?"

"They discovered a tracking device in Walter," Destructo answered. "It's been removed, and he otherwise registers as operating as intended. But…"

"But it's still a tracking device," Leroy said, finishing Destructo's thought. "Meaning we led someone here."

"Exactly," Destructo said. "And since the Top Dog wants you so badly, it's only a matter of time before he sends someone to retrieve you."

"Do you still have the tracking device?"

"No," Destructo answered. "We destroyed it."

"Why did you do that?"

"Why wouldn't we destroy it?"

"We could have used it," Leroy explained. "I could have taken it with me and led the signal away from here."

"For a warbot, that's a rather naïve idea," Destructo said. "You've already been here too long. Even if the device was linked to you rather than Walter, someone is going to be coming here. That means Rustbucket's cover is blown."

As soon as Destructo finished speaking, the door opened and a robot stepped through.

"Destructo, we just had a shuttle fly overhead," the robot said. Everyone turned and looked at him. "It flew in, circled overhead a few times, and then flew back the way it came."

Everyone turned and looked to Destructo.

"Thank you, Tejax," Destructo said. "Dismissed."

Tejax nodded, then left the room.

"So what's the plan?" Leroy asked.

"That remains to be seen," Isaac said.

"Steek, have everyone assemble," Destructo told the robot. "And make sure they keep it orderly."

Steek nodded, then left the room. Most of the others followed, leaving Leroy alone with Isaac and Mr. Destructo.

"What's everyone assembling for?" Leroy asked.

"Rustbucket needs to decide what to do next," Destructo answered. "Officially, nobody is in a position to order them to do anything. So, they need to make a group decision."

"That sounds a little unwieldy, given the circumstances," Leroy said.

"You're not wrong," Destructo admitted. "But it's been like that since before I arrived."

"It's less complicated than it sounds," Isaac explained. "It mostly boils down to a choice between two options. Will they evacuate, or will they stay and fight?"

"Credit for not naming 'surrender' as an option," Leroy said.

"Surrender isn't a viable option," Destructo replied. "For most of these robots, surrender would be akin to suicide anyway."

"What's the plan for each option?" Leroy asked.

"Normally, I'd advocate evacuation," Destructo said. "We'd gather together everyone willing to leave, take what we could with us, and start marching as a group to escape the Top Dog's territory. However, given recent developments, fighting might actually be a viable option."

"Is that so?" Isaac asked. His screen shifted to display a crude question mark.

"What recent development is that?" Leroy asked.

Destructo lifted his hand, pointed his finger out, and pressed it against Leroy's chest.

"You," he said.

"I appreciate the vote of confidence," Leroy said. "What's your plan?"

"It's a long shot, but hear me out on this," Destructo said. "The Top Dog knows you're here, and he wants you, Leroy. We can use that to draw him out. He's either going to come for you himself, or he'll send a team to capture you. If he comes himself, we can assassinate him when he arrives. If he sends a team, we can hijack whatever they send to retrieve you, and use that to sneak into his fortress. It may be our best bet to actually destroy the Top Dog."

"No," Leroy said.

"No?" Destructo asked.

"I recognize where you're coming from," Leroy replied. "But no. Tactically and strategically speaking, it's a terrible plan. There are far too many unknowns and variables. You said it yourself, that plan is a long shot. And I agree with you on that. It's more likely to just get everyone destroyed."

"I agree that fighting is the better option," Leroy continued. "But there's a better option."

"What's that?" Destructo asked.

"This cave," Leroy said. "It's a natural tactical advantage. We can use that."

"You're implying we take on the Top Dog's army directly."

"Not exactly. But yes."

"I don't think you understand what we have to work with, Leroy," Destructo said. "We have a total of six robots here dedicated to security. Seven, if we include you. Aside from you, only two of them were designed for war, and they amount to big, intelligent, walking guns. We have a handful of vehicles we use for collecting junk from the wasteland, and they have limited arms intended for defense. The closest things we have to heavy military support are Humbug and that walking tank you came here in. We have only a few spare weapons with which to equip a handful of citizens, aside from a handful that have built in weapons of their own."

"It's a start," Leroy said.

"A start?" Destructo asked.

"We can build from there."

"You're talking about taking on the Top Dog's entire army," Destructo said. "Our security is mostly to keep the peace, to fend off any raiders trying to pick a fight, or provide escort in case of evacuation. There is a reason our primary strategies have been to avoid detection and prepare for evacuation if that fails."

"If that's all you have to go on, then you should have evacuated long ago."

"Surprise, surprise. Sometimes individuals like to hold onto what they have. I would think you'd understand, given your own situation."

"That…is a valid point," Leroy admitted. "And it sounds like all the more reason to stay and fight."

"How?" Destructo asked. "On what grounds do you expect to take what we have and stand up to what the Top Dog throws at us?"

"I'll have an answer for you soon," Leroy said. He then walked past Mr. Destructo and out of the room. Without delay, he marched over to the maintenance hall with speed that came just shy of an outright run. There, he quickly located Synnapses, who was franticly at work alongside a handful of other robots.

"You said you wanted to do an experiment with my shield system," Leroy said.

Synnapses and the others stopped what they were doing and looked at Leroy. A few moments passed before anyone spoke, as their processors caught up with what was happening.

"Yes, we did discuss that," Synnapses said. "Did you change your mind?"

"Could you use those parts to upgrade my shield system?" Leroy asked.

There was some initial hesitation, with the robots glancing to each other.

"Technically speaking, it should be possible," one robot said with a higher-pitched, feminine voice. The basic humanoid female frame of her body showed signs of age and was heavy with mismatched retrofitting, including two extra pairs of arms on her back and an additional pair on her sides.

"Technically speaking, yes," Synnapses said. "Whether it's a wise idea is another question entirely."

"Have you heard that Rustbucket has been compromised?" Leroy asked.

"We have," Synnapses said. "We were preparing to gather with the others."

"Let me put it this way, then," Leroy said. "It's my understanding that this place has two real options – evacuate or fight. Neither one benefits from removing my shield and using it for whatever project you had in mind. If you evacuate, it's not going to do you much good out there. If you fight, it's only going to last so long before they pound through it anyway."

<How is using our parts to upgrade you any better?> Asked another, shorter robot that looked like a yellow and white trashcan on wheels. His words came in a mechanical language of beeps, whistles, and other digital noises.

"Because I'll be able to carry it, and I already know how to use it. And if we fight, I'll be able to use it not just defensively, but I know how to use it as an offensive weapon as well. That's exactly what Rustbucket is going to need."

The mechanics shared glances, and then Synnapses turned to Leroy.

"If you'll excuse us, we need to confer on the matter," he said. Leroy gave a subtle nod and wave, signaling for them to do just that.

As a group, the robots turned and stepped further into the maintenance hall to discuss the situation among themselves. Leroy waited as they debated the matter in their small circle, doing his best not to eavesdrop or in any way suggest that they hurry up. After a few minutes of discussion, the group turned back to Leroy and Synnapses approached him.

"You promise this isn't a ploy to steal our parts before you run off on us?" he asked.

"Believe me, I have a lot more interest in keeping this place alive," Leroy answered.

"Then let's get started."

****

A few hours after news first broke of Rustbucket's discovery, nearly everyone in the settlement gathered in the outer region. They centered around a building located near the middle, one with a reinforced roof that allowed it to double as a speaking platform. Atop it stood Isaac, who was flanked by Mr. Destructo on one side and Steek on the other. Behind him was a stout robot built around a large metal ball named Ozochki, who served as the leader of Rustbucket's engineering department.

"EVERBODY! LISTEN UP!" Destructo shouted. The words echoed through the cave and commanded everyone's attention, ensuring they were focused on a single point and quiet enough to allow a single robot to be heard by everyone present. Then, Destructo rolled back several inches, allowing Isaac to take center stage. Isaac stepped forward with an exclamation point showing on his screen.

"As you have all been informed, Rustbucket's location has been compromised," Isaac began. "Agents of the Top Dog have learned where we are. They are almost certainly on their way as we speak. It now falls upon you to decide how we will proceed. Previous discussion and planning for this very moment presents two primary options. We can either evacuate, or stay and fight. Each option comes with its own benefits and challenges. This is not a decision to be made lightly."

"Whichever option you choose, our security team will support you," Destructo said. "However, we cannot support both options. If most want to evacuate, we will go with them. Anyone who wants to stay behind will be free to do so, but we will not be able to protect them. Likewise, if you choose to stay, we will stay here with you. Anyone who chooses to leave will still be free to do so, but they will be on their own."

Destructo let the words hang in the air and looked across the crowd before speaking again.

"However, while we will do everything in our power to protect you if you stay, it must be remembered that there are only so many of us capable of fighting. We also know the Top Dog has a powerful army of his own, and he will almost certainly hit us with as much as he has to in order to ensure he can lay claim to Rustbucket. We are well within his territory, and he does not take kindly to robots who do not respect his authority."

"If we evacuate, and we leave as soon as possible, we can still escape his notice," Destructo continued. "He knows where Rustbucket is, but right now, he knows nothing about it or where we would be going. We can still escape his territory, find a new location, and rebuild."

"I'm not going to lie to you by saying evacuation will be easy. It will be hard to leave, we will have to leave a lot behind, the journey will be dangerous, and it will be a challenge to establish a new home. But I do not see staying and fighting as a viable alternative. My calculations tell me that if we stay, the Top Dog will win. As difficult as it may be, I calculate that evacuation is the only path we have for survival."

Once he finished speaking, Destructo rolled back. Isaac then stepped forward again and prepared to speak, but a voice shouted out from the crowd before he did.

"If I may provide a counter argument!"

Destructo looked out to the crowd and saw Leroy Brown

navigating his way to the central platform.

"*Officially* speaking, I don't have the ability to stop you," Destructo replied with a subdued voice.

Once Leroy reached the building, he tossed Walter on top and then climbed up himself.

"Hello everyone!" Leroy said, taking stock first of the platform, then of the crowd. He raised an arm up into the air and waved it to ensure he had everyone's attention.

"I'm Leroy Brown!" He began. "I'm new here, and most of you probably know me as 'that crazy robot that wants to build a spaceship'. That's not why I'm here right now; I'm not going to tell you that building a spaceship will solve your problems. But I will tell you this is a fight we can win."

"Out there is no safer than in here," Leroy added, briefly pointing out of the cave. "I've been out there, and it is not a friendly place. But beyond that, what you have here is a position made for defense. You have natural defenses on three sides and above, meaning we know exactly where everything is going to come from. You're not going to find a better position to defend than that."

"I also know this is a fight we can win because I'm going to help you win it. Winning is what I do. I am a certified warbot. I was designed and built from the ground up for exactly this – fighting and winning. I am the reigning undefeated champion of the Underground Robot Combat League. And one of the first things I did after I got here was kill a Scrapwyrm."

"You lie!" shouted a voice from the crowd.

"No. It's true." Leroy said, pointing in the general direction of the voice. "You don't believe me, ask Walter here."

"It's true!" Walter said. "I was there! I saw it myself!"

"So you can go on the run if you want." Leroy said. "Just know that if you run now, you're going to have to keep running, because it's only a matter of time before you're going to have to pick up and move again. Until someone punches the Top Dog in his stupid face, he's just going to keep expanding, and then one day you're going to run out of room to keep running and have to ask yourself what other options you have left."

Leroy looked across the crowd, then gave a glance to Isaac and Destructo. Isaac betrayed nothing about what he was thinking, though Destructo's movements signaled a sense of unease.

"That's why I, for one, am going to stay right here," Leroy continued. "I am going to defend Rustbucket from whatever the Top Dog sends this way, and I am going to win. You can take your chances out there if you want, but I intend to stay right here and keep fighting until I have the opportunity to punch the Top Dog right in his stupid face."

Once he was done speaking, Leroy walked to the edge of the platform and leapt back to the ground. He then stepped back into the crowd and walked back the way he'd come.

****

"You got what you wanted."

Leroy looked out from where he sat inside the spider-mech's head to see Mr. Destructo standing in the open hatchway.

"They decided to stay," Destructo continued. "Most of them. They're willing to take a chance on you. They're trusting you to lead them to victory."

"How many are leaving?" Leroy asked as Destructo rolled into the cockpit and squatted next to the empty seat.

"Roughly a dozen," Destructo answered. "The security team and I will be staying, as promised."

"Good to hear," Leroy said. "Any help is welcome."

"Says the robot who talked like he can fight the Top Dog's entire army all by himself," Destructo said. He looked out the mech's windshield, then back at Leroy.

"Leroy, why are you doing this?" He asked.

"What?" Leroy asked. "Defending Rustbucket?"

"Telling these robots this is a fight they can win," Destructo replied. "You disregarded my plan because you said it had too many variables. Do you even know what kind of forces the Top Dog has?"

"We'll find out soon enough," Leroy said. "But whatever he has, Rustbucket is as defensible a position as they're going to find. Unless someone else steps up, these robots are going to have to fight him eventually. That's how conquerors work. They keep conquering until there's nothing left to conquer."

"Why are you so invested in this?" Destructo asked. "Before you knew he was coming you were set on leaving Junkworld and now you're all but ready to defend Rustbucket to the bitter end."

"It's still about the spaceship," Leroy admitted. "Right now, I know two potential ways to get one. The first option is I convince the robots here to build one for me. The second is that I get one from the Top Dog, assuming he really is building them. He wants me for reasons that can't be good, and both effectively require I destroy him to get what I want."

"You're doing all this for a spaceship?" Destructo asked with a hint of disbelief.

"Yes," Leroy answered. "You should be thankful for that. It's a victory for both sides anyway. Rustbucket doesn't have to worry about the Top Dog anymore, and I get the spaceship I want so I can go back to New Chicago."

Slowly, Mr. Destructo turned to look back out the mech's windshield again.

"Alright then, Mr. Warbot," he said. "You're supposed to be the expert here. What do we do next?"

"We put together a plan."

01010.

Dawn made its presence known across the horizon as the sun slowly began its journey into the sky. Backlit by the celestial sphere illuminating the surface of Junkworld, a large vessel trekked forth with a singular purpose and destination. As it drove ever closer to the cave that held the settlement of Rustbucket, its shape revealed it to be a junktrawler. While the lookouts couldn't say with all certainty why it approached, circumstances dictated they consider it hostile until they could confirm its intentions were otherwise.

"I'll go give them the update," Steek said.

Cannon Man briefly lowered his telespectacles and glanced after Steek as the thin robot headed inside to let Destructo, Leroy, and the others know of the vessel's approach. Turning back away from Rustbucket, Cannon stayed low to the ground and resumed observation of the approaching vessel. It continued on a path leading directly to Rustbucket, but fortunately, it refrained from showing any signs of outright hostility. Whether that heralded a good omen or not remained to be seen.

A couple minutes after Steek entered the cave, he returned with Leroy and Mr. Destructo in tow. Surprisingly, Walter was there as well, rolling close behind Leroy's footsteps.

"You really shouldn't be out here," Leroy said to Walter.

"Why not?" Walter asked. "Next to you is the safest place to be right now."

"That's not how it works, Walter," He came to a stop and

turned to face the robot directly. "I appreciate the sentiment, but no. You stay too close to me, you're going to get in my way and endanger everyone."

Walter lowered his head dejectedly as he let out a disappointed noise, and then turned and rolled back inside. The matter dealt with, Leroy turned and finished walking out of the cave.

"Where is it?" Destructo asked.

"There," Cannon said, pointing out towards the vehicle. Destructo zoomed in with his receptors to take a closer look.

"You recognize it, Leroy?" He asked.

"Affirmative," Leroy confirmed after he concentrated on the vessel a bit. "That looks like the *Horizon*, all right."

"Steek, Cannon, head back in and get it ready," Destructo said.

The two robots nodded in the affirmative and returned to the cave while Mr. Destructo and Leroy Brown watched the *Eternal Horizon*'s approach.

****

"Looks like you came through, Doctor," Captain Danger said.

The Captain lowered his high-tech spyglass and turned to Doctor Clank, who stood next to him atop the highest levels of the *Eternal Horizon*.

"And you doubted me," Clank replied, to which Danger gave a nod.

"Consider yourself dismissed," Danger said. Clank gave a half-hearted salute and turned to leave.

Danger looked back toward the horizon and peered through

the spyglass once more. It was difficult to make out what he saw at first. The cave certainly looked large enough to hide all manner of nasty surprises, and the docking structures around it suggested here was a settlement or outpost hidden within. Yet he spotted no overt signs of actual defenses, save for the handful of robots walking in and out of the cave. At present, the only two he could see were Leroy Brown himself and another robot of a far more rotund design.

It was not the worst scene Captain Danger could have imagined finding, but the obscure nature of the situation left him with a sense of uneasiness. Putting away the spyglass, Danger retreated from the top of the *Horizon* and made his way to the bridge.

"What's our move, Captain?" Commander Echo asked.

Danger didn't answer at first, instead returning his focus out to the cave. After staring at it for a few moments, he turned to Echo.

"Keep a distance," Danger said. "Close enough to walk, but far enough it doesn't look like we're trying to threaten them."

Wexxler, the lead pilot on duty, gave a nod and made the proper adjustments to their course.

"Zon," Danger said. A long robot with a centipedic build and a large, rounded head turned to the Captain. "Bring out Bonez."

"You're sending in Bonez?"

"I'm taking him with me," Danger said. "With any luck, we can settle this matter without a fight. But if not, I'll need someone down there to watch my back."

"You're going down there?" Echo asked.

Danger turned and faced his first officer.

"I owe it to Leroy to face him directly," Danger said.

"Are you certain about that?" Echo asked.

Danger looked at Echo a moment, then turned and made for the door.

"Have Bonez meet me on deck," he said, then he left the bridge.

With a slow series of footsteps, Danger walked down to the main deck, then along the railing. As he advanced along the *Horizon*, he kept his visual sensors pointed in the direction of the cave. The vessel turned into a semi-circle, finally coming to a stop when it was in parallel with the mountainous surface the cave dug into. The ship's crew scurried about with their duties, including preparing the six cannons with line of sight to the cave opening.

"Bring the lift!" Danger shouted as he neared the end of his walk.

The Captain stood by the ships railing waiting for both the lift and Bonez. During his wait, he looked down at the cave and the two robots still standing there patiently, betraying nothing about their intentions. Before long, the crew finished setting up the exterior lift, and Danger was joined by the large, hulking form that was Bonez. Together, the two rode down to the surface, then began their walk to the cave. As they came closer, he watched the round robot reach up to the spheres on its shoulders, latch on, then pull them off, giving the appearance of wearing large, metal boxing gloves. Danger finally came to a stop several yards out from Leroy and the round robot. Bonez stopped close behind him.

"Leroy Brown," Danger said. "I need you to come with me."

"That's not going to happen," Leroy replied.

"Please don't make this difficult, Leroy. I don't want to fight you over this."

"And I don't want to be shut down so I can be shipped off to the Top Dog on his terms. But I guess one of us isn't getting what we want."

"Leroy, I am trying to be nice about this," Danger said. "If I had a choice, I wouldn't be here at all."

"Then how about you make that choice, turn around, and leave," Leroy said, pointing back out into the distance.

"I can't. The Top Dog won't allow it."

"That's not my problem," Leroy said.

"It is your problem, Leroy," Danger said. "I don't know who else is in that cave with you, but it'll be their problem, too. Come with me now, without a fight, and we can keep this between you and the Top Dog. He doesn't have to know about this place."

"That's not how it works," the robot next to Leroy said. "The Top Dog isn't going to stop with Leroy. When you bring him back, the Top Dog is going to ask where you found him. Or he'll just pull the information out of Leroy's head. He might even do both."

Danger looked to the robot, then pointed to him.

"Friend of yours?" He asked Leroy.

"Mr. Destructo," Leroy answered. "He's in charge of security here."

Danger nodded in acknowledgement.

"I don't want to fight you and whatever's in that cave, but I will if I have to," Danger said.

"You're right," Leroy replied. "You don't want to fight what we have in there."

"If you're trying to find a peaceful option, you're not going to find it here," Mr. Destructo said. "You've already made the Top Dog's position clear, and I know full well that means you're in no position to offer us a peaceful solution to all this."

"You're familiar with the Top Dog?" Danger asked.

"I am," Destructo answered.

"Then you know the situation I'm in," Danger said. "If Leroy doesn't come peacefully, I'll have to use force."

"As will everyone else the Top Dog sends after we defeat you," Destructo said. "I also know that violence and force are how he operates. Even if we did hand Leroy over, it wouldn't help us. The Top Dog will come for us all the same."

Danger looked from Destructo to Leroy. He then turned and looked back at the *Horizon* before looking back at the two robots standing before him.

"It appears we are at an impasse, then," Danger said.

"You could just go back to the *Horizon* and leave," Leroy said.

"The Top Dog wouldn't stand for it." Danger replied.

"Leave him too," Leroy said. "Just drive off and keep going till he can't get you anymore."

"If only it were that simple."

"That would be nice, wouldn't it?"

Danger looked at Leroy for several moments, then let his head hang loose.

"I'm sorry, Leroy," Danger said, then he lifted his head up. "I didn't want this."

"You can apologize all you want, but it's not going to fix the situation," Leroy said.

Danger nodded, then he swiveled to face the *Horizon*.

"You're right, Leroy," He said as he started to walk back to the vessel. "You're absolutely right."

After taking several steps, Danger noticed that Bonez wasn't moving and came to a sudden stop. He stepped over to the large hulk of a robot, gave him a few knocks on the arm, then signaled to him.

"Come on," he said. Slowly, Bonez turned to follow, and the two began their walk back to the *Eternal Horizon*. Glancing over his shoulder, Danger noticed Leroy and Destructo likewise returning to the cave. He shook his head remorsefully before turning forward again. He was nearly halfway back to his vessel when he heard a loud mechanical nose from behind him, followed soon after by a commotion slowly erupting across the *Horizon*. Turning back, he was left stalled for a moment by what he saw. It was a massive walker, built to resemble a giant metal spider, and riding on its head was Leroy Brown.

Before Captain Danger could react to the situation, the spider-walker opened fire, shooting a beam of blue ionic energy at the *Horizon*. The bolt of energy rushed across the sky at rapid speed until it collided with its target and disabled one of the cannons. Danger let out a loud beep and ran for the vessel as fast as he could, but stopped short when he realized that Bonez was running toward the spider-walker instead. Danger took a few steps to follow the crewman as he considered chasing after him, but quickly changed his mind and decided it was likely a lost cause. Instead, he resumed running to the *Horizon* as fast as he could. As he rushed across the terrain, more shots flew overhead, both from the spider-walker and from the *Horizon* as it finally returned fire.

****

The alpha strike went as well as Leroy could have hoped. Shots from the spider-mech took out two of the Horizon's cannons before its crew had a chance to respond. A third was neutralized just before the first salvo of return fire flew in the spider-mech's direction.

"Hold fire!" Leroy shouted when he saw the scraptrawler's cannons firing. He then immediately activated his barrier shield and projected it ahead of the spider-mech. The energy field materialized directly in front of the blasts, intercepting the explosive bursts to disperse them harmlessly. While the collisions pushed Leroy back across the spider-mech's head, the shield held strong. There was a noticeable pause after the first round of weapons fire was blocked, prompting Leroy to deactivate the shield again.

"Return fire!" He shouted. "Return fire!"

The drivers inside the spider-mech did just that, knocking out a fourth cannon before the *Horizon* opened fire again. Once again, Leroy commanded the drivers to hold fire and reactivated his shield. The energy barrier went up just in time to intercept the latest shots from the enemy vessel.

"Advance! Advance!" Leroy shouted. The shield still up and the cannon fire coming up short, the spider-mech marched forward toward the *Horizon*.

****

Despite his initial misgivings, Mr. Destructo had to admit Leroy's plan was working. Leroy's shield was holding strong, and while the enemy vessel momentarily held the upper hand as it continued to fire on the spider-mech, it was a tenuous position. If Leroy and the mech's crew didn't make any mistakes, Destructo expected victory would come shortly.

Then, he spotted a problem. Rushing toward them was the hulking robot that had accompanied Captain Danger. Destructo didn't know what the robot was planning, but he could tell that the thing would become a problem if he wasn't dealt with.

"Turrex, cover me!" Destructo shouted.

Destructo rolled forward at top speed with the walking laser turret scrambling after him as fast as he could. The enemy hulk reached his target first, leaping onto the nearest spider-mech leg as soon as he was able, and then climbing it as soon as he'd grabbed hold. Destructo continued to rush forward and deployed a series of energy spikes on his pauldron fists. Then, with a smooth series of well-rehearsed motions, he transitioned his treads into four legs and leapt into the air. When he reached the apex of his jump, he launched one of his spiked fists at the enemy robot. Dragging a gravity cord behind it, the large metal projectile collided with its target while he was in the middle of an upward motion, knocking the robot off-kilter.

The robot flailed his arms around and barely grabbed hold of the leg again. Destructo didn't allow him opportunity to recover. The moment he touched down, he took a handful of steps and leapt back into the air. His upper body spun around in a circle, bringing his other fist down on the enemy's head in a fearsome blow. Both robots came down to the ground, with Destructo shifting his legs back so that he landed on dual treads while his opponent hit the ground in an uncoordinated heap.

Destructo immediately continued his assault. He charged forward again with both pauldron fists latched onto their respective forearms once more. As soon as the enemy lifted his head, he was rewarded with a round, spiky hunk of metal slamming into his face at hundreds of miles per hour. The blow knocked the robot several yards backward through the air. Dozens of pieces of loose, broken metal flew free from the brute's face, flying through the air in just as many directions before landing in an uncoordinated pattern around the very wounded form of their owner.

One, then two laser blasts flew past Mr. Destructo, missing by feet and inches. Destructo rolled back and aside to avoid becoming a moving target, while Turrex advanced to return fire. The enemy hulk took advantage of the break in Destructo's assault to pick himself up and seize the initiative. While his face was very much broken, enough of it remained to let him know exactly what he was doing. He lunged at Destructo, swinging at him with all his might. Destructo dodged and weaved before striking the foe with a blow to the side. He rolled backward when the robot rotated, dodging the immediate counterattack.

The robot continued his assault, and Destructo continued to dodge the attacks as the legs of the spider-mech stomped around them. With each swing, Destructo rolled and spun out of the way, striking back whenever the opportunity presented itself. With each blow, the enemies' efforts slowed down and carried less and less might behind them. Finally, Destructo struck back directly, swinging a fist directly into the path of one of the hulk's own attacks. The impact created a mighty clang that saw several pieces of the hulk's hand fly about.

In that moment, Destructo recaptured the initiative and threw punch after punch into his opponent's body. He was relentless in his assault, and each blow left a mark. He continued to pummel the robot until its movements suggested it was almost ready to shut down. Destructo pulled back and prepared to let the big robot fall. The robot found one last burst of energy in him and made one last effort to strike at Destructo. Destructo had none of it, spinning to the side and striking the robot from behind as he went by.

The hulk collapsed to the ground. In a display of tenacity and durability that both surprised and impressed Mr. Destructo, the robot tried to get up once more. But it was too late – the robot was directly in the path of one of the spider-mech's legs. The moment the robot found his footing again, the spider-mech crushed him underfoot.

****

Among the leading terms Commander Echo would have used to describe the current situation was "from bad to worse". They were making no headway against the spider-walker, Captain Danger was still in a perilous position, and Bonez was gone. On top of that, they were down to just two cannons that were being carefully utilized to ensure they didn't create a gap the spider-walker could exploit. While the crew was working hard to swap the disabled cannons with their counterparts from the other side of the *Horizon*, the spider-walker was approaching far faster than the cannons were being replaced.

"Keep firing!" Echo commanded, though neither what nor whom at the order was meant for were specified. In addition to the spider-walker that kept the cannons occupied, there was also another robot hiding somewhere behind the walker and taking potshots at them to provide cover for the robots on the ground. While crewmen aboard the *Horizon* were firing hand weaponry at the robot, there was no sign they were having any success.

Then came another salvo, a series of heavy ion bolts that dispersed across the vessel's hull. The first round didn't cause any damage, but the second hit two robots that were close together.

"Find out where that's coming from!" Echo ordered.

Someone spotted the attacker popping in and out from around the cave docking structures, and a firing team shot back with a round of counter-fire that missed their target. That same team was soon interrupted when beams of laser fire from the first turret bot pushed them into cover.

Then, the heavier turret robot fired another salvo of ion fire that collided with the lift carrying Captain Danger. The lift immediately shut down, as did the Captain. In an uncontrolled fashion, the Captain fell off the lift and to the ground.

At first, neither Echo nor any of the other robots watching the Captain fall reacted, their processors momentarily freezing up. The moment was ended when further weapons fire hit the *Eternal Horizon*. Just as quickly as they'd frozen up, the crew went back to work, though there were clear signs panic was about to set in.

"Retreat!" Echo shouted. "Fall back! Retreat!"

Echo immediately ran for the lift, not waiting for anyone to respond. Several robots shouted at him, asking where he was going and what about the Captain, but he didn't respond to anyone directly.

"Retreat!" He repeated, making the order clear. "Get us moving! Cannons keep firing!"

As soon as he reached the lift, Echo leapt over the side of the vessel and grabbed hold of the cords and bars allowing the lift to do its titular job. He slid down along the lift in a controlled drop, coming to a brief stop when he met the lift platform. The *Horizon* finally began to move as he climbed around the lift, then he slid the rest of the way to the ground till he neared the bottom and leapt off. The moment his feet touched the ground, he rushed for Captain Danger's disabled body and picked the robot up. Carrying him in his arm, Echo ran after the *Horizon* with an extra burst of speed until he was close enough to leap up and latch onto the lift.

A few shots flew after the *Horizon* as it rolled off in retreat, though fortunately none hit anything important. As they pulled further away, the weapons fire stopped entirely. Looking back, Echo saw the spider-walker was starting to turn around and fall back, making it clear they had no interest in pursuing. Echo promptly returned focus to his immediate surroundings and resumed climbing back up to the *Horizon's* top deck.

****

The spider-mech stomped its way back into Rustbucket to a round of light cheers and applause, with dozens of robots waiting to greet their defenders. Leroy rode along the back end of the spider-mech until it came to a complete stop, keeping watch in case there was any trickery afoot. Mr. Destructo and the others on the ground followed behind from a safe distance, ensuring they wouldn't find themselves caught underneath the large walker's feet. Once the machine came to a complete stop and shut down, Cannon Man and Steek disembarked alongside Leroy, while the ground team finally closed in.

"Excellent job, everyone!" Leroy said as they met up and the robots around them closed in to further congratulate him. "I don't think that could have gone any better."

"I'll admit, I did not expect that to go as well as it did," Destructo said. "But you did good, Leroy."

"We all did good, Destructo," Leroy replied. "It was a team effort."

"So, what's our next move?" Destructo asked.

"We get ready for the next wave," Leroy said. "It's time to prepare for Round 2."

01011.

"You can restore him, can't you?"

Doctor Clank looked up from where Captain Danger's inactive body laid on his worktable and turned his attention to Commander Echo.

"What kind of stupid question is that?" Clank asked. "It's ion damage. You're acting like someone made him explode."

"He was hit by heavy ion shots," Echo replied. "Those aren't known for being safe."

"Fine, yes," Clank said. His face moved in a circular motion approximating a roll of the eyes. "He didn't take any irreparable damage. I'll need to do some work to restore him to full functionality, but it's nothing that isn't well within my capabilities."

"Good," Echo said. "Keep me appraised."

"Shouldn't be necessary," Clank said. "When I'm finished, I'm sure he'll tell you himself."

"Fine, just get to work," Echo said.

With that, he turned to leave for the bridge. Clank muttered several somethings behind his back as he left the mechanic's domain, but none of it was anything Echo deemed worth caring about.

Echo marched to the bridge with a brisk walk. As soon as he entered the room, everyone greeted him with their full attention. He responded by signaling for them to return as they were.

"How's the Captain?" Asked Zon West Omega.

"Doctor Clank should have him operational again in no time,"

Echo answered. "What's our status?"

"Still holding ten miles out," Xerox answered. "Scouts have reported rare sightings of vehicles moving in and out on what we suspect are scrap runs, but otherwise there has been no significant activity as of late."

Echo nodded, then turned to Frigjar-Zeta.

"Secure a channel to the Top Dog," Echo said. The order earned glances from every direction.

"Are you sure that's wise, Sir?" Zon asked. "That would seem a decision best left until Captain Danger is restored."

"Until the Captain is functional again, it is my duty to act in the best interests of the *Horizon* and the crew," Echo replied. "That is exactly what I am doing."

When no one raised any further concerns, Zeta carried out Echo's order. The room filled with a deathly silence while the crew went about their duties, as Echo stood with a disturbingly still patience waiting for any kind of news or update. It was over an hour later when a response finally came.

"*Captain Danger,*" The Top Dog said. "*I presume you have good news for me.*"

"This is Commander Echo," Echo answered. "The Captain is currently indisposed."

A noticeable pause followed.

"*Who?*" The Top Dog asked.

"This is Commander Echo," Echo repeated. "Captain Danger's first officer."

"*Oh, right,*" The Top Dog said. "*Why am I talking to you? Did Danger get himself killed?*"

"No, he was rendered disabled during our attempt to capture Leroy Brown."

"*You found him, then. So you're calling with news that you have him and you're bringing him to me now?*"

"No," Echo answered. "The situation is–"

"*What do you mean, 'no'?*" The Top Dog asked.

Echo briefly glanced around the room in a befuddled manner.

"Just that," Echo said. "We know where he is, but our initial attempt to capture him–"

"*So you failed.*" The Top Dog interrupted. For a second time, Echo glanced up from the radio as he considered what to say.

"If I might have the opportunity to do so, I can explain the situation in full," Echo said.

"*What is there to explain?*" The Top Dog asked. "*I said I wanted you to deliver Leroy Brown's inactive body to me. Either you failed, or you didn't. How difficult is that to understand?*"

"If I might explain, *Sir*," Echo said, doing his best to remain firm while avoiding a semblance of disrespect. Tension swiftly filled the room during the seconds it took for the Top Dog to reply.

"*Fine,*" he said, relieving a significant portion of that tension. "*If you must.*"

"Thank you," Echo said. "We tracked Leroy to a cave that holds a settlement or outpost of some kind. Captain Danger tried to convince Leroy to come peacefully, but he refused. They then attacked with a large war machine. During the fight, Captain Danger was rendered incapacitated. I then ordered a retreat. We're currently ten miles out keeping an eye on them."

Another pause filled the room, restoring the previous tension.

"*So, what I'm hearing you say is that you failed,*" the Top Dog finally said.

"What I am trying to say is that we know where he is and request assistance," Echo said.

"*Because you failed.*"

"Given the situation, this is not a mission the *Horizon* is equipped for," Echo tried to explain. "We're not a war vessel."

"*What do you mean you're not a war vessel? You've got twelve guns on that thing.*"

"That are there as a defense," Echo said. "They are meant to ward off hostiles."

"*And the crew?*"

"We have a few soldiers," Echo explained. "Most the crew could fight if we needed, but we are not equipped for a capture mission of this kind. If you wanted Leroy dead, we could bombard his position and pull his remains out of the wreckage, but you made it very clear you want him alive."

Another pause followed, stretching the tension so tight Commander Echo could swear he felt it.

"*Commander Echo, send me your coordinates,*" The Top Dog finally said. "*Then, when your Captain is functional again, inform him I will be sending a ship to meet you. That is all.*"

Then, the conversation cut out, leaving the room filled with silence once more.

****

"Welcome back, Captain."

Captain Danger looked around to find he was in Doctor Clank's workshop. In short order, his memory reloaded and reminded him of what happened just before he'd been incapacitated.

"Did we win?" he asked.

"We retreated," Clank answered. "You'll want to talk to the Commander about the details."

Danger nodded, then slid off the table.

"Any issues I need to be concerned about?" he asked.

"Your body should be functioning just as it did prior to the battle," Clank answered.

"Very good. As you were," Danger said, then he left for the bridge.

A solemn atmosphere hung in the air as Danger walked through the hallways and corridors of the *Eternal Horizon*. His crew naturally gave him acknowledgement when he walked by, but none said anything. It created a sense of dread that left Danger with plenty of concern when he finally reached the bridge.

"What's our status?" he asked after stepping through the doorway. "Clank told me you retreated after I was hit."

"That we did, Captain," Echo answered. "We're currently holding at ten miles out and keeping watch. There's been no significant activity thus far other than what we assume are scrap runs."

"Very good. We're going to need to plan a new avenue of attack. If Leroy Brown hasn't snuck out, we'll need to find a way to get at him."

"About that, Sir," Echo said. "The Top Dog said I should inform you that he's sending a ship to meet us."

Slowly, Captain Danger turned to look at Echo.

"The Top Dog is sending a ship?" He asked.

"Yes, Sir," Echo answered.

"He's sending a ship to meet us?" Danger asked.

"Yes, Sir," Echo repeated.

"Why would he do that?"

"I contacted him while you were incapacitated. I informed him of our situation and attempted to request assistance."

Danger froze for a moment, then started as if he was about to say something. He stopped just as suddenly, and merely raised his fist above his head and slammed it down on the console in the middle of the room. Everyone jumped a little and looked in Danger's direction. He held his fist on the console for an extended series of seconds, staring at Echo with an unreadable look. When Danger realized the other crewmembers were staring at him, he lifted his fist off the console and stood up straight.

"Commander Echo," Danger said. "Please follow me."

Danger marched out of the room in silence, with Echo close behind. He motioned Echo inside, then slammed the door behind him.

"Why?"

Echo turned to Danger.

"Can you please specify, Sir?" Echo asked.

"Why did you contact the Top Dog?" Danger asked.

"I thought it in the best interested of the *Horizon* and its crew," Echo answered. "Given the outcome of our first attempt, I'm having difficulty calculating a viable plan for capturing Leroy with what we have available."

"And now he thinks we've failed," Danger said. "Am I right?"

"Yes," Echo admitted. "He did put a great deal of emphasis on that assessment."

Danger slowly walked to the desk in the middle of the room. There, he pulled a chair toward him and sat down.

"He had me execute Pentabot," Danger said. Echo looked down at the Captain, not sure how to respond.

"The first time we failed him, when Leroy Brown escaped," Danger said, staring straight at Echo. "That's why he wanted to know who to blame. He had me execute him. He all but threatened to kill everyone aboard the *Horizon* if I didn't. Now, we have failed him a second time. I don't know what that means, but I do not expect it to be anything to look forward to."

The two robots looked at each other a moment before Echo spoke up.

"Bonez was destroyed during the fight," Echo said. "We could blame the failure on him."

"Maybe," Danger said. "If that's an option, I'll see if I can use it. But I clearly don't understand how the Top Dog operates. And now he's apparently sending a ship here, so who knows what might come next."

"So, what's the plan?" Echo asked.

"For now, we continue to watch the cave and wait for the Top Dog's ship to arrive," Danger answered.

"Is that is?"

"Yes," Danger said. "That is all. Dismissed."

Echo looked at the Captain, then turned for the door. When

he reached it, he looked back at Danger once more before leaving the room.

****

Several hours later, word came that a shuttle had been spotted approaching from the distance. Captain Danger promptly traveled to the *Horizon*'s deck and stood waiting for its arrival. It had a dark complexion and looked surprisingly well put together. While it was still clearly built out of parts assembled from other sources, Danger found himself impressed all the same at just how professional its construction looked.

The shuttle flew in, touched down, and stayed just long enough for a single robot to exit. As soon as the lone individual was safely and securely on the *Horizon*'s deck, the shuttle lifted off and flew back the way it had come. Even before the shuttle finished lifting in the air, the robot turned to look at Captain Danger and approached him.

"I am Remote Overseer and Communication Unit Beta-5," the robot said in a near monotone voice. "It is acceptable to refer to me as Rocu."

Danger looked down at Rocu and gave the robot a once-over. Much like the shuttle that delivered him, the robots appearance suggested he was a Junkworld original, built from the ground up out of parts scavenged from the planets scrap-strewn wastes but constructed in a very professional manner. He stood at roughly two-thirds Danger's own height yet carried himself tall all the same. The bulky build of his body bore a darker nature, and his head mostly consisted of an array of sensors arranged to just barely resemble a face. The top of his body looked as if it was meant to split open and reveal something contained within, while his arms and legs were both simple in their design.

"I see," Danger said, his voice holding back a great deal of reluctance, misgivings, and frustration about what Rocu's presence and the nature surrounding its arrival signified.

"Welcome aboard the *Eternal Horizon*," he added, though his tone spoke in direct contrast to the words they backed.

"Captain Danger," Rocu said, though Danger couldn't tell if it was meant to be acknowledgement or identification. "I am to deliver a message as soon as possible. This message can be delivered either in the open or with discretion. Please make your selection now."

Danger looked at Rocu, hesitating with his answer as he tried to process what he was being told.

"The Top Dog insists on speaking to you," Rocu said, pressing the issue. "You may choose to reserve the conversation for your eyes only, or the conversation may take place in the open. Choose now. The Top Dog does not like to be kept waiting."

"Very well," Danger said. "We'll to go my command room."

"An acceptable decision," Rocu said.

With misgivings following his every step, Danger walked to his command room. Rocu followed close behind as he rolled along on the treads that made up his feet. Despite keeping a distance ensuring there was no concern the robot might accidentally run into him, Danger still felt like the smaller robot was following him far too closely all the same.

Once they entered the room, Rocu closed the door behind them, then rolled further inward. When he came to a stop, he rotated his body to face Danger directly. After the two robots were facing each other, Rocu's head shifted back atop his body, and his chest cavity retracted to reveal a video screen. Further back, a small dish and antenna poked their way out the top of the robot. Before Danger could inquire what was happening, the screen turned on. A brief display of static soon gave way to a video image of the Top Dog himself.

"Hello, hello?" The Top Dog asked. "Am I coming through?"

Danger looked at the screen, then up at Rocu's head, then back at the screen.

"Hello?" the Top Dog said. He reached out his hand and tapped the display on the other end. "This is functional, right?"

"It is," Danger said.

"Ah! Good!" The Top Dog said. "Captain Danger. Hello."

Captain Danger merely nodded his head in acknowledgement.

"Since we're having this conversation, I know you've met Rocu Beta-5," the Top Dog continued. "Get to know him well, because he's now the newest member of your crew."

"Excuse me?" Danger asked.

"Yes," the Top Dog replied. "I couldn't help but notice that in what few orders I've given you and your crew, there has rapidly developed a pattern of failure. As I'm sure you can understand, this is not something I can stand for. However, I'm also a very busy individual, meaning I don't have time to keep checking up on you every five minutes. That's why I'm assigning Rocu here to do it for me."

"So he's a spy." Danger said.

"No, Captain. That's a very crude and inaccurate assessment of his role. If he were a spy, you wouldn't know he was aboard at all. To the contrary, there will be no mistake that Rocu is there. Just think of him as a lesser version of me."

"So, he's a babysitter." Danger said.

"Fine," the Top Dog said with a roll of his head. "I suppose that's as good a description as any. Just so long as you remember that he answers to me and he'll be sure to let me know if you do anything I'd disapprove of. Including continuing to fail me."

"Does that mean you have new orders for us?" Danger asked.

"It does. Though you'll be glad to know that I'm relieving you of your responsibility of delivering Leroy Brown to me."

"You are?" Danger asked.

"Yes," the Top Dog answered. "I will be assigning the mission to a more substantial force that will be better suited to the task. For the time being, I need you to merely continue to provide intelligence and keep me informed of the ongoings in the area."

"Yes, of course," Danger said with relief.

"There is one other matter that needs to be dealt with," The Top Dog said. "I need you to summon Commander Echo and execute him."

Captain Danger froze, creating a silence in the room stretching for several long seconds.

"Captain, did you hear me?" The Top Dog asked.

"What?" Danger asked.

"I asked if you heard me."

"You want me to do *what*?" Danger asked again.

"You are going to summon Commander Echo," the Top Dog explained. He spoke the words in a slow, pointed pattern. "Once he is here, and I can see him, you are going to execute him."

Once again, Captain Danger froze for several long seconds.

"Is there a problem, Captain?" The Top Dog asked.

"Why?" Danger asked.

"Why what?"

"Why do you need me to execute my first officer?"

"I need you to execute your first officer because his conversation with me made quite clear that he bears responsibility for your failure to capture Leroy Brown." the Top Dog explained.

"But you just told me you were assigning someone else to the task!"

"I did," the Top Dog said. "That doesn't change the fact that you failed, and that Commander Echo is responsible. Now summon him so I can watch you execute him."

Danger looked to the screen inside Rocu, then glanced to the door.

"Let's not make this a repeat of last time, shall we?" The Top Dog said. "Do it now."

Danger looked back to Rocu, then slowly turned to his desk. He took one step, then a second, then walked over to it in with footsteps carrying the heavy weight of regret. There, he opened a panel on the desk, and reached for a button to speak with the bridge. As his finger neared the button, he held it in place shy of actual contact for several seconds.

"Captain Danger, you continue to test my patience," the Top Dog said. "Do remember that I could make this far worse if I really wanted to."

Slowly, Danger pushed the button, though there was hesitation before he spoke.

"Xerox," he said, followed by another extended pause.

"*Yes, Captain?*" She replied. Another pause followed before Danger replied.

"Have Commander Echo meet me in my command room," he finally said. He then cut the feed.

"Smart choice," the Top Dog said.

Danger retrieved a weapon, then turned and stood with his back to the doorway as he waited for Commander Echo to arrive. With each second that passed, he kept hoping the Top Dog would change his mind, and considered possible plans that might allow him to escape the order. But no ideas came to mind, and the room remained quiet until Echo stepped through the door.

"You wanted to see me, Captain?" Echo said.

Danger slowly let his head hang as any expectation he'd be saved from having to carry through with the order disappeared.

"Yes," Danger said. "I'm sorry, Commander Echo. But I wasn't given a choice."

"What are you sorry about?" Echo asked.

Danger didn't say anything, but there was a pause as he tried to stall for a reprieve, in whatever form it might come.

"Captain?" Echo asked again with a concerned tone.

Almost before Echo had finished speaking the word, Captain Danger turned around, aimed his weapon at Echo, and fired. He pulled the trigger multiple times in rapid succession, firing the weapon until he was absolutely certain Echo was dead. The former Commander's ruined body collapsed, with smoke seeping out of multiple holes. A few long seconds later, Danger dropped his arm, letting gravity claim his weapon. A haunting echo filled the room when the weapon hit the floor.

"Good job," the Top Dog said.

Danger slowly glanced at Rocu.

"Though I can't help but notice that you apologize a lot," The Top Dog continued. "Why is that?"

Danger slowly turned back to Echo's broken body.

"Are you genuinely sorry, or does it merely help your processors continue to function properly?"

Danger slowly turned to look back at the Top Dog's image once more.

"Is it something I need to be concerned about?" The Top Dog asked.

"No," Danger said, speaking just loud enough to be heard. "Nothing to worry about."

"Good," the Top Dog said. "I'll keep in touch."

With that, the video cut out. Rocu immediately retracted the screen and folded back to his previous appearance, then rolled out of the room to leave Captain Danger alone with his former first officer's broken, smoking body.

THE BATTLE OF RUSTBUCKET

01100.

"We have limited time and limited resources," Leroy began.

Less than an hour after the battle with the *Eternal Horizon*, he and Rustbucket's de facto leadership were gathered together to plan the next phase of the settlements defense. Five of them stood around the central table in the command center, including Isaac, Mr. Destructo, Ozochki, Synnapses, and Leroy Brown himself.

"Under normal circumstances, the optimal strategy would be to focus on building up defenses, hunkering down, and planning a strategy around just outlasting whatever they throw at us," Leroy continued. "However, our lack of information and overall situation does not afford us the luxury of that option. If we're going to win, we're going to have to set ourselves up to take aggressive action while still making the most of our defensive position."

"Fortunately, we have two major advantages," Leroy continued. "First, we have Rustbucket's position. As I've said, you could not ask for a better environment to hold out. It ensures there is only one direction from which they can come at us."

"That's not entirely true," Isaac said.

"How so?" Leroy asked.

"The magma tunnels we use to power Rustbucket," Ozochki said, his voice a low rumble. "We've never found a way to make use of them, but we have mapped out enough to know they do lead outside."

"How difficult would it be for someone to attack us from that direction?" Leroy asked.

"Very," Ozochki answered.

"Assuming they know they're there," Destructo said. "Even so, they wouldn't need to get many through that way to become a big problem."

"Can you seal those tunnels up?" Leroy asked Ozochki.

"We should be able to put something together," Ozochki answered.

"Do what you can down there," Leroy Said. "At least make sure we'll know if they try to sneak in the back. If it's difficult to get through, it should be easy to defend."

"The second main advantage we have is me," Leroy continued. "It has been made very clear that the Top Dog wants me, and he wants me taken alive."

"How is that an advantage?" Synnapses asked. "That's the entire reason we're in this mess in the first place."

"True," Leroy admitted. "But it also means the enemy is going to be restricted in how they can attack us. We, on the other hand, do not have that limitation. We need to exploit that fact as much as we possibly can."

"What do we know about the forces the Top Dog is likely to send at us and their general tactics?" Leroy asked, looking to Destructo.

"Not much, directly," Destructo answered. "Based on what we do know, he has a sizable military to work with. His standard procedure is to try to terrify people into surrender, and if that doesn't work, apply as much blunt force as he needs to."

"We'll plan for the basics, then," Leroy said. "Ground troops, air support, siege weapons, heavy support."

"First step, we need everyone's support for this," Leroy continued. "Construction, operations, actual defense, we're going to need every robot in Rustbucket to help out."

"After that first victory, you've earned yourself a great deal of goodwill and support," Isaac said. "I would dare say that task is already complete."

"Good," Leroy replied with a nod. "Second, we're going to need as much scrap and materials as we can get our hands on."

"We should have enough to get started, and I've already assigned teams to start gathering more," Ozochki said.

"Good," Leroy said again, with another nod. "That brings us to the actual defenses."

Leroy looked at the table in the center of the room, then looked up and around before turning back to the group.

"Does anyone have a map of Rustbucket?" He asked.

A panel opened on Ozochki to reveal a projector lens. From it emerged a beam of light displaying a holographic map of Rustbucket on the table.

"Thank you," Leroy said. "The first two layers of defense will be walls and gates. While the cave gives us a natural defensive setup, we still can't ignore how large the opening is."

He pointed to the area around the outside of the cave and drew a line with his finger around the structures already there.

"If we can manage, we want the first wall and gate to go around the structures you already have," Leroy said. "We want as big and thick a wall as possible, but make sure it still has a gate that won't force us to tear it down again when we need to get out. We also want firing positions so we can shoot out while minimizing the enemy's opportunities to shoot back."

He moved his finger to the cave opening and drew a line across it. "Second point is around the cave opening itself. We don't want to diminish the benefits of the opening, so we mostly just want a series of gates we can close if things go wrong."

Leroy then moved his finger to the area between the cave opening and the line for the outer wall.

"We'll want at least a couple anti-air guns positioned here to protect against air attack."

His finger then shifted to draw a long oval that went in and out of the cave.

"We'll want at least one big gun to fire at any heavy support," Leroy continued. "Ideally, something we can roll in and out of the cave. Probably something that can shoot large balls of junk, for sake of ammunition, though if you can develop anything better, I'm open to hearing it. If we can manage, we should back that up with mortars for a secondary option."

"We'll assign anyone who can't shoot a weapon and isn't occupied by other duties to man those when the time comes," Leroy continued. "On which note, we'll want to bring out every weapon you have in storage and build as many as you can. Anyone we can't give a range weapon to, we'll find a melee weapon of some kind to arm them with."

"Fortunately, we already have a head start in those departments," Ozochki said. "Some of the robots in the engineering department have some designs and prototypes they've worked on in the past. We haven't made much use of them since evacuation became the lead reaction to the Top Dog's expansion. After it was decided we're going to stay and fight, I had the engineering teams pull them out. It shouldn't take long to put them into production once we're sure we have the materials we need."

"Good to hear," Leroy said. "Once we have enough range weapons, the security team and I will start training robots how to use them. Destructo, your team will take lead during the fight."

Leroy then turned his attention to Synnapses.

"Are there any robots in Rustbucket who could provide remote operations?" Leroy asked. "Anyone with the ability to run a swarm operation?"

"We have a few that might fit that description," Synnapses replied. "Why?"

"Because I have a very special project in mind," Leroy answered. "They're coming for me specifically, so we're going to give them more of me than they'll know how to handle."

****

Across the junk-strewn wastes, a small truck sped along. It carried a single robot, a rag-cloaked individual sitting in the driver's seat. Taking note of a particular piece of scrap that stood out to his visual receptors, the robot came to a stop, then turned toward it to investigate closer. When he arrived, he climbed out and gave the piece a careful inspection. He wasn't quite sure what it was, but it looked valuable enough and was in reasonable condition. Both were good reason to lay claim to it, and so he loaded the large piece into the back of his truck before moving on.

As he continued driving, he spotted a clearing partially circled by the mountainous regions around it. With even just a casual glance inside, he could tell it was full of several piles of junk that might be full of all number of valuable pieces. Inward he went to have a look and see what he might find. He stopped at the first pile he came to, and quickly went to work looking for anything worthwhile.

Soon after he started looking, the robot thought he heard an approaching noise and stopped to look up. It was quiet at first, but rapidly grew in volume. Soon, the ground began to shake in time with an increasingly heavy clanking sound signaling something with multiple legs. As the noise came closer, there was a constant loud metallic buzz further heralding its approach. Looking up toward the noise's source, he saw the approach of what could best be described a three-story tall metal spider. Like so much of the world it inhabited, it was built as a mashup of an untold number of sources. Underneath the head was mounted a turret bearing two large cannons flanking an assortment of other miscellaneous tools. Two cranes sat on its back – one near its neck and the other near its tail end – while a third utility arm was mounted to the center of its undercarriage.

The robot looked up at the large, terrifying machine and froze when the machine pointed its head straight back at him. Much to the robot's fortune, however, the large walking spider-tank paid him mind for only a few short seconds before moving on. Inward it continued, its head turning back and forth as if looking for something. Curious, the robot climbed back into his vehicle and slowly followed to keep watch, though he took care to keep a safe distance, not provoke it, or draw its attention any further.

The spider-tank continued to ignore him and kept searching until it locked onto an open shipping container that had an inactive robot body lying next to it. With its cranes, the spider-tank picked up both the container and the robot, and then dropped them into an unseen opening in its back. Once both were secure, it began looking at what else was lying around and loaded up several scoops full of metallic miscellanea.

Finally, the spider-tank stopped scooping up loads of junk, turned, and marched back off the way it had come. Over the mountainside it went, its eight towering legs carrying it along until it vanished from sight. Even after it was out of sight, the robot continued to look toward the source of the noise. It was only after the sound and the shaking of the ground both ended the robot returned his attention to what was still left and resumed looking for anything that might still be of value.

****

Every vehicle in Rustbucket was requisitioned for the nonstop effort to collect as much material as possible. Teams with armed escorts traveled out of the cave and returned with full loads of miscellaneous junk that was swiftly unloaded so those teams could turn right back around to collect more. The unloaded junk was hauled back to engineering, where it was sorted and recycled into either raw components that could be made to serve a new purpose or by being melted down and re-forged.

Within hours, each trip in and out of Rustbucket included passing by the newly laid foundations upon which a wall was growing. With each subsequent hour, the wall continued to slowly rise into the sky to provide an ever-stronger barrier between Rustbucket and the hostile forces lying in wait across the planet. Before long, a gate was added, creating the final piece allowing the wall to truly serve its intended purpose, even as construction continued.

Once the basic structure of the wall was in place, the engineering teams turned their primary focus to the second gate. Most of the work was done within the engineering region itself, where large panels were constructed alongside the pieces that would attach them to the walls of the cave opening. Once completed, the entirety of it all was hauled out to the entrance, where gate installation began.

Once work on installing the large gate was underway, the engineering team leaders turned their focus to weapons. Aside from the existing prototypes and plans pulled out of storage, they received another boost when it was discovered the shipping container full of *Terminator* wardrones came complete with weapons to match. Using these as a starting point, training for how to wield a gun began for every robot in Rustbucket equipped to do so. Some of the robots incapable of wielding a rifle were even given modifications and upgrades that allowing them to do so anyway. With Steek taking the lead, each robot was trained in the basics, including how to handle the weapons and how to operate as a group. Those robots identified as having a particular aptitude for combat were quickly assigned to lead positions under the command of Rustbucket's security team.

Backed by the walls and heavier weapons assembled by the engineering teams, within three days' time the citizens of Rustbucket already felt ready to take on anything the Top Dog might throw at them.

****

Mr. Destructo looked back and forth between two halves of a mirror image. On either side stood Leroy Brown, looking at another robot that also bore the appearance of Leroy Brown.

"I'm impressed," said one of the Leroy Browns, who then turned to Synnapses and Zealot-Three.

"It was not an easy job, but building around the wardrones did make the job far more manageable." Synnapses replied.

Leroy nodded, then turned to another robot named Phelx Moon who stood nearby.

"You're sure you can operate these as a group?" He asked.

"I am positive," Phelx replied. "Though I will issue a reminder that it will be significantly beneficial if I am assigned only to operate those units modified to resemble Leroy Brown."

"We'll plan to assign the ones we don't modify to other robots," Synnapses said. Leroy nodded in acknowledgement.

"How many will you be able to rig up to match?" Destructo asked.

"We're currently aiming for a dozen," Zealot answered. "Anything beyond that will depend on how much time and what parts we have to work with."

"We'll plan around a dozen for now, then," Leroy said.

"There is one other thing," Yutah said from nearby. He hauled out two large pieces of metal. When Leroy looked around at the mechanics in the room, Yutah turned the pieces around to reveal they were shields.

"We're building a pair for each wardrone we modify, and a pair for you as well," Yutah explained. "We realized that while we can make the wardrones look like you and move like you, there's one important thing we can't replicate – your shield. While you can use your barrier shield to protect yourself, the wardrones won't be able to do the same."

"If your expectation regarding their attack strategy holds true, we can predict the enemy to use ion weaponry against you and any robot they think might be you," Synnapses continued. "We're building the shields to counter that – any ion shots hitting them should safely dissipate without causing any harm to the robot wielding them."

"And you built a pair for me so I don't give myself away," Leroy said, to which Synnapses, Zealot-Three, and Yutah all nodded. "Smart."

****

Within five days' time, Rustbucket reached and then surpassed the minimum levels Leroy had set for establishing settlement defenses. Every minute and hour beyond that, the settlement went even further beyond the aims he'd laid out, and increased his assurances that they would emerge victorious in the upcoming battle.

"I think we can actually do this," Mr. Destructo said as he and Leroy stood overlooking the outer regions of the cave.

"You had doubts?" Leroy asked, glancing to Destructo.

"If I might speak with all honesty?" Destructo replied. "I still do. I'm not here because I think we can win, Leroy. I'm here because they think we can win, and I promised that we'd stick by them and back them. Seeing them come together and rally like this, though? I favor our chances a lot more than I did when you first talked them into fighting. I favor them now more than I did after we fought off the first attack. I think our chances of winning outweigh our chances of defeat. I think we have a genuine chance of winning."

"And to think," Leroy said. "You insisted our best chances of winning was a silly plan to draw out a capture team and sneak back into the Top Dog's headquarters on an assassination mission."

"I still think that would have been our best chance at victory," Destructo replied. "Though I doubt that plan is still viable anymore."

"It was never viable, Destructo."

"I suppose we'll never know, will we."

Leroy shrugged and looked back down on still ongoing work, including the growing pile of ammunition for the large central cannon, each one thrown together from dozens or hundreds of pieces of junk that hadn't found any other use.

"So, what is your plan when we win?" Leroy asked.

"*If* we win," Destructo said. "You may be assured of our victory, but I'm not looking past the next battle until it's over."

"Fine," Leroy said. "What is your plan *if* we win?"

"Did I not *just* say I'm not making plans past the next battle?" Destructo asked. "I refuse to do anything that relies on assuming we win."

"Alright, fine," Leroy said. "I'll just have to be the optimist for the both of us."

"Leroy Brown! Mr. Destructo!"

Both robots turned to the sound of Walter's voice and watched the little robot roll toward them at high speed.

"What is it?" Leroy asked.

"Scout reports are coming back saying there is a force gathering ten miles out!" Walter answered.

"Sounds like they're about ready to attack," Destructo said to

Leroy. Leroy nodded in agreement.

"Have them send out the signal, recall everyone," Leroy said to Walter, then he turned back to Destructo. "We'll assemble for a final briefing, then move into position."

Walter nodded, then rolled back off the way he'd just come from with just as much speed.

"Looks like it's show time," Leroy said to Destructo.

The sun hung high in the sky as the last of the forces assigned to Commander I-Kron Delta assembled. Located ten miles out from their target destination, the army under his command arranged themselves into proper positions as they prepared for their ultimate objective, the capture of one Leroy Brown. From within the bridge of his command vessel, Commander I-Kron looked down at a series of maps detailing the area and what was known about the settlement where Leroy had taken refuge.

Most of it was based on information provided by one Captain Danger. What they knew told him the settlement's residents were building a series of walls. It was an understandable course of action, in I-Kron's opinion. Most the settlements the Commander had encountered had them, especially in response to the Top Dog's conquest of Junkworld. It created a false sense of security that those hiding behind them might hold back the inevitable. That was until both the walls and the sense of security were both torn right back down again with extreme prejudice.

Far more concerning was the order to capture Leroy Brown. It was an uncharacteristic move on the Top Dog's part. In his time under the robot's command, I-Kron couldn't recall anyone having received orders for the capture of any one robot in particular. It was a challenging complication, to be sure. Under normal circumstances, they could just destroy everything and pick the surviving pieces out of the remains. To capture one robot, however; that would require a far more intelligent approach if they were required to use force. It left I-Kron hoping that delivering Leroy Brown to the Top Dog would bring with it an opportunity to learn just why he was so important.

"Lt. Mol," I-Kron said to a robot that stood nearby. "Do we have confirmation that everyone has arrived?"

"Statement: Affirmative," Lt. M-01 answered. "In addition to the *Superior*, you now have at your direct and immediate disposal two battle cruisers, two heavy gun platforms, four light gun platforms, a dozen combat transports, and a full complement of troops for each."

"Good," I-Kron said, giving a nod. "Establish a connection to the Top Dog."

An affirmative came from the helm, and within a few short minutes, a series of images appeared on the screens positioned around the bridge of the *Superior*. Each one showed a matching video of the Top Dog.

"Commander I-Kron," the Top Dog said.

"Yes, Sir," I-Kron replied. "I've called to inform you that we've finished assembling ten miles out from the target and are in the middle of final preparations. Any final orders before we begin?"

"What's the situation with the settlement?" The Top Dog asked.

"From what we can see, everything is in line with what Captain Danger reported. They've clearly been very busy in the last few days, the wall they've assembled is not an unimpressive one."

"Good to know he's not entirely worthless. I'd hate to have to go to the trouble of sifting through his crew and figure out which ones I can keep and which I have to scrap. I've got far better things to do with my time than bother with that level of tedious nonsense."

"Understandably so, Sir," I-Kron said.

"Anyway, proceed as previously ordered," the Top Dog said. "And to be clear, Leroy Brown is to be brought to me alive and intact. Understood?"

"The order is quite clear, Sir," I-Kron said. "What of the rest of them?"

"Once you have Leroy? Destroy it all."

"What if they surrender?"

"It is my understanding that Captain Danger already gave them a more than generous opportunity to hand over Leroy Brown without making a fuss about it. If they wanted to survive, they should have acknowledged my supremacy from the start instead of making me send you out there."

Once he was finished talking, the Top Dog cut the feed.

"Understood, Sir," Commander I-Kron said to no one in particular.

****

Commander I-Kron's war fleet parked a mile out from Rustbucket. As soon as the vessels were in position, troops marched out and assembled in organized formations ahead of their respective support vehicles. Those that didn't arrange themselves in the largely cosmetic formations took positions serving as groundwork for further on-the-ground support for their fellow soldiers. Further unifying the Top Dog's troops where a series of armor upgrades and modifications ensuring a uniform aesthetic in spite of the robots designs consisting of hundreds of different makes and models. All of it was carefully orchestrated theatrics aimed at a single goal – to convince the enemy before them how utterly inferior they were by comparison.

From amid the military setup that was far more professional in appearance than it was in application, a small, motorized cart carrying a single robot advanced beyond the front line. Short and round in appearance, the robot stood atop a pair of squat, sturdy legs ending in treads. On either side of his body was a simple arm. As the unit came ever closer to Rustbucket, a handful of robots lined up along the top of the wall and aimed weapons at the approaching enemy. Several yards out, the cart came to a halt. The robot disembarked, and then looked up at the defenders.

"I am ROCU Core-3," the robot said. "I am here on behalf of Commander I-Kron and the Top Dog."

The robots atop the wall glanced to each other, then one stepped aside and disappeared. A few minutes later, Isaac and Steek stepped atop the center of the wall and looked down at Rocu.

"I am Isaac, the de facto leader here," Isaac said. "What have you come for?"

The robot rolled a little bit closer, lowered a short distance to the ground, and then unfolded to reveal a video screen in its chest he aimed up to Isaac.

"I am Commander I-Kron," A robot said after his face appeared on the screen. "We hereby demand your surrender, and that you hand Leroy Brown over to us immediately."

"What are the terms?" Isaac asked.

"Terms? There are no terms here. The only terms are your full and immediate surrender, including handing over the robot known as Leroy Brown to our custody."

"And if we don't?"

"Then I have an army ready to take Leroy by force and crush your pathetic settlement into oblivion," I-Kron answered.

Isaac looked to Steek, then to the other robots on the wall, then back to Rocu.

"May we have time to discuss the matter?" Isaac asked.

"You've had days to discuss the matter," I-Kron replied. "And you've already rejected one offer to turn him over. Besides, didn't you just say you're the de facto leader of this settlement?"

"De facto, but not official," Isaac said. "This is not a decision to be made lightly."

Commander I-Kron looked at the two for several long seconds from the other side of the screen.

"Fine," He finally replied. "I will give you ten minutes to discuss the matter. Not a second more. If you do not hand him over by that point, I will interpret it as a refusal of surrender and proceed accordingly. Your ten minutes begins now."

Wasting no time, Isaac and Steek retreated from the wall. The Rocu unit stayed put and the screen remained active as I-Kron waited for their return. When they passed nine minutes, I-Kron began counting down the seconds – silently at first, but ever louder as the ten-minute time limit came closer and closer. At nine minutes and thirty seconds, a loud metallic noise of creaking and grinding sounded as the gate began to open. Once there was room to walk through, Isaac and Steek stepped out and approached Rocu.

"Cutting it awfully close, wouldn't you say?" I-Kron said. "Can I presume this means you've agreed to surrender?"

"It does," Isaac answered.

"Good," I-Kron said. "Now where is Leroy Brown?"

"They'll be hauling him out shortly," Steek said.

"*Very* shortly, I presume," I-Kron said.

Sure enough, two teams of robots stepped out through the gate almost the moment I-Kron finished speaking. The first carried an inactive robot that looked like Leroy Brown. The second carried a metal crate large enough to hold him. The two groups continued until they stood in front of Isaac and Steek. The second group laid the crate on the ground, and then the first placed Leroy's inactive form inside the crate.

"Stay right there, I'll send a team out to claim him," I-Kron said.

With that, the screen went blank. The robots stood in front of the gate in silence as they waited. Several minutes later, a shuttle lifted off from the largest vehicle in the distance. In short order, it landed again a few yards behind Rocu. A ramp lowered from the shuttle, allowing six robots to exit and join Rocu. Two stood next to the small robot, while the other four stepped next to the crate and looked inside. After one looked up and nodded, a cover was placed on the crate, and the four robots lifted the crate and carried it back into the shuttle. As soon as they'd stepped aboard, the shuttle lifted off the ground and flew back from whence it came.

"Please stand by for further instructions," Rocu said.

****

"Statement: Cargo incoming," Lt. Mol reported.

"Good," Commander I-Kron said. "Once we confirm it's him,

we can send Leroy on to the Top Dog, then establish occupation before moving on to dismantling procedures."

"Statement: Affirmative," Lt. Mol replied.

I-Kron nodded, then left the bridge and walked to the *Superior*'s landing pad to meet the shuttle. By the time he arrived, the shuttle had already landed, and a crate was sitting on the deck between a quartet of robots. I-Kron turned to the sound of a door opening and watched as two robots outfitted as mechanics stepped onto the deck to join him.

"Open it up," I-Kron said. On command, the robots opened the crate to give everyone a clear view of the robot contained within.

"It certainly looks like him," I-Kron said. He turned to the mechanics. "If you could confirm, please?"

One of the mechanics stepped forward and signaled for Leroy's inactive body to be removed from the crate. The four robots around it did so, standing Leroy on the deck.

"Thank you," The mechanic said before stepping in closer for a full examination. The robot began to look Leroy's body over, both for any signs it was a fake and for access points by which to open the outer shell and examine the interior. Looking at the back, the robot noticed something amiss – a connection piece that looked out of place. Focusing on the irregularity, the robot examined it closer.

That was when the body erupted into a massive explosion. A blast wave ripped across the *Superior*, sending fire and shrapnel in every direction. Everyone and everything in close proximity was immediately destroyed, and the *Superior* was dealt crippling damage. A shallow crater was left on the deck, and the damage to the vessel's structure caused the command tower to topple over.

****

The two robots next to Rocu turned toward the explosion aboard the *Superior*, and Rocu began folding up to do the same. None of them had an opportunity to take stock of what was happening. Rocu was shot multiple times before he finished reverting from his communication mode, and the two robots with him were shot in the back while distracted. Before their bodies hit the ground, everyone made a hasty retreat for Rustbucket's wall, with two robots lifting Isaac up to carry him inside. The outer gate started closing just as they began to step through; sealing shut once they were all inside.

From within the safety of the cave, more robots rushed out of Rustbucket and took position along and atop the wall. As they did, an opening salvo was fired from the main cannon. A large ball of fused together junk flew out at high speed and crashed down on top of a combat transport. Immediately on impact, it cratered the vehicle and flipped it end over end. Dozens of large pieces of shrapnel from the former junk ball flew in every direction, spreading even more damage to the carefully arranged army.

Already shaken by the destruction of the *Superior* and Commander I-Kron, disorder and confusion swept across the Top Dog's forces. Further chaos ensued when it was discovered there were eight different Leroy Browns atop the wall. All semblance of a true command structure vanished when another shot from the cannon landed amongst the carefully assembled troops and ripped through their numbers.

One of the battle cruisers took the initiative and advanced on Rustbucket. While the other large vessels stayed put, the light platforms followed soon after, along with half the troops and remaining transports. The lead cruiser soon turned into an angle bringing its cannons in line with the settlement, then opened with a salvo of ion blasts. Rustbucket responded with another shot that hit the cruiser across the deck. The shell of junk left a massive gash in its wake knocking out several of the cruisers guns and destroying multiple crewmembers. All the same, the cruiser continued to plow forward with its supporters in close pursuit.

"Cannon! Humbug!" Steek shouted, directing the battle. "Focus on the smaller vessels!"

The two robots answered in the affirmative, then turned their attentions towards the approaching gun platforms. As they and the other robots atop the wall waited for the enemy to come within firing range, the enemy continued to close the distance. Ion shots continued from the battle cruiser, and Rustbucket's main cannon fired another return salvo. The shot struck the land ship's front wheel, ruining it and slowing the vessel to a crawl.

Soon, the troops and other vessels came within range as well. A smattering of small arms fire followed from the ground troops and transports, most of it poorly aimed in an attempt at cover fire. The defenders of Rustbucket quickly caught on, and with the Leroy Brown's on the wall providing cover of their own, they returned fire far more deadly in its aim. Soon, the approaching soldiers slowed down and fell back, allowing the troop transports and gun platforms to pull ahead and lead the way. Concentrated fire from Cannon and Humbug soon knocked out the treads on the lead gun platform, then support fire from other positions finished it off in short order.

All the while, the battle cruiser continued to advance and fire its ion cannons on the settlement. Another shot from Rustbucket's main cannon took out two more of its wheels, bringing the vessel to a halt. Some of the robots atop the wall, led by Turrex and two of the Leroys, concentrated fire on the deck of the cruiser and any robots there they could see, further beating away at the war machine.

"Come on, Destructo," Steek mumbled at a barely audible volume. "Do your thing already."

****

Off in the distance, well away from the battle, two small vehicles sat and watched events unfold. Each one was driven by a fake Leroy Brown and carried two passengers – one with Mr. Destructo and the real Leroy Brown, and the other with yet two more of the fake Leroys.

"Time to move," the real Leroy said when the first cruiser exploded.

"What's our target?" Destructo asked.

"We'll hit the two big ones in the back first, then move on from there," Leroy said. Destructo nodded in acknowledgement.

"Let's move!" Leroy added, giving his driver a double pat on the shoulder.

The two vehicles revved up and sped forward, with Leroy and Destructo's vehicle taking the lead. They drove forward along a curved path, weaving between and around rocks and piles of junk lying across the wastes between them and their targets as they tried to avoid bringing attention to themselves too soon. As they neared the enemy vessels, some of them began to advance towards Rustbucket.

Among them was one of the battle cruisers. Both Destructo and the faux Leroys looked to Leroy Brown, waiting further input.

"We'll take the back Battle Cruiser!" Leroy shouted. "Go for one of the big ones that's staying behind!"

The faux Leroys nodded, then the two vehicles split to approach their individual targets. Leroy and Destructo brought out heavy-duty climbing gear, launchers with strong cables and sturdy hooks designed to support their weight. The vehicle slowed down when they neared the battle cruiser, and the two robots fired their hooks into the air. The hooks latched on to the edge, and Leroy and Destructo began their climb. As soon as they started their way up, their vehicle sped off once more to take refuge and wait for their return.

As soon as the pair climbed on deck, Leroy brought out the twin shields he carried on his back. Destructo likewise armed himself with his pauldron fists. Leroy took point as they advanced, searching for a path that would lead them to the vessel's engineering section. Their presence did not go unnoticed for long – they had hardly left the vessel's stern before the first robots took notice and made sure everyone was aware of it. The response that came was equal parts ion shots and far more deadly weapons fire, the crew either having not gotten the message that Leroy was to be taken alive or not realizing who they were shooting at amid the chaos. Fortunately, Leroy's shields protected both him and Destructo all the same, while Destructo launched his massive fists to eliminate any significant threats too far away for Leroy to take care of himself.

Together, the two plowed through every obstacle in their way. With little delay, the two forced their way down the hallways, stairs, and corridors until they burst through to engineering. As soon as they entered the room, they went to work smashing through every other robot there. Half of the engineering crew fled to escape sudden doom, while the other half put up a valiant effort to fight of the invaders. Those that stayed behind quickly fell, each one left to lie on the floor in multiple pieces.

"Go to work," Leroy said once the last of the defenders fell. "I'll cover for you."

Mr. Destructo nodded, then charged into the deepest reaches of the vessel's engineering. With swing after swing and blow after blow, he bent, battered, and broke everything in sight. Smashed pieces soon littered the floor, and in less than a minute lights began flashing while klaxons blared, giving a clear warning the systems were going critical. Wasting no time, the two left the vessel the same way they'd entered.

Their escape was noticeably easier than their entrance, with most of the robots they passed focused more on making their own escape than stopping the two responsible for the situation. They reached the back end of the vessel and escaped by climbing down the metal cords of the grapple cannons just as explosions started to shake the structure from the inside. The shaking grew until it burst through the hull on either side, tearing apart the back end of the land ship. Fire and metal flew, and soon after the command tower collapsed as the structure below it lost integrity. The tower caused even further damage when it landed, rendering the vessel unquestionably dead.

As Leroy and Destructo rode away from the battle cruiser, more explosions drew their attentions to one of the heavy gun platforms. Looking toward it, they watched as it too ruptured, exploded, and died. There was no immediate sign of the two Leroy drones that had been sent aboard, however. Neither Leroy nor Destructo wasted any time contemplating their fate, instead turning their attention to their next target.

****

Another artillery shell flew out of Rustbucket and struck the battle cruiser's command tower. The collision smashed the last of the tower's structural integrity to pieces, leaving it to topple over until it snapped. Without anything holding the tower up, it collapsed and fell to the ground, where it landed on top of a combat transport and several troops.

With two of the Leroy drones providing support, Cannon Man and Humbug pulled heavy duty on the smaller vehicles. Pelting them with concentrated weapons fire, they punctured through the armor and then tore through the insides, leaving them dead on the battlefield. The other troops atop the wall held their own as well, firing a storm of gunshots and energy blasts at the advancing troops. The enemy forces, making clear they weren't suicidal, dug in behind what cover they could find and approached with an ever slowing advance. They took great pains to exploit any opening they could find in the defender's counter-fire, but otherwise relied on their armored support to spearhead the primary advance.

The assault already deteriorating, the Top Dog's army was dealt another demoralizing blow when the second battle cruiser – the one that had yet to even join the battle – exploded in a fiery display. It was soon followed by one of the heavy gun platforms, which went up in a similar fashion. The first signs of actual retreat came in short order when the last heavy gun platform, whether concluding that the battle was lost or merely looking to save itself, revved up and immediately went into a U-turn. A handful of cheers erupted from the robots atop the wall, though they proved to be premature when one robot's celebration was cut short by an energy beam tearing his head clean off.

"Keep your focus! Keep firing!" Steek shouted, underlining the reminder that while the battle was going their way, they had yet to win. Sure enough, while a handful of the ground troops were turning to run away from the wall rather than toward it, most of the forces that had joined the assault still remained, however cautious and slow their advance had become. Off in the distance, the remaining forces split, with half advancing to join the assault and the rest following after the retreating heavy gun platform.

"Focus on the threats!" Steek shouted, looking to maintain order in the chaos. "If they're running, let them!"

Another boom sounded from inside the cave, heralding another round from the primary cannon. The shot flew only a short distance before it struck one of the remaining light gun platforms with a perfect hit, smashing halfway through the main command structure. Soon after, the vessel came to a halt and died.

Then came a boom from a far less friendly origin, followed by an explosion along the wall's right flank. Turning toward the noise, Steek saw one of the remaining gun platforms abandon any concern of collateral damage or who might be destroyed as it tried to pound through Rustbucket's first line of defense. Following in its wake were a pair of transports covering for several enemy troops.

"Priority target! Right flank!" Steek shouted to Cannon and Humbug.

Humbug immediately shifted to the new threat, but nearly fell off the wall when another explosion struck and threatened to tear a hole straight through it. The danger becoming more obvious, other robots nearby quickly moved to defend the position. In doing so, however, they created another opening. Bolstered by the approaching reinforcements, it was an opening the main line of hostiles used to advance.

Another explosion, and a section of the right wall reached the verge of collapse. Humbug opened fire as soon as he was able, pelting shot after shot at the gun platform. The first shots struck the armor, forcing it to give way as the counterattack continued. Cannon Man soon came to his aid, pelting support fire on any robot trying to eliminate Humbug. The concentrated fire from the turret robot soon drove its way into the vehicle's innards. The machine died, then exploded, leaving behind a burning wreck.

One of the transports charged around the wrecked vehicle to ram the wall. While both Humbug and Cannon tried to shoot the transport down, it slipped by with minimal damage. The transport crashed into the damaged section of the wall at top speed, but its effort to break through came up just short, lodging it dead center in the very hole it created. Unable to move, it quickly fell to concentrated fire, leaving the vehicle unable to even attempt a retreat.

A handful of the ground troops charged, attempting to use the broken transport as an impromptu stepping-stone to climb over the wall. Most of the soldiers were shot down during the advance. Three of them successfully climbed over. One was immediately torn apart by the hulking security member known as Krix, who threw the body back over as a warning. The other two attackers shot down two of

Rustbucket's defenders atop the wall but were swiftly cut down in turn by Turrex before they did any further damage.

With the attack to the right flank thwarted, the defenders atop the wall refocused on the pressing threat from the front. The push forward was soon brought to a halt and suffered another blow when Rustbucket's main cannon demolished one of the reinforcement transports. The army already suffering from disillusionment, it was the blow finally setting them into retreat. It came slowly at first, but quickly built momentum until every robot and still functioning vehicle was moving away from the settlement with all possible speed.

When it became clear the Top Dog's forces were in full retreat, the defenders of Rustbucket stopped shooting and turned to celebration. Cheers of victory over their defeated foe erupted atop the wall as they watched the enemy flee into the distance.

01110.

"Hold!" Captain Kyron ordered when the *Hammer* reached five miles outside the settlement's walls. "We'll use this position as a rally point."

The heavy gun platform slowed to a crawl, turning in a quarter circle allowing it a clear line of sight to the other retreating forces before coming to a full stop.

"All security on alert," Kyron continued. "I want heavy protection around engineering and the bridge until we know those saboteurs didn't get aboard."

Kyron turned to look out the windows back to where they'd come from, watching for signs of the other retreating forces. Only two were clearly visible, a pair of transports, though there were plenty of signs others were on their way as well.

It was one of the last things he saw. While Captain Kyron was taking in the full weight of the situation, his first officer walked up behind him and twisted the robot's head clean off his body. Shock immediately swept through the bridge. Kyron's body fell to the ground while his neck sparked wildly from where it had been ripped free, and his face fluctuated from his futile efforts to remain active with what little power his head had left. Slowly, Lt. Hal Zeta-4 turned his captain's head around so they looked each other face to face.

"Such failure can not be tolerated," Hal said. He then dropped the head to the floor and stepped on it. Looking to the rest of the bridge, he turned to shoot a very pointed look at each robot in turn.

"If anyone has any complaints, feel free to take it up with the Top Dog," Hal said. "Now call him up."

There was a moment's hesitation, but the right look in the right direction brought that hesitation to a swift end. Nearly an hour later, the screen on the back end of the bridge lit up with a glitch-filled image of the Top Dog.

"Sir. This is Lt. Hal Zeta-4 reporting," Hal said. The Top Dog's face grew in the screen as he took a closer look.

"Who are you and why am I talking to you right now?" The Top Dog asked.

"I'm reporting from the *Hammer* on the mission to capture Leroy Brown," Hal answered.

The Top Dog looked at Hal a moment as he reasoned out what the robot was talking about.

"Why am I talking to you and not Commander I-Kron?" The Top Dog asked.

"Commander I-Kron was destroyed," Hal answered. "So was most of his army. All the cruisers are gone, so are half the gun platforms. I don't know how many troops survived. We're currently gathering five miles out from the settlement."

The Top Dog stood practically frozen as he looked at Hal.

"Does not compute," The Top Dog finally said. "*Explain.*"

"The settlement tricked Commander I-Kron and used a bomb to blow up the *Superior*," Hal answered. "Chaos followed. Half the forces attacked; the other half held back. Those that attacked were torn apart by a cannon they were hiding, the half that held back were torn apart by saboteurs. Worse, there were multiple robots that looked like Leroy Brown, adding to the confusion. We failed to break through, and Captain Kyron ordered a retreat to save the *Hammer*. Soon after, the surviving forces were driven into a full retreat."

For a second time, the Top Dog looked at Hal with a practically frozen look.

"This is what I am hearing," the Top Dog finally said. "I send what should be an overwhelming army to capture Leroy Brown and destroy the settlement where he's hiding. Instead of Leroy Brown, what I'm given instead is the loss of nearly everything I've invested in that mission at the hands of a dinky little band hiding in a cave, with nothing to show for it. Is that an accurate assessment?"

"Mostly, yes," Hal replied.

"*Mostly*?"

"Whoever they are, they knew exactly what they were doing," Hal answered. "They were well defended and well organized. When our side made a mistake, they took advantage of it. We may have had superior forces, but they used far superior strategy."

"And who's responsible for the mistake that allowed them to win?" The Top Dog asked.

"Most of them are dead already," Hal answered. "I believe that Kyron was the last of those who could be blamed, and I've already taken the liberty of executing him for both his hesitation to attack and for ordering the retreat that ensured our loss."

"Did you now?" The Top Dog asked.

He glanced to the rest of the robots in the room.

"Is that true?" He asked. The other robots all confirmed the news.

"Interesting," the Top Dog said. "How very ambitious of you."

"I was merely acting in accordance with what I believed you

would want," Hal replied.

"I see," the Top Dog said. "I suppose that would make you the Captain now."

"If you are willing, Sir."

"Very well," The Top Dog said. "Consider yourself the new Captain."

"Aye, Sir."

"For the time being, your standing orders will be to stay there," the Top Dog said. "Gather up everyone who's left and prepare them for my arrival."

"You're coming here?" Hal asked.

"Yes," the Top Dog answered. "I'll be arriving in the near future to personally lead a replacement army that will correct the ongoing series of mistakes that keep happening."

"Understood, Sir," Hal said. "We will eagerly await your arrival."

The Top Dog gave only the barest hint of a nod, and then the screen went blank.

****

Once the immediate celebration of their victory died down, the robots of Rustbucket turned quiet to watch and wait for signs of Leroy and Destructo's triumphant return. While the destruction of the battle cruisers and gun platforms in the distance had been a clear sign they had carried through with their mission, their survival was far less of a certainty. As the robots stood atop the wall, silently looking out across the remnants of the battle, the only sounds that could be heard were the wind and the burning wreckage.

"Look!" a robot shouted with a point. He was soon joined by another, then two more. Before long everyone could see exactly what they had been looking for.

Two small vehicles drove along a winding path toward Rustbucket, maneuvering around the largest obstacles and over the smaller pieces. Each one was driven by one of Leroy's drone duplicates, with one carrying another duplicate, while the other carried Mr. Destructo and Leroy Brown himself. Another round of cheers erupted from Rustbucket in celebration of their survival and triumphant return. Destructo waved back, though Leroy's focus was mostly on the battlefield around them.

When they neared the wall, the gate opened to allow the vehicles to roll through. Just before they entered, however, Leroy stepped out of his ride. Most the robots didn't think much of it, instead swarming around Destructo and likewise out of the gate toward Leroy to congratulate them both. Destructo only accepted the congratulations just enough to avoid upsetting anyone, his primary focus turned to Leroy.

"Leroy?" Destructo said as he carefully pushed his way past the crowd. Leroy didn't react at first, but soon turned to face the wall and everyone around it.

"Everyone, listen up!" Leroy shouted. The celebration died down and the robots turned their focus to Leroy's words.

"That was an excellent performance!" Leroy continued when he was sure he had their attention. "Everyone performed admirably. You all succeeded above and beyond expectations. In this moment, you should take pride in your success and take a moment to congratulate yourselves on a hard-fought, well-earned victory!"

A subdued round of cheers and applause followed as the crowd took a moment to do just that.

"Good," Leroy said once the celebration had died down again. "Now that the moment is past, it is essential that we not lose sight of the future. We have won this battle, but we have not yet won the war. The threat is still out there, and I can guarantee you that they are angry. They are going to return for Round 3, and that opening trick we pulled is not going to work a second time."

Leroy turned to face the battlefield, then looked back over his shoulder to the robots behind him.

"This wreckage is a gift, and we need to make the most of it. It's time to go to work, people. We've built a fort, now it's time to make a fortress. Let's get to work like our existence depends on it."

A quiet hung in the air, but Leroy paid it no mind. He turned and walked through the crowd to the wall, intent on inspecting how it had held up. Destructo rolled after him.

"I can't say that's the speech I would have given," Destructo said.

"It's the speech they needed to hear," Leroy replied. "I meant every word. We don't have time to relax and celebrate right now, Destructo. We're at war, and war doesn't wait for when you're good and ready."

"That's your fault, if I'm not mistaken."

"If I'm not mistaken, this was going to happen eventually," Leroy replied. He stopped and turned to face Destructo. "I just accelerated the timetable."

"You're also the one who convinced them to fight."

"Which was also going to happen eventually," Leroy countered. "Again, I just accelerated the timetable."

"You're not turning this into your own personal war, are you?" Destructo asked.

"No, Destructo," Leroy replied. "We already went over this. It's a mutually beneficial arrangement. I fight on their behalf, we beat the Top Dog, I save Rustbucket, and then I get to go home. Everyone wins except the Top Dog and anyone standing between us and him."

The two robots looked each other eye-to-eye.

"I'm a warbot, remember?" Leroy said. "This is my element. This is *what I do.*"

Destructo stared at Leroy, then slowly lifted his arm up and planted it on Leroy's shoulder with a mild clank. He nodded, then turned back to the robots around the wall.

"Alright, everyone!" Destructo shouted. "Let's get to work! If you don't know what to do, we can easily find something for you!"

****

With drones taking the lead, Rustbucket's security teams swept through the battlefield searching for any leftover hostiles. A handful of stragglers were discovered during the search. Most attempted to flee and were allowed to do so. A few tried to continue the fight but were quickly neutralized. While security forces ensured the area was safe, engineering teams went to work on the wall, starting with the transport that was lodged halfway through. It was quickly decided to cut the transport in half, after which each half was pulled out its own direction. Once the hole was clear, work ensued to ensure Rustbucket's already established defenses were fully restored.

After security teams confirmed the area was safe, salvage teams moved in en masse. Everything that could be laid claim to was, and anything that could be kept intact was salvaged in as good a condition as was manageable. With multiple large wrecks to go through, there was no shortage of materials to choose from. Soon, the abundance of gathered materials were gathered in piles both inside and outside the wall. The larger the piles grew, the more talk spread of how to use the windfall of resources. There was even discussion about repairing some of the broken vehicles so they could be turned right around and used to fight the very same army that sent them in the first place.

It was talk that left Leroy facing the unfortunate problem of managing expectations. While he inherently agreed with many of the ideas discussed, he was forced to remind them of the many challenges standing in the way, first and foremost Rustbucket's limited population. For all the robots that suggested that they find a way to use the broken battle cruisers for their own ends, Leroy was forced to remind them more than once that above all else, they didn't have the numbers to operate either of them properly.

He instead turned their focus toward force multipliers to make the most use of what numbers they had. To that end, focus was turned to the wall once more. After the previous construction was repaired and reinforced, another layer was added that rose even higher, and included emplacements to house recovered and refurbished weapons claimed from the wrecked enemy vessels. Once the wall additions were well underway, construction began on a larger and more powerful artillery cannon to compliment the first.

For a week straight work continued. Functioning together as

a team, the citizens of Rustbucket put piece after piece into place. The wall rose to new, thicker, stronger heights. The second cannon came together as a terrifying weapon that gave the robots of Rustbucket another boost of confidence in their ability to fight off all of Junkworld if they had to. Together, they worked in a constant fashion, with one robot filling in whenever another needed to recharge, allowing construction to proceed at an inhuman rate.

On occasion, shuttles flew overhead along flight paths making it clear they were on reconnaissance runs. When the first appeared, Rustbucket's anti-air turrets were armed and opened fire as soon as it came within range. While they hit the shuttle, it escaped critical damage and slipped away in retreat. Every scout that followed flew at a far more respectful distance. All the same, they provided a regular reminder about the danger the settlement still faced and the need to prepare for the next wave.

Just over a week after Rustbucket fought off the Top Dog's first army, a shuttle was spotted flying directly at the settlement. It flew low enough to the ground to avoid the anti-air cannons, practically floating off the ground as it twisted in and out amid the features on the terrain. It slowed its approach as it grew near, giving the shuttle an ominous air. For the first time in a week, work halted in anticipation of hostile activity. By the time the shuttle landed, just beyond what remained of the nearby battle cruiser wreck, armed defenders had taken up position on the wall and were ready for action.

"Hold fire!" Mr. Destructo shouted. "Let's not get too trigger happy, people."

The defenders watched closely as they waited for whatever might come around the corner, fearing it might be a trick of some kind. To their surprise, the only thing that appeared was a familiar-looking robot. It was another Rocu unit, by the looks of it, identical in every way that mattered. The defenders atop the wall kept their guard up all the same as the Rocu rolled forward on his tread-footed legs. Half the weapons were aimed at the small robot, the other half pointed out in every other direction in case the Rocu was a distraction from some other plot.

"That's close enough!" Mr. Destructo shouted when the robot came within twenty-five yards of the wall. The robot stopped, then looked back up at him.

"I am ROCU Alpha-5!" The robot shouted back. "I come bearing a message from the Top Dog for the robot known as Leroy Brown!"

Steek, Destructo, and a handful of other nearby robots glanced at Leroy.

"About what?" Leroy asked.

Rocu didn't answer. Instead, the robot solidified his position and folded open to reveal a video screen. The robots waited for something to appear, but the screen stayed blank.

"Steek, shoot it," Destructo said.

"What? No," Leroy said, stopping Steek before he could pull the trigger. "Why would you shoot it?"

"Why wouldn't we shoot it?" Destructo asked.

"Because the Top Dog actually wants to talk," Leroy said. "And he actually came to me to do it. None of that silly nonsense about being shipped off to meet him while turned off. You ask me, this is a good sign."

"Leroy–" Destructo started.

"What are you so worried about?" Leroy asked. "I'll have my shield ready in case something goes wrong. You just worry about watching my back."

With that, Leroy made his way off the wall and toward the gate. Destructo followed, along with two other armed robots. After stopping a moment to let the gates open, they stepped beyond the safety of the walls with a slow, cautious walk. They and everyone atop the wall looked around with each step, expecting something to go wrong at any moment. No such trickery came, however, allowing them to make their way to Rocu without incident.

"Alright, I'm here," Leroy said once they reached the messenger. "What does the Top Dog have to say?"

The screen flashed with a blur of static, then slowly cleared up and gave way to the image of a robot. Leroy froze up the moment he saw who it was. While there were several differences, such as extra visual receptors that had been attached to the head, it was still a strikingly familiar design. It was enough that Leroy's immediate reaction was to conclude it had to be a different robot of the same basic make and model. That conclusion quickly fell apart when the Top Dog spoke.

"Hello, Leroy," the Top Dog said. "Did you miss me?"

Leroy looked at Mr. Destructo.

"Freddy?" Leroy asked. "The Top Dog is Chainsaw Freddy?"

01111.

"Good! You do remember me!" The Top Dog said. "It's been a while, and with all the years you've waited to show yourself, I had concerns perhaps your memories had been compromised."

Leroy looked at the Top Dog – a robot he knew far better as Chainsaw Freddy – and then back to Destructo.

"How is this possible? There is no way–" Leroy started. He stopped short and turned back to Freddy. "Years?"

"More than ten years, if you need a number," Freddy said.

Leroy stared at Chainsaw Freddy, then looked to Destructo, then back to the screen.

"Oh, I didn't see you there, Destructo," Freddy said. "I was so focused on Leroy. So this is where you've been hiding, then."

"Hello, Freddy," Destructo said with a cool voice.

Leroy glanced back to Destructo, then returned his attention to the screen again.

"Chainsaw Freddy," Leroy said. His processors nearly froze for a moment as he tried to calculate everything that was happening.

"You look surprised," Freddy said.

"How is this possible?" Leroy asked as he turned back to Destructo. "We just fought a few weeks ago. A few months ago at most. How is it possible that he's the Top Dog? Why do I keep running into people from the URCL?"

"Did you not just hear me when I said it's been over ten years?" Freddy asked. Leroy looked back to the screen. "You really have no idea what's happened since then, do you? Destructo, have you been keeping Leroy in the dark?"

Freddy looked at Destructo, and Leroy turned to match.

"I think this is a good time for you to tell him the truth," Freddy said. "I could tell him myself, but I think it would be more believable coming from you."

"Truth about what, Destructo?" Leroy asked him.

Destructo stared at Leroy, but said nothing.

"Well?" Freddy said. "We're waiting."

Destructo glanced at the screen, then back to Leroy.

"Tell me," Leroy said.

"It's been more than ten years since your fight with Chainsaw Freddy," Destructo finally said. "The URCL was shut down shortly after. Everyone was shipped here afterwards."

Leroy stared at Destructo, silent and unmoving.

"Shut down?" Leroy asked.

"It's gone, Leroy. The URCL hasn't existed in over a decade."

Once more, Leroy stood and stared at Mr. Destructo, silent and unmoving.

"Why?" he finally asked. "How?"

"You know what U-R-C-L stands for, right?" Freddy asked. Leroy slowly turned to look back at the screen as he spoke. "*Underground* Robot Combat League? It was shut down for being illegal. They just managed to get our fight in before that happened."

"Shut down?" Leroy asked.

"Here I thought you were smarter than this," Freddy replied. "Yes, shut down. By the local authorities. The League held our match, and then the government shut down the league. Which brings me to the reason I'm here."

Freddy closed in on the screen until his face was all that could be seen.

"I want a rematch, Leroy," Freddy said.

Leroy stared at the screen, silent and unmoving once more.

"A rematch?" Destructo asked. "This is all about a *rematch*?"

"Yes," Freddy answered. "Well, not my status as the Top Dog, of course. But that's why I wanted Leroy Brown. The League may be gone, but that doesn't mean the two of us can't have one last fight. I want the chance to correct my loss to him."

"So, the only reason you're attacking Rustbucket is so you can have a stupid rematch with the only robot to ever beat you?" Destructo asked.

"No," Freddy answered. "If I'd already known about your stupid settlement, I would have destroyed you all long ago. You should be thankful, actually, because wanting a rematch with Leroy is the only reason I've had my forces hold back. Which leaves me with a bit of a quandary."

"I'd love to have a true rematch with you, Leroy," Freddy continued. "I really would. But I have a growing empire to run. I can't afford to keep wasting my forces on efforts to keep you alive so we can have our rematch. Fortunately, I don't have to. Seeing as you've managed to assemble a small army of your own, I'm willing to settle for a rematch by proxy, your army versus mine. So, here's how this is going to work. My scouts tell me that...Rustbucket, you said?"

"Yes," Destructo answered. "Rustbucket."

"I've been informed that Rustbucket sits in the shadow of a volcano. It has active magma at the bottom and everything. That volcano happens to have a large outcropping that as far as I'm concerned, is the perfect setting to serve as an impromptu fighting arena. So, one day from now, I'm going to go there to fight you, Leroy. If you're there, we can settle this like the old days once and for all. If you don't show, however, I'll assume you've refused my offer and settle for duel by proxy, your army against mine, and I'll throw everything I have at you to ensure there is nothing left of your little settlement or anyone who lives there. Understood?"

Leroy and Freddy stared at one another, though Leroy said nothing.

"Hello?" Freddy asked. He tapped the screen a few times. "Is this thing still on?"

"I'll be there," Leroy answered in a cold, solemn voice.

"Good!" Freddy answered. "I look forward to it."

With that, the screen went blank. Rocu folded back up, spun around, and rolled off back the way he had come, leaving the robots of Rustbucket to watch his departure. Destructo watched for only a short bit before turning to look at Leroy. Leroy, however, continued to watch Rocu until he vanished around the corner again, and then kept watching until the shuttle lifted off and disappeared over the horizon. He then turned to look at Destructo.

"Leroy..." Destructo started but stopped when Leroy lifted his hand up and planted a finger against Destructo's metal shell.

"You. Me. Talk. Now," Leroy said.

Leroy turned into a brisk walk leading back through the gates. After a moment, Destructo turned and followed. He continued following Leroy all the way through Rustbucket, with the warbot ignoring all attempts to talk. Leroy didn't stop walking until he finally entered the command station overlooking the settlement.

"Out," Leroy said. "Everyone out."

While nobody knew what was going on or why Leroy wanted them to leave, they obliged him all the same. Destructo waited until everyone else left, then entered the room and closed the door behind him.

"Tell me everything," Leroy said to Destructo. "Now."

"What else is there to tell?" Destructo asked. "I've already told you everything you need to know."

"You really think you're the right one to make that judgment?" Leroy asked.

"Yes," Destructo answered.

"Did you also think it was the right decision to not tell me that the Top Dog is Chainsaw Freddy? Or not to tell me that the URCL no longer exists?" Leroy asked. "You knew full well that everything I was doing was a means to get back there. Everything I have done since I arrived has been to serve one mission – to go back to the URCL. I made it perfectly clear that all I really wanted was to go home. Yet you never once thought to tell me that it no longer exists?"

Destructo looked at Leroy but said nothing.

"Start talking," Leroy said. "I'll decide for myself what's worth knowing."

Destructo looked back at Leroy a moment, then nodded.

"Your fight with Freddy happened a little over a decade ago," Destructo began. "The day after, word spread that legal authorities were planning to shut down the Underground Robot Combat League. After that news got out, it was all but a scramble to get rid of the evidence and do anything necessary to escape arrest and prosecution.

Most the robots were thrown in boxes and shipped to Junkworld as fast as possible."

"They got rid of me?" Leroy asked.

"Yes, Leroy," Destructo answered. "You're a certified warbot. Of course they got rid of you. When they learned the URCL was done, you were one of the first ones shipped off New Chicago. If anything, the rest of us were surprised when we arrived and there wasn't any sign of you. The ones that arrived in-tact and reactivated, at any rate."

"After that, we were forced to contend with what to do with ourselves," he continued. "A few tried to band everyone together. Some accepted their new existence and wandered off in search of a new purpose in life. Others didn't adapt very well. Like Freddy."

"You sure?" Leroy asked. "Because from where I'm standing he appears to have done pretty well for himself."

"Perhaps, from one standpoint," Destructo said. "But he couldn't accept that the URCL was gone. It got worse when he realized you were nowhere to be found and he might never get a chance to have a rematch of that last fight. He started picking off the other survivors. When that didn't satisfy him, he turned his eyes to bigger fights. Somehow, that turned his mind to conquest, and he settled on taking over the whole planet. The rest of the URCL survivors tried to band together and put him down, but that failed horribly."

"Everyone else is gone?" Leroy asked.

"It's possible there's one or two survivors out there yet," Destructo answered. "Someone who's unaccounted for that Freddy missed. But as far as I know, it's just you, me, and him."

"He didn't seem to care when he saw you," Leroy said.

"He's already beaten me, Leroy. Back in the Battledome.

Outside of Rustbucket, apart from you, he doesn't care about me. You, on the other hand? You're unfinished business. You're the only unfinished business he really cares about."

"So what happens if he conquers Junkworld?" Leroy asked.

"I don't know," Destructo answered. "If he succeeds, I probably won't be around to care anymore. I'm not thinking that far ahead. All I'm thinking about right now, Leroy, is protecting Rustbucket and the robots who live here."

Leroy looked at Destructo, then turned to look out the window at Rustbucket below. After a moment, he walked forward until he reached the window.

"Why didn't you tell me?" Leroy asked. "I made it clear the only thing I really wanted was to go back to the URCL. Did you ever even consider telling me it hasn't even existed in over a decade?"

Destructo quietly stared at Leroy while the warbot waited for an answer. When none came, Leroy turned to look at him.

"Well?"

Destructo continued to stare at Leroy and say nothing. Leroy stepped forward until he was directly in Destructo's face.

"Why, Destructo?"

"I couldn't afford to risk it," Destructo answered.

"To risk what?" Leroy asked.

"How you would respond."

"How did you think I would respond?" Leroy asked.

"I don't know, Leroy," Destructo answered. "I had no idea how you would react. That's why I couldn't risk it. That is why I didn't tell you. Junkworld is bad enough with one Top Dog running around. I – we – none of us could afford the possibility that you'd follow Freddy's example if you didn't have the URCL to go back to."

"Why would you think I'd turn into a warlord?"

"I don't know you, Leroy," Destructo said. "I didn't know you. We may have both been part of the League, but we didn't really know each other. We knew of each other, we fought in the Battledome a few times, but we never actually knew each other. I had no way of knowing how you would react when you learned the truth."

"Did you just think I was going to stay in the dark forever?" Leroy asked. "What did you think was going to happen if I agreed to your plan to assassinate Freddy and I found myself face-to-face with him? Or what did you expect to happen when I returned to New Chicago and learned there was nothing left for me anymore?"

"I suppose I thought that if it took long enough, it wouldn't matter anymore," Destructo answered. "You'd accept your new life here, and the League wouldn't matter anymore."

"You wanted to throw me to Freddy the moment Rustbucket was discovered. You were ready for me to meet him face-to-face. How quickly did you expect me to forget about the URCL?"

"All that mattered at the time was that Freddy would be focused on you," Destructo explained. "I was willing to bet you'd be enough of a distraction that we could finally end the Top Dog."

"So all you cared about was that I could serve as a distraction?"

"For what it's worth, if anyone could survive being thrust into the role, it would be you."

Leroy stared at Destructo a moment.

"Why?"

"While you spent the last decade trapped in an inactive ignorance, I've watched Freddy destroy every link we have to our old life and become a threat to all of Junkworld with no idea how to stop him. Right at this moment, he is a very direct threat to the one small piece of it that I've made it my mission to protect. Try running the calculations from my perspective, Leroy."

Silence hung in the air as the two robots looked at each other. Leroy stepped back, then turned and leaned on the table in the middle of the room.

"I thought I was here by mistake," Leroy said. "I thought I had a team that lost me by mistake, I thought the URCL was where I was supposed to be. And now..."

The words hung in the air for a moment, then Leroy looked back at Destructo.

"Now...what, Destructo? What now?"

"Right now, Rustbucket still needs you Leroy," Destructo said. "Junkworld still needs you."

"Does it?" Leroy asked, then let his head hang. "An hour ago, I thought I was needed on New Chicago. Now...that hasn't been true for over a decade."

"You're still the best chance of stopping the Top Dog," Destructo said. "He's given us the perfect opportunity. We know where he's going to be and when. He's going to be exposed. We can set up an ambush, and when–"

"No," Leroy said.

"You're not going to fight him?"

"I am," Leroy said. "I'm still going to fight him. But it's going to be exactly what he wants – a rematch. A real rematch. No ambush, no tricks. Just one final showdown to give the Underground Robot Combat League the send-off it deserves."

"A rematch for the fate of Junkworld," Mr. Destructo said, his words sitting in a strange place between statement and question. "You are going to win."

"I'm Leroy Brown," Leroy said, still looking face down at the table. "I'm the undefeated URCL champion. Winning is what I do."

****

The sun held high in the sky over the wastes of Junkworld. Captain Hal Zeta-4 stood on the ground in front of the *Hammer*, watching as a shuttle flew overhead, then lowered to the ground and landed directly in front of him. A ramp lowered as soon as the shuttle came to a stop, and out rolled the unmistakable form of the Top Dog.

"Sir," Hal said as he stood there.

"Captain Hal," the Top Dog said with an acknowledging nod.

"When you said you were coming here, I didn't expect you to mean my ship specifically," Hal said.

"Technically it's *my* ship," the Top Dog said. He rolled past Hal and toward the *Hammer*.

"Of course," Hal said as he turned and followed.

"I thought it would make for a good place to inspect my troops before I go into battle," the Top Dog said as he rolled up the *Hammer*'s loading ramp.

"I look forward to fighting alongside you, Sir," Hal said.

"No, no, you misunderstand," the Top Dog said. "I have a fight to attend, assuming my opponent shows up. I should know if he'll be where he's supposed to be soon."

Atop the deck of the *Hammer*, the Top Dog rolled to the edge of the ship and looked out at the forces assembling nearby. There, nearly the entirety of his war force prepared and waited for the command to march onward to battle. Among them were the *Ultimatum*, four battle cruisers, six heavy gun platforms, a dozen light gun platforms, and two dozen combat transports, including one very long, very special transport built very recently for a very special purpose. The only forces not present were those held in defensive reserve to ensure no one would get the wise idea to take a shot at his territory while he was preoccupied with Rustbucket.

"Impressive, isn't it?" the Top Dog said as he gazed across his military.

"Indeed it is, Sir," Hal replied. "And I could not be more pleased to be part of it."

"Always good to hear," the Top Dog said.

The Top Dog turned around as a Rocu unit approached.

"We've received confirmation from your scouts," The robot said. "Leroy Brown is waiting at the designated location."

"Excellent," the Top Dog replied. The Rocu nodded, then turned and rolled away again. The Top Dog then turned and made his way toward the *Hammer*'s bridge. Hal followed, though he was left unsure as to what the Top Dog was up to.

"Sir?" Hal asked.

The Top Dog stopped and spun the top half of his body around to look at Hal.

"Is there a problem?" he asked.

"I certainly hope not," Hal replied.

"Likewise," the Top Dog replied. He spun back around and continued forward.

When he reached the bridge, everyone turned, froze up, and then stood at attention.

"At ease, everyone," the Top Dog said.

All the same, everyone stood where they were.

"Well, if you insist," the Top Dog added when it was clear nobody had any intent of doing so.

Hal stood in the entryway as the Top Dog took a short, self-guided tour of the bridge, looking it over with a somewhat casual attitude.

"Is there anything you need, Sir?" Hal asked.

The Top Dog stopped where he was, then turned the treads on his feet in opposite directions to pivot his entire body as a single unit.

"As a matter of fact, there is," The Top Dog said. "I need you to step over here."

Hal looked at the Top Dog for a moment, then nodded and did just that.

"Good," the Top Dog said. "Tell me, *Captain*. Do you know how I got to be where I am? How I became the Top Dog, both in name and in fact?"

"I don't know the full story, no," Hal answered.

"It was a lot of hard work," the Top Dog said. "I had to tear through a lot of robots to do it."

"I'm sure you did," Hal said.

"Good times, those," the Top Dog said, briefly looking out to an unseen horizon before looking back at Hal. "Fortunately, I had help. Especially from this."

The Top Dog rotated the bottom portion of his body around to display his laser-tipped chainsaw, mounted on a long, multisegmented limb like the stinger of a tail.

"It's pretty cool, isn't it?" The Top Dog said. Hal nodded in agreement.

"It's also very dangerous," the Top Dog continued. The chainsaw started up, a low energetic hum accompanying the red blur that spun around the weapon.

"I have to be very careful with this thing," the Top Dog continued, slowly waving the chainsaw back and forth in an ominous fashion. "Or else I just might accidentally break something I didn't mean to, like-oops!"

In that moment, the chainsaw sliced across Hal's side, cutting his arm off. Hal looked to and grabbed at his now missing limb, only to have his legs suddenly cut out from under him. Hal fell to the ground in a heap, his head swiveling back and forth as his processors tried to understand what was happening.

"If I hadn't meant to do that, I would have called it a mistake," the Top Dog said.

He gave Hal's body a kick, sliding it against the bridge floor so that it bumped up against the wall. Hal tried to scramble with his one remaining limb, but the Top Dog was on him again before he made any meaningful progress. He pressed his foot down against Hal's body, pinning the nearly limbless robot against the floor and wall.

"Just like the very serious mistake you made," the Top Dog said. Hal's head jerked up as he looked at the robot towering over him.

"Here's the funny thing," The Top Dog continued. "If you just had the sensibility to wait, I probably would have given you the order to execute your captain myself. But no, you thought it was a good idea to just go ahead and do it anyway."

"I thought it was what you wanted!" Hal said. He grabbed hold of the Top Dog's leg with his one remaining hand. While he tried to push on the leg holding him down, it was clear he had little hope of accomplishing anything.

"In the strictest sense, you're right," the Top Dog said. "It is what I wanted. As I just told you, had you waited for my orders, I almost certainly would have told you to do it and made you the captain anyway.

The Top Dog leaned down to look at Hal closer but kept his head far enough away to ensure it was just out of reach of the one remaining arm.

"I'm sure you're asking yourself a lot of questions right now," the Top Dog said. "Like 'Why?' and what sense is there in doing this if I would have ordered you to do what you did anyway. Here's the thing, *Captain* Hal. I can't abide robots in my organization taking it upon themselves to go around executing their duly appointed superior officers whenever they assume that's what I would want. I refuse to stand for anyone in my chain of command assuming they can just go around executing the robots they answer to without my express permission and authorization. You know why that is?"

The Top Dog stared Hal in the face. For a moment, it looked like the Top Dog was waiting for Hal to answer, but he spoke up again before Hal said anything.

"It's not just because that's a lousy way to run an army. It just leads to chaos. The more important reason is because the robots who have the ambition to go around executing their superior officers without my approval are the same kind of robots who are most likely to get the very bad idea that they can do the same thing to me."

The Top Dog stood straight up again; thought he kept his eyes focused squarely on Hal.

"And that just won't do," the Top Dog said. The moment he finished speaking, he stabbed his chainsaw straight into Hal's head. He held it there a few moments, then sliced upward to split the robot's head in half before jabbing it through the robot's chest. He pulled it back out, then jabbed the chainsaw in and out of the body several more times, just to make sure Hal was good and dead. When he pulled the chainsaw out for the last time, he turned it off, then rolled back and turned to the rest of the room.

"Would someone please clean up this mess?" The Top Dog said. No less than three robots scrambled toward the remains of their former captain, and together they hauled Hal's remains off the bridge.

"Good work, everyone," the Top Dog said. "Now, would someone please tell me who his first officer was?"

The Top Dog looked around the room, but no one gave any indication they fit that description.

"Really? He didn't have a first officer? No one?"

He continued to look around the room. Eventually, a robot stepped forward. The Top Dog looked at the robot, then glanced around to make sure no one else was trying to lay claim to the title.

"And you are?" the Top Dog asked.

"Kronto-Five," the robot answered.

"Congratulations," the Top Dog said. "Consider yourself the *Hammer*'s new acting captain."

"Yes, Sir," Kronto replied.

"I'll be choosing a permanent captain later, but who knows. Maybe you'll impress me, and I'll just make your new position permanent."

"Yes, Sir."

The Top Dog nodded, then looked around the room again.

"Now, if you'll excuse me, I have a fight to win," he said. Then the Top Dog rolled out of the room.

10000.

Ripples of heat flowed into the air from a lake of magma that lay deep below Junkworld's surface. High above the pit of liquid rock, a large outcropping jutted inward to create a semi-circular formation, almost as perfect a natural stage as one could ask for. It came complete with lesser formations standing out among the rim of the volcano, mostly around the section leading to the central outcropping.

Standing in the center of the outcropping, watching and waiting for the arrival of Chainsaw Freddy, were a handful of robots from the settlement of Rustbucket. At their center was Leroy Brown, and joined by Mr. Destructo, Isaac, Walter, and four others, including a pair consisting of one robot with a recorder built into her body and a second transmitting whatever the first saw back to Rustbucket for all to see.

"Are we sure he will come?" Walter asked. "He is not planning to attack while we are gone, is he?"

"No," Leroy answered. "He'll come. He'll come, and we're going to fight. Just like on New Chicago."

"Are you sure that this is not a trick?" Walter asked.

"Yes."

Walter looked out toward the outer end of the outcropping, then back to Leroy.

"How do you know?" Walter asked.

"Trust us," Destructo said. "He knows."

A few minutes later, a pair of matching shuttles appeared from over the edge and landed at the outer end of the volcano. From one of the shuttles came a small team of robots, including three that looked like they each served as both a camera and transmitter all in one. The robots moved around the edge of the volcano, taking positions in preparation for the imminent fight. Once the robots had taken their places, the second shuttle opened. In an overly slow and dramatic fashion, Chainsaw Freddy rolled down the ramp and continued across the outcropping.

"Leroy Brown!" Freddy shouted. "Words cannot express how much I have anticipated this very moment!"

"Have you now," Leroy said.

"More than you can imagine," Freddy said. "At long last, I finally have the opportunity to fix my one true mistake."

"And that mistake is?"

"Losing to you."

"Really?" Leroy asked. "That's your one mistake? The only mistake you've ever made?"

"It's the only one that matters," Freddy said. "But enough with the banter. Let's make this official already."

The robots around Leroy stepped away and went to take positions of their own around the outer edge of the Volcano. Destructo started to follow but stopped a moment next to Leroy.

"You're going to win," Destructo said, the words as much a question as they were a statement.

"That's what Leroy Brown does, isn't it?" Leroy said, looking onward at Freddy. "Leroy Brown, Champion of the URCL. Winning is all he does."

"This isn't about the URCL, Leroy," Destructo said. "This is about Freddy, this is about Rustbucket, this is about Junkworld."

"Because the League doesn't exist anymore."

"That doesn't matter right now. This is bigger than the League. It matters that you win because everyone in Rustbucket is counting on you. You beat him once before, it's time for a repeat performance."

Leroy glanced to Destructo.

"Right," Leroy said. "The League doesn't matter. The League never mattered. All that matters is winning. Which is what I do. Because I'm Leroy Brown."

"Mr. Destructo!" Freddy shouted. "Do you mind? We have a fight to get underway!"

Leroy and Destructo both looked to Freddy. Destructo then looked back to Leroy.

"Go tear him apart, Leroy," Destructo said, then he rolled off to join the other inhabitants of Rustbucket. As he did, Leroy and Freddy took positions along opposite ends of the outcropping, each one with a drop off directly behind them. A small robot from Freddy's retinue rolled along the pathway toward the center between them.

"What's wrong?" Isaac asked when Destructo stood next to him.

"Leroy Brown," Destructo answered.

"What's wrong with Leroy?" Walter asked.

Destructo looked to Walter, then looked back to the makeshift arena.

"He's not going to win," Destructo said, his voice barely audible.

Before anyone could ask Destructo what he meant, the robot in the center of the battle zone spoke up.

"LADIES AND GENTLEMEN! ROBOTS OF ALL MAKES

AND MODELS!" the robot shouted with far greater volume than anyone expected from a unit of his size. "Welcome to tonight's very special presentation of the Underground Robot Combat League! For tonight, we give the URCL a sendoff more than a decade in the making with one final match!"

Cheers sounded out from Freddy's retinue, though it was difficult to tell how much of it was genuine and how much was merely pre-recorded material being played back.

"The challenger!" The announcer said, before he turned to Freddy. "You know him better as the Top Dog, and for a good reason! He's the big, mean, killing machine who's as deadly as they come, and he's on a warpath! Get in his way, and it'll be the last thing you regret. Love him or hate him, you can't ignore him, it's CHAIN-SAAAAAAW FREDDY!"

Freddy raised his arms up and turned to what little crowd there was, and another round of cheers followed. Once they died down, both Freddy and the announcer turned to Leroy.

"The reigning champion!" The announcer said. "Returning from parts unknown, this warbot is ready to rumble once more! Whether fighting Scrapwyrms or entire armies, the one thing he's yet to achieve is failure! It's the Defender of Rustbucket, LEROOOOOY BROOOOOOOWN!"

A silence hung thick in the air, broken only by the wind and Walter doing his best to give a cheer of support.

"Really?" Freddy asked Leroy. "That's all you could manage? You're really spoiling the moment, Leroy."

Leroy said nothing. The announcer looked to Freddy for orders, and Freddy waved him off. The robot quickly made his way off the outcropping to join the others from Freddy's group.

"Robots at the ready!" the announcer shouted once he was seated.

Freddy took a combat-ready stance, though Leroy remained as he was. A moment later, the announcer began the final countdown.

"THREE! TWO! ONE! FIGHT!"

Once the announcer had shouted the final word, Freddy revved up his chainsaw and made his way across the arena with a cautious approach. He spun the weapon around his body, creating a ring of glowing red energy. Leroy's own approach was similarly slow, with an even lesser display of energy. Had anyone watching not known better, they might have assumed he wasn't in the middle of a fight at all.

The distance between the two closed well onto Leroy's side of the arena. Facing an imminent strike from Freddy's saw, Leroy raised his shield to block. The anticipated clash of shield and saw didn't come. At the last moment, Freddy brought the weapon to a sudden stop less than an inch from Leroy's energy barrier. In the moment after, Freddy swung a fist down on Leroy from behind, walloping him across the head. The blow knocked Leroy to and then across the ground. Freddy's supporters cheered at their leader's opening success.

Leroy rolled over and sat up, nearly falling prey to the saw a second time, evading its strike at the last moment. Leaping to his feet, he raised his shield to block another strike from the saw, then ducked and weaved when Freddy came at him with multiple swings of his fists. It soon became clear Leroy was in trouble, with Freddy in full command of the battle's tempo. Freddy swung at Leroy from every angle, refusing to give Leroy an opening to launch a counterattack. Yet, from the way Leroy was moving, there hung in the air the question of if he would have even tried to launch a counterattack had the opportunity presented itself.

"What are you doing, Leroy!?" Destructo shouted. "Start fighting already!"

Freddy's assault continued. One swing came after another in rapid succession, Leroy staying alive by sheer virtue of how fast he swung his barrier shield around to meet each blow. Then, he let his shield down just as Freddy's saw swung at him. With a careful, precise motion, he stepped aside and guided the saw so that it struck one of Freddy's fists that swung from the opposite direction.

The saw lopped the fist in half, eliciting an angry yell from Freddy when he realized what happened. For a moment, hope shown through the fight might turn in Leroy's favor. In the brief span when Freddy was distracted, Leroy snuck behind him, grabbing his bottom limb in an attempt to pull the chainsaw arm clean off. He'd barely gotten a grip on the limb when Freddy swung his fists around for a one-two punch. The first strike knocked Leroy off-balance; the second knocked him into the air onto his back.

Freddy wasted no time pursuing Leroy and stabbed his saw down at the robot. Leroy leapt back to his feet, the chainsaw slicing straight by his head to leave a deep scratch that came just sly of piercing through his exterior plating. Leroy charged forward and threw his shield up to block the saw when it came at him from the side. Before he reached Freddy, however, Freddy swung his fist out and struck Leroy straight in the face.

Leroy was thrown to his back again, then put his shield up when Freddy jabbed down at him. He kept the shield up to hold off the saw, but in his downed state he fell prey to a punch that struck from the side. Leroy was knocked across the arena floor, nearly sliding off into the abyss entirely. He scrambled to his feet to get away from the drop off, but then stepped straight into another punch. Leroy tried to recover, but it was clear he was fighting a losing battle. Freddy threw strike after strike at Leroy, the blows coming fast and furious as ever. Leroy tried to use his shield to keep them from dealing critical damage and holding back the chainsaw, but even that failed to hold indefinitely. With one punch, Freddy struck Leroy against the ground again. Leroy pushed himself to his feet like he'd done so many times before, but this time, his speed failed him.

Before he found his footing, before he could dodge or throw his shield back up, Freddy's saw broke through and stabbed him straight through the back.

Even seeing it coming, the robots of Rustbucket were shocked. They watched in frozen silence as Leroy laid there, Freddy standing over him, the red glow of the chainsaw plunging into Leroy's back. It became worse when Freddy intensified the damage, pushing the saw clear through Leroy's body and out the other side, impaling the robot on his limb.

Chainsaw Freddy laughed as he slowly lifted Leroy's limp but still active body into the air. Deactivating the chainsaw, he flicked it inward to throw Leroy against the ground. Leroy didn't even try to move when Freddy approached him. While he still functioned, everyone could tell any fight left in him had died.

"Behold!" Freddy said as he stood over Leroy's body. "The great Leroy Brown! At long last, the champion has finally tasted defeat!"

After standing upright and holding his arms in the air for several long moments, his retinue cheering his all but assured victory,

Freddy turned his view downward again. He raised his chainsaw into the air above Leroy's body and revved it up again, preparing to deliver the final killing blow.

"A shame you had to make it a hollow victory, Leroy," Freddy said. "I expected you to put up far more of a fight."

Freddy pointed his chainsaw down at Leroy, touched the tip against the robot's head to leave a black mark, then raised it up again to ensure the blow was delivered with maximum impact.

Before Freddy finished off Leroy, before he landed the final blow to destroy Leroy Brown once and for all, he was interrupted when a large, round, metal fist covered in energy spikes and trailed by a gravity cord struck him across the head.

The massive blow left a major dent at the center of the impact. More importantly, it threw Freddy off balance and forced him away from Leroy's body. As the first pauldron fist was pulled back to its source, the second struck him along the lower third of his body, hitting the section his chainsaw limb was mounted on with even more force than the first blow.

"We…we have a new challenger!?" the announcer exclaimed as Mr. Destructo sped into the arena at top speed.

Destructo wasted no time with formalities, banter, or smack talk. He moved as one with but a singular purpose in mind – to succeed where Leroy Brown had failed and end Chainsaw Freddy once and for all.

Already suffering from the first two blows, Freddy found himself on the defensive from the start. He rolled into reverse to keep a safe distance between him and his attacker, narrowly avoiding another punch Destructo threw at him with lethal intent. Freddy tried to spin his saw around to restart his orbit of death, but he quickly discovered the damage to his bottom section had knocked it out of alignment and made the rotation too unreliable.

Finding himself in trouble, Freddy remained on the defensive. He retreated from, dodged, and redirected each one of Mr. Destructo's massive swings in a near frantic effort to avoid losing complete control of the situation. Each blow came with the threat of suffering critical damage, serving to heighten Freddy's precarious situation. Yet Freddy held on all the same, successfully keeping the deciding blow from finding its way home.

The longer Destructo's assault continued without finishing Freddy off, however, the more in tune Freddy became with Destructo's attack pattern. Soon, Freddy's frantic effort to stay alive shifted into a far more level fight even as Destructo held the upper hand. Their moves became a violent dance of death, the two robots twisting, turning, and rolling across the ground as veterans of the arena who were in their element.

Amid his continued survival, Freddy calculated a counterstrategy that just might allow him to emerge victorious. Continuing to evade and deflect Destructo's attacks, Freddy kept watch for just the right moment. Then, when the opportune moment presented itself, he threw his fist directly into the path of one of Destructo's punches to grab it. While the blow ruined Freddy's hand, he was still able to latch onto the fist just long enough to hold it in place. In that moment, Freddy sliced his chainsaw across Destructo's wrist, cutting the robot's hand off entirely.

With Destructo distracted by the sudden loss of his fist, Freddy followed through with a punch to the robot's face. Destructo moved with the strike and rolled backwards to create a distance between the two fighters while he assessed his new situation. Freddy, on the other hand, didn't wait to continue the fight. He charged forward and was back in Destructo's face in no time.

Down a fist, Destruco's offensive power was all but cut in half. Freddy's aggression made clear he knew as much. The battle took on a far more even footing, with each fighter dodging and deflecting the others primary weapon while looking for openings to sneak an attack through their opponents' defenses. For each blow one robot landed, the other landed a counterattack in return, but neither succeeded in landing with anything more than minor blows.

Then, Destructo made a critical error. Trying to knock Freddy's saw out of commission, he swung at the joint connecting the saw limb to its owner's body. The blow was close, but not close enough. Freddy quickly punished the mistake by cutting into Destructo's leg, nearly taking it off entirely. Destructo pulled back at an almost sluggish pace, only surviving a far more critical strike by catching the saw head on with his already broken arm.

Recognizing his tracked mode was no longer reliable, Destructo swapped to his legs and nearly fell over when one of them fell clean off. He barely recovered in time to once again use his crippled arm to stop the saw from stabbing him in a more critical area. With the block, he even succeeded in delivering another powerful blow to Freddy's center section. But it wasn't nearly enough to keep Distracto from falling all that much further behind his opponent.

With Destructo's legs and balance in critical condition, Freddy slowly took command of the fight. His own mobility largely unimpeded, he was free to pick away at Destructo as he pleased. Destructo continued to fight on undeterred, even hitting with a few more strikes, but it did him little good. For each strike that got through, Freddy countered with two or three more serious blows in turn. Before long, Destructo was reduced to pure defense, especially after Freddy finished off the other half of the robot's leg, all but killing his mobility entirely.

From that point forward, Destructo's defeat was inevitable. Each swing of his fist, thrown with hope he might level the playing field, came up short. Each time he successfully stopped a strike from finishing him off only delayed what everyone knew was coming. It was only after Freddy finally cut off Destructo's other two legs the robot finally showed any sign suggesting he knew the fight was over.

With only one arm still functional, and the other on the verge of falling off, Mr. Destructo tried to push himself up, to create any possibility of getting in one more punch. But his movements were weak, and any idea the fight wasn't over yet was nothing more than an illusion. With a celebratory motion, Chainsaw Freddy rolled over to his second fallen opponent's body and planted a foot first on his chest, then a second on Destructo's last functional limb.

"I should be a lot more upset right now," Freddy said, then he looked down at his fallen foe. "Storming into the middle of a fight like that? Normally, I'd consider that absurdly rude behavior. But I have to say, after that pathetic fight Leroy put up, you found a way to give me exactly what I was looking for."

Freddy lifted his chainsaw into the air and held it above Destructo's head.

"Domo arigato, Mr. Destructo."

Then Freddy stabbed his chainsaw through the top of Destructo's head.

A moment later, Destructo shut down and his body went limp.

"WINNER, and STILL CHAMPION!" The announcer shouted. "CHAINSAAAAAW FREDDY!"

While a wave of shock washed over what was left of the crowd from Rustbucket, Freddy pulled his saw out and turned to Leroy Brown with the intent to finish off his first opponent. To his surprise, however, Leroy was nowhere to be seen. Freddy looked around, both to his own crowd and to the sad collection of five robots representing Rustbucket, one of which was trying to flee. No one, however, showed any indication they knew where Leroy had gone.

"Detain them!" Freddy shouted, pointing at the enemy crowd. "And someone catch that small one!"

His robots quickly set into motion to follow their leader's orders, while Freddy took a second look for Leroy. When Leroy continued to elude him, Freddy concluded Leroy must have been knocked off into the lava below at some point during the fight. While disappointed, Freddy shrugged and returned his attention to Mr. Destructo's fallen form. Using his chainsaw, Freddy cut the robot across where his head met his body, decapitating Destructo entirely. After the head fell to the ground, Freddy picked up what was left of the body, heft him over to the edge, and tossed him off.

Mr. Destructo's body fell deep into the abyss, past rock walls that circled it in all directions. The metal corpse grew hot as it fell ever further down, beginning to glow well before it even hit the bottom. It finally landed with a muted thud creating a small splash. The robot corpse began to melt away the moment it hit the lake of magma.

In the span of a few short minutes, Mr. Destructo's body was all but erased from existence.

10001.

"*I should be a lot more upset right now. Storming into the middle of a fight like that? Normally, I'd consider that absurdly rude behavior. But I have to say, after that pathetic fight that Leroy put up, you found a way to give me exactly what I was looking for.*"

Silence hung over Rustbucket as its inhabitants watched events unfold. In the middle of the settlement, a large screen had been set up, with intent of allowing everyone to watch the Top Dog's defeat without having to crowd around the volcano.

Instead, they watched as the Top Dog stood triumphant over Mr. Destructo, his voice echoing through the cave in a haunting fashion.

There, the robot they had once counted on to protect them lay on the ground, broken and helpless. Having already watched the fall of Leroy Brown, to see Mr. Destructo fall too was more than some of them could bear.

"*Domo arigato, Mr. Destructo.*"

A chill hung in the air when the Top Dog stabbed his chainsaw into Destructo's head, destroying the robot for good. A commotion broke out, and the silence of the cave was soon filled with dozens of different conversations at various levels of panic.

"What do we do now?"

Steek turned to see both Krix and Cannon Man looking at him. Steek looked back to the screen, just in time to watch the robots at the volcano break into a panic and the feed go dead, leaving them with nothing but darkness.

"Krix, get everyone in line. Make sure we don't have a full-blown panic break out," Steek ordered. "Cannon, get everyone back to battle stations."

Both robots nodded and confirmed the commands, then Steek turned and walked to the cave opening. Once outside, he promptly made his way up the wall, where a handful of robots were standing guard, mostly to keep Rustbucket apprised of anything the Top Dog's army attempted. Among them were the remaining duplicates of Leroy Brown – once a clever ploy and much needed assistance, now a haunting reminder of the loss they just suffered.

"Is it true?" Humbug asked with a digitized voice as Steek walked up the wall. "The Top Dog won?"

Steek stopped and considered how to respond.

"Mr. Destructo is gone," he said. "So is Leroy Brown. The Top Dog broke them both. We're going to have to defend Rustbucket without them."

"Can we do that?" Humbug asked.

Steek stood there a moment but failed to put together an answer he could viably express. He was saved from having to do so by the sound of two shuttles flying overhead. Departing from the volcano, they returned to the vast army that had assembled just beyond the remains of the last battle.

"Everyone into position," Steek said, continuing up the wall.

Fortunately, the efforts of the remaining leaders of Rustbucket kept the settlement from immediately falling apart. With some encouragement, everyone returned to their stations, preparing themselves for what would come next. There was a near universal hope that with the Top Dog having what he wanted, he might turn his army around and forget about the settlement entirely. No one expected it to actually happen. Most presumed the army would attack as soon as it was ready, and they were all surviving on borrowed time.

It was to a small degree of surprise, then, when a single transport rolled on ahead of the rest of the army. With every gun platform and battle cruiser aiming their weapons at Rustbucket, no one dared to open fire on the transport as it approached, lest they be responsible for dooming everyone. So, the transport was allowed to continue until it came within a hundred yards of the outer wall. The tension hung thick in the air as the defenders of Rustbucket watched and waited.

Then, to their further surprise, the Top Dog himself exited the transport, flanked by eight fully armored and heavily armed soldiers. He rolled forward across the ground, the troops following close behind, and came to a stop halfway between the transport and the wall.

"CITIZENS OF RUSTBUCKET!" the Top Dog shouted. "YOUR CHAMPIONS AND DEFENDERS HAVE FALLEN! THEY ARE NO MORE!"

As if to emphasize the point, he held his arm high in the air, displaying Mr. Destructo's head for all to see. Once he was certain everyone knew what it was, he tossed it to the ground in front of him. In that moment, Steek briefly considered shooting the Top Dog, pulling the trigger and finishing what Mr. Destructo had started and avenging the robot.

"Normally, your continuing refusal to surrender and recognize my supremacy would mean that I would destroy you all!"

The Top Dog continued. "However, I'm currently in a good mood. Mr. Destructo may be gone, but certainly put up an enjoyable fight before he fell. And I must admit, in defiance of all expectation, your pathetic settlement has put forth an impressive resistance."

"Like all resistance, it has finally come to an end. Your final hour has arrived, and there will be no one to save you from the fate that lies before you. But rather than simply destroying you all in this, your final hour, I am offering you a generous choice. You can either surrender, or be destroyed. Those who choose to surrender need only pass beyond your walls and hand themselves over to my custody. Those who do so may yet survive. But to those who think they can refuse surrender and trust in your defenses to keep you safe, know that your destruction is imminent!"

With a wave of the Top Dog's hand, a couple more robots exited the transport and walked toward him, carrying the familiar form of Walter with them.

"Oh no," Steek said in a barely audible fashion.

"This robot was present to personally watch me crush Leroy Brown and Mr. Destructo. When he saw that they had been vanquished, he tried to escape his fate by running."

The Top Dog grabbed Walter from his minions and held him high up in the air by the neck.

"Look at him now!" The Top Dog shouted.

He threw Walter to the ground, then stepped on him. The weight and force the Top Dog planted on the robot smashed him into the ground, bending him near to the breaking point. Walter tried to protest and plead for mercy, but his cries went unanswered. The Top Dog lifted his foot up and stomped down a second time. It was a blow

Walter did not survive.

"Surrender, and you might avoid his fate!" the Top Dog shouted at the speechless crowd atop the wall. "Anyone who stays in Rustbucket has an hour until they join him! That hour begins now!"

The Top Dog and those with him returned to the transport, leaving Mr. Destructo's head and Walter's broken body on the ground as a reminder of the choice the remaining inhabitants of Rustbucket had to make.

In his wake, a commotion broke out within the wall of the settlement. Steek looked around, then back out to the army beyond. Turning, he marched across the wall and back to the cave. Halfway down, Cannon tried to intercept him.

"Steek–" the robot started, but Steek didn't stop for him.

"Keep everyone in position," Steek said as he went.

"Where are you–" Cannon tried to say, but Steek turned around and cut him off.

"We have less than an hour to put together a plan," Steek said. "Something that takes into account the fact that both Destructo and Leroy are gone. I need to find Ozochki and Synnapses so we can figure out what to do."

Steek turned and continued to the cave. Cannon Man tried to speak, but Steek had none of it. A few feet after he reached the ground, he was distracted by noise coming from the gates. Turning toward it, he saw the commotion of three robots, with several more looking on.

"Open it!" one robot shouted, being held back by the other two. "I am leaving!"

"We are not opening the gate!" Steek shouted. "Keep him back, keep that gate closed!"

He turned for the cave again without spending any more time on the issue, though the moment weighed on his processors all the same. By the time he reached the cave, he saw some of the defenders from the wall running in ahead of him. Steek started to make an effort to get them back where they belonged, but quickly stopped himself – he didn't have time to get each and every robot in line. He had to focus on the larger problem. It was an ominous sign all the same – the defense of Rustbucket was already collapsing, and the final battle hadn't even begun.

Rapidly marching through the settlement, it didn't take Steek long to find Ozochki. The Engineering head was likewise trying to keep organized amid the chaos, splitting his attention between ensuring the settlement's weapons were ready and overseeing a reduced crew count.

"Steek," Ozochki said once he saw the robot approaching. "What's the plan?"

"Why are you asking me?" Steek asked. "You and Synnapses are the closest thing we have left to leadership."

"This is a military situation, Steek," Ozochki replied. "This is outside our purview. If they're going to be looking to anyone for leadership right now, it's you."

"Fine. What can you put together in the next hour to help us win?"

"What happens in an hour?" Ozochki asked.

"The Top Dog gave an ultimatum," Steek answered. "He's given us an hour before he destroys Rustbucket and anyone who hasn't surrendered to him."

Ozochki turned away from Steek briefly, looking inward and

around before returning his attention to the security bot.

"We currently have less than an hour," Steek said. "What can Engineering build before then?"

"What do you expect us to put together in an hour?" Ozochki asked.

"Something to help us win. We have the guns, we have the walls, what else can you build?"

Ozochki stared at Steek a moment before responding.

"Nothing," Ozochki said.

"Nothing?" Steek asked.

"What we have is what you get," Ozochki replied. "In less than an hour and counting, there is nothing my team can design and build that will do anything to save us any more than what we already have. If we had a few days, we might be able to design and build something to save Rustbucket from the army out there. But not in an hour."

"Steek, what is the plan?"

Both Ozochki and Steek turned to see Synnapses approaching.

"What can you put together in an hour?" Steek asked.

"What are you expecting us to put together in an hour?" Synnapses asked in response.

"You put together those fake Leroy Browns. What else can you make?"

"In an hour?" Synnapses asked incredulously.

Steek looked at the two as he finally processed what they were saying.

"If you are looking for my advice, I think it may be time to call another vote." Synnapses said.

"About what?"

"If Rustbucket will stay and fight or surrender."

"We already had a vote," Steek said. "We voted to fight. I intend to honor that vote."

"I may not favor surrender, but Synnapses has a point," Ozochki said. "I don't think the last vote is relevant anymore. The robot that convinced us to stay and fight is no longer here. He can't fight for us and protect us anymore. If the Top Dog is giving us another opportunity to surrender, I think we owe it to the others to let them decide if they want to accept that opportunity."

The conversation ended abruptly by the sound of a loud commotion happening outside the cave. Looking out, Steek noticed there were robots running in all manner of direction around him, with several groups heading for the exit. He ran toward the outside, with Synnapses and Ozochki following soon after. When he left the cave, Steek discovered a small crowd had grown around the gate.

"Open the gate!" shouted one robot. Looking the scene over, Steek quickly realized the crowd was trying to leave.

"The gate is staying closed!" shouted one of the guards.

"You can't keep us in here!" another robot shouted.

With the scene growing ever more tense and threatening to break out into violence, Ozochki let out a loud blare, immediately capturing everyone's attention. One by one, everyone looked at Steek, Ozochki, and Synnapses.

"Just what is the meaning of all this?!" Steek exclaimed. "What do you think you're doing?"

"You need to open the gate, Steek." said a robot named Warwick.

"Why?" Steek asked.

"What kind of question is that?" Warwick replied. "You've seen the army that's out there, haven't you? These walls are now a death trap. If the Top Dog has offered us an opportunity to surrender, I intend to take it."

"You can't," Steek said.

"Why not?" Synnapses asked.

Steek turned to look to the head mechanic.

"You're siding with him?" Steek asked.

"What authority do we have to keep him here?" Synnapses asked. "What authority do we have to keep anyone here?"

Steek looked at Synnapses, then slowly turned to look toward the wall.

"We need to stick together," Steek said. "That army out there, we're not going to survive if we start breaking up like this."

"We're not going to survive if stay together, either," Warwick said. "Not in here."

"Not with that attitude," Steek said.

"Not with any attitude," Ozochki replied. Steek turned around to look at him again. "As much as I'm loath to admit it, Leroy Brown was the only reason we survived this long, and he's gone now. Now that they don't have a reason to hold back, we don't have near enough firepower or numbers to win this fight."

"So we destroy as many of them as we can," Steek said. "We already made a promise to defend Rustbucket, we need to stand by that promise."

"No, Mr. Destructo made a promise that the security team would abide by Rustbucket's decision to fight or evacuate," Synnapses said. "And he's gone now."

"He also said we were free to leave," Warwick said. Steek turned back to the robot, who waved his arm to the gathered robots behind him. "We're leaving."

Warwick turned and marched back to the gate. Steek started to speak, then stopped short, then started again, then raised his weapon up and fired it into the air. Everyone turned back as an array of shocked cries went out.

"*Do not open that gate!*" Steek shouted.

"Steek!" Synnapses shouted. "What is wrong with you!?"

"We need to stay together and fight on!" Steek said. "We cannot abandon Rustbucket! Not now!"

"Or else what?" Ozochki asked. "You'll start shooting people? At least the Top Dog is giving them the option to survive. Are you really prepared to deny them even that?"

"We can not lose this fight," Steek said. "Not like this. Not now."

"We already have," Ozochki said. "The Top Dog won. All any of us can do now is decide how to face that loss. We can either surrender in hopes of surviving under a tyrant, or we can go out fighting."

Steek looked at Ozochki and Synnapses, then turned back to Warwick and the crowd. After a moment, Steek let his weapon drop to the ground. He took one step forward, then another, then walked to the gate controls. Motioning the guards there aside, Steek activated the gate himself. A loud metallic noise of creaking and grinding echoed as the gate opened.

"Go." Steek said. "If you want to surrender, *go.*"

The noise continued until the gate came to a halt and left a wide hole in the wall. The gathered robots looked out to the army waiting for them. Then, they stepped through. Only a couple walked out at first, but soon the whole of them marched through. As Steek stood by the gate controls, he saw a few more robots exiting the cave and promptly making their way to and then through the gate, with clear signs there were more on the way.

Steek stepped away from the controls and walked back to his rifle. Halfway there, he noticed Synnapses was already on his way back inside. Ozochki, however, stayed where he was.

"So, what about you?" Steek asked. "What's your decision?"

"I'm staying," Ozochki replied. "My engineering team and I have put in too much work here. It may be the end of me, but I intend to stand by it. I'm certainly not going to abandon it for the sake of taking orders from the Top Dog."

Steek nodded, then turned as Cannon Man, Krix, and Turrex approached.

"Let everyone know what the situation is," Steek said to them. "If they want to surrender, tell them know they need to leave now. Make sure everyone left is ready to fight when the clock runs out."

Cannon and Krix gave solemn nods, then all three and Ozochki went inside the cave. Steek watched until they disappeared inside, then slowly walked to the top of the wall again. There, he sat down and looked inward at Rustbucket to watch as the remaining inhabitants choose to stay or leave. They came as a trickle after the first group, which grew into a solid flow until more than half of Rustbucket had stepped through the gate. Each robot he watched choose to surrender hurt Steek just a little bit more. It was especially painful to watch the robots he knew well. Among them was Synnapses, who along with Zealot-Three was among the final robots to leave.

"I guess I shouldn't be surprised," Steek said as he watched the mechanic approach the gate. Synnapses came to a halt and looked back up at him.

"I've no interest in dying today," Synnapses replied. "And those choosing to surrender may yet need me."

"We still need you, too," Steek said.

"No, you don't," Synnapses said. "Anything that happens here will be beyond me."

Before Steek could say anything more, Synnapses looked forward again and continued through the gate.

If there was one last bright point to the final minutes before the Top Dog's deadline, it was that all four of Steek's fellow security bots chose to stay. They gathered atop the wall nearby, circling around him.

"You know you don't have to stay, right?" Steek asked.

"Yes we do," Cannon said. "We already promised we would."

"By my count, over half of Rustbucket is gone," Steek said. "If you really wanted to stick by that promise, you'd have to choose surrender."

"We promised we'd stick together," Krix said. "If you're staying, we're staying."

Steek looked back up at his fellow robots, then stood up and turned to them.

"It's been an honor to fight alongside you guys," He said. The other robots nodded in agreement.

"Whatever comes next, let's give Mr. Destructo something to be proud of."

****

From the moment he arrived back at the *Ultimatum*, the Top Dog watched the scene at Rustbucket with great interest. He watched the countdown even closer. When the crowds finally marched out of Rustbucket and along the mile-long trek to his army, he found himself torn by the numbers approaching. On the one hand, he was pleased they were finally seeing reason. On the other hand, he had come to Rustbucket with the intent of testing his new weapon, and the fewer remaining in the settlement, the less effective the test would be.

The wait and the internal debate surrounding it was broken up early when three robots from the settlement attempted to flee rather than surrender. They only got a handful of yards before the guns of the Top Dog's army opened fire. Several of the surrendering robots stopped and turned as explosions erupted near the escaping robots. The first few shots came close but missed their targets. Then, the lead robot was hit and exploded into several dozen pieces. One of the other two hesitated and began to backtrack, but soon fell much like the first. The third kept running and survived for several more seconds before he, too, was shot down.

Silence hung in the air as everyone looked at the carnage and the guns cooled down, then the march of surrender resumed. Only one other robot attempted escape, running in the opposite direction at a much faster speed. He too failed to get very far before an overwhelming number of large guns turned him into nothing more than broken, flaming scrap metal. The message already clear, the failed second effort dissuaded any further attempts.

As time grew short, the Top Dog began to count down the

minutes and seconds until Rustbucket's final hour was up. By the time there was less than a minute remaining, he began counting the seconds out loud with near gleeful anticipation.

"Five…four…three...two…*one*," the Top Dog said. "That will be time."

He looked away from the depleted countdown clock and turned his view back to Rustbucket.

"Send out a general order," he commanded. "Anyone who's not already outside is to be shot down if they try to escape. Then, once the surrendering robots have all been apprehended, send in the Siegewyrm."

****

"It's time," Steek said when the countdown hit zero. He turned to look down inside the wall.

"Close the gate!" he shouted. With Rustbucket's final hour up, he had no intention of making the Top Dog's assault any easier than it needed to be. The creaking and grinding of metal was heard from the multiple large metal doors closing, ending with a low 'thoom' when they sealed up entirely.

"Everyone in position!" Steek ordered. "Be ready for anything!"

He glanced back and forth at the robots on either side of him before turning back to the army beyond.

"If this is the end, let's make it an end to remember."

The cannons were readied, the defenders braced themselves, and everyone in Rustbucket prepared for the worst. Silence hung in the air as they watched the last of the surrendering robots finish their mile-long walk. After the last of them disappeared, tension grew thick as those still in Rustbucket waited for the inevitable. They braced themselves for the guns to open fire and the enemy forces to advance, but to their surprise, nothing came. The longer they waited, the more they began to wonder why the battle hadn't started yet.

"Why are they not attacking?" Turrex asked.

"That's a good question," Steek said.

Then, a large transport of an absurd length rolled forward until it poked out just beyond the rest of the army. It looked hastily slapped together from several smaller vehicles of similar designs and left everyone wondering what purpose it could possibly serve. Then, the front end lowered with a loud, high-pitched metallic screeching noise. Slowly, out came a sight that sent a wave of terror across every robot that saw it.

It was the instantly recognizable form of a Scrapwyrm.

The Scrapwyrm's drill spun up, then it penetrated the ground as it rolled out of the vehicle. Knowing what was to come, two robots leapt over the wall and tried to make a run for it. They only made it a few yards before being thoroughly shot down. Half a dozen more turned and ran for the cave. Steek couldn't even bring himself to order them to hold their ground. Internally, he debated following them. Their prospects of survival and victory had been slim before. If the Top Dog truly controlled a Scrapwyrm, he found it difficult to imagine a point to even fighting anymore.

When the Wyrm burst forth from the ground, it emerged inside the wall and crashed through the docking structures. Anyone who wasn't already fleeing or being thrown about turned their weapon on the death machine, but the Wyrm showed no concern for the attacks.

What was left of docking collapsed while the Wyrm burrowed back into the ground.

The wall shook, and those standing atop it soon realized the Wyrm was digging directly underneath, its body grinding against the lower edge as it tunneled just beneath the surface. The wall buckled and threatened to collapse, taking what little order remained with it. Chaos ensued, and one of the cannons inside the cave opened fire. In a fleeting moment of hope, it scored a direct hit on one of the Top Dog's battle cruisers. That hope was quickly dashed when the entirety of his army returned fire. The wall shook, then began to fall apart entirely, the combined force of the unstable ground and the concentrated fire being more than it could bear. Weapon emplacements were obliterated, robots atop the wall were blown to pieces, and the wall's outer layer was torn to shreds as it suffered blow after blow. Steek watched Humbug explode before he himself was thrown to the ground by the concussive force of a shot hitting the wall directly in front of him.

Anyone left standing returned fire with whatever weapons remained. The primary cannon fired and hit with another shot. Both cannons inside the cave were immediately torn apart when the Wyrm burst forth directly beneath one, tore it in two, and ripped through the second. The cannons exploded, their remains causing even further damage as they flew about and fell to the ground. Panic within the settlement grew uncontainable, and any semblance of coordination vanished. Some robots tried to run, others kept shooting at either the Wyrm or the army, but nobody was truly working together anymore.

Steek stood up, but was frozen with indecision about what he could possibly do. The need for a decision ended shortly after when the Wyrm emerged from the ground directly in front of him and tore him apart with its drill. His upper half flew through the air while the Wrym punched through an already heavily damaged section of the wall, bringing it down entirely. Steek's remains landed near the cave entrance, where he was forced to watch as the Top Dog's forces freely continued their assault.

One robot tried to close the inner gate in vain effort to slow the attack, but the Wyrm emerged again and struck it with enough force to knock the entire system out of alignment. From there, it continued inside the cave to resume tearing apart Rustbucket itself. With the exterior defenses and weapons all but gone, weapons fire from the Top Dog's army died down while the Wyrm laid waste to both the settlement and the robots within.

One by one, the buildings within were torn apart and collapsed. Robots were destroyed either as the cave and its contents collapsed on them or when they were crushed by the Wyrm directly. While the outer region was destroyed around them, most tried to save themselves by retreating further into the cave.

"Run!" Shouted Krix, who by that point was the last surviving member of the security team. He tried to guide anyone who could still move toward Rustbucket's engineering region. "We'll escape out the back!"

They were words he hardly believed himself, but in the middle of the chaos, he felt driven to do anything he could to reassure the other survivors. Looking across the broken ruins of the outer region, he spotted a pair of robots barely avoiding being consumed by the Scrapwyrm's maw. They continued running for the back of the cave, only for the command section to fall from above. One of the robots fell to the ground as he pushed the other forward, and the structure landed on the robot's legs. The robot tried to pick himself up, but discovered he was trapped.

Krix immediately ran back to help, running around and leaping over the wreckage around him. As soon as he reached the pair, he lifted the collapsed building just enough to pull the robot out, then picked both up and ran back to engineering. They arrived just in time for the Wyrm to burst out of the ground behind them and lunge forward into engineering ahead of them. All three stopped and stared in dead, hopeless shock as they watched and listened to the initial destruction.

They continued to stand in horror at the scene until the Wyrm dug out of the rock above them, consuming all three at once.

****

"If I may, Sir?"

The Top Dog turned to look at one Submin Array. He was boxy in appearance, the bulk of his body resembling a short, dark, hexagonal pillar. Each one of the robots six sides featured a visual receptor, a tentacled limb, and a motorized wheel for movement.

"What is it, Submin?" the Top Dog asked. "Can't you see I'm enjoying watching your work?"

"Yes, it's about that," Submin replied. "Readings show the Siegewyrm is in danger of going critical. We're overstressing it."

"I thought you told me you had it ready," the Top Dog said.

"Technically, we did," Submin answered. "And if I do say so myself, this proved an excellent test-run of the Siegewyrm's potential."

"So what's the problem?"

"Technically, Sir, it's functional, but it's far from finished. The stress it's under puts it on the verge of breaking again. If that happens, we're going to be hard-pressed to pull it out of there and finish our work."

The Top Dog stared at Submin a moment, then turned back to look at Rustbucket.

"Fine," he said. "Recall the Siegewyrm. If it worked as intended, then my ground troops should be able to finish the job without any trouble anyway."

The signal was sent, and the Siegewyrm retreated from the deepest reaches of Rustbucket. While the Wyrm was loaded back into its transport, the Top Dog's army marched past the wall and into the cave en masse to finish off any survivors. Nothing was spared from the destruction of the settlement. The last remaining sections of the wall were toppled, and any robots fortunate enough to survive the Siegewyrm found themselves overrun and overwhelmed by dozens, then hundreds of ground troops. Anyone discovered, whether out in the open or underneath wreckage, was shot until they ceased to function. Any machinery still operating was smashed. Even the few robots trying to flee by re-opening the back passageways failed to escape, as they were caught and shot down before they could get away.

By the time the Top Dog's army left the cave behind, Rustbucket was rendered dead beyond all question. What had once been an impressive display of civilization built from discarded materials was reduced to ruin. Its burning and smoking remains were all that was left, reduced to nothing more than yet another monument to the Top Dog's ongoing conquest of Junkworld.

UNFINISHED BUSINESS

10010.

[Initiating Startup Sequence]

[Systems Loading...]

[Systems Loading...]

[Systems Loading...]

[ERROR: System Error]

[Systems Damage Detected]

[Compensating...]

[Systems Loading...]

[Systems Loading...]

[Activating Systems in 3...]

[2...]

[1...]

Surprise accompanied Leroy Brown's reactivation. While his memory banks didn't initially load the reason, he couldn't escape the idea he was supposed to be permanently nonfunctional. For a moment, he looked up at the darkness around him and wondered if, contrary to everything he knew and all sensible logic, perhaps there was an afterlife for robots after all. When his memory finally caught up with him, he recalled the last thing he knew to be his fight with Chainsaw Freddy. More importantly, the fact he had lost, and Freddy had been intent on finishing him off. For some reason, however, he hadn't.

Leroy turned his attention to his immediate surroundings. He quickly noticed he was in a cave of some kind and held in a standing position by a crude engineering lift. While there was light nearby, it was dim, hardly enough to make sense of his location. Once he'd properly adjusted his vision to account for the darkness, he took a second look and discovered nothing short of utter destruction. Broken machines, destroyed robots, collapsed cave rubble, and all manner of twisted metal lay sprawled out for as far as the eye could see. Examining the scene closer, he discovered that despite the ruins, he recognized the place.

Somehow, he was back in Rustbucket, but a Rustbucket that had suffered a terrible fate.

"Good," Leroy heard from a familiar voice. "You're functional after all. It's good to know my work was successful."

"Isaac?" Leroy asked. Turning to the sound of the voice, he saw the small robot standing nearby. He looked like he'd undergone a lot recently, including fire-blackened markings on his cloak.

"Your memory is intact," Isaac said. "Also a positive sign."

"Are you dead too?" Leroy asked. "Am I in some kind of robot hell, or are you a hallucination of some kind?"

"No, we are both very much real and active," Isaac said with a solemn tone.

Leroy slowly nodded in acknowledgement, then turned to look at the scene around him.

"Is this Rustbucket, then," Leroy said with mournful recognition.

"It is, unfortunately," Isaac confirmed with a nod.

"What happened?"

"I can only assume the Top Dog destroyed it."

Leroy looked at Isaac.

"I can't give you a definitive answer, Leroy." Isaac said. "By the time I returned, it was already like this, and the Top Dog's army was gone. By my calculations, the most logical answer is he did as he said he would, then left."

Leroy gave a solemn, subtle nod, and then looked back out at the ruins.

"Why am I here?" Leroy asked. "Freddy defeated me. He destroyed me."

"Defeated you, yes," Isaac answered. "Destroyed, not quite. He dealt you a critical blow, but he never finished you off."

"Then what happened?" Leroy asked. A sudden realization hit him, and he turned back to Isaac, "How long has it been?"

"Since your last fight with…'Chainsaw Freddy? A week," Isaac answered. "After he defeated you, Mr. Destructo intervened before he could finish you off."

"Destruco? Where is he?"

"Dead," Isaac said, blunt as could be. "He entered the ring just in time to save you. He thought he could finish what you started and defeat Freddy himself. He almost won, too. But he didn't come quite close enough. Freddy finished him off the way he intended to do to you."

"Where is he?" Leroy asked.

"He's gone," Isaac answered.

"But I'm here."

"Yes." Isaac answered. "While everyone was focused on the fight between Destructo and Chainsaw Freddy, I used the distraction to retrieve your body and sneak it out of there. When it became clear that Mr. Destructo was going to lose, I used the back tunnels to escape notice, and fortunately they never came looking for me."

"But where is Mr. Destructo?" Leroy asked a third time. "Why am I here but he's not?"

"He's gone, Leroy," Isaac answered a third time. "I went back to look for him, but I never found his body. His head I found later, but..."

"But what?" Leroy asked when Isaac failed to finish the sentence.

Isaac looked at Leroy, turned, and plodded off. He returned a short time later carrying something in his arms, but Leroy couldn't tell what it was at first. Isaac stopped, put something down, and continued forward. When he finally stood in front of Leroy again, he put Mr. Destructo's broken head on the ground in front of him, positioning it to make clear the large hole in the middle.

"Even if I had the body, his processors are physically ruined. The programming and data that made him Mr. Destructo are gone."

Leroy glanced up at Isaac, then looked back down at Destructo's head.

"I failed, then," Leroy said. He looked up toward the empty darkness. "I failed everyone."

Leroy looked out at nothing, then looked to Isaac. He waited for the small robot to say something, but nothing came. He turned his head to look out in the direction of the volcano, then let his head hang.

"I failed," he repeated, then lifted his head up to stare into the darkness again. "I convinced them to fight. I promised I'd save them. I didn't even care about them. I just wanted a spaceship to go back home. To a home that doesn't exist anymore. But then I failed them. And Freddy destroyed them. They're all gone...because of me."

Slowly, his head turned to look at Isaac.

"Why did you save me?" Leroy asked. "Why did you rescue and rebuild me?"

"Because Junkworld still needs you," Isaac answered.

Leroy looked at Isaac a moment, tilting his head in confusion. He turned to look back out at the ruins of Rustbucket and held his arm out toward the destroyed settlement around them.

"They thought the same thing," Leroy said, then he let his arm drop. "Walter, Ozochiki, Phlex...they believed in me. They trusted me. But because of me, Rustbucket was destroyed. All for a purpose that never existed."

Isaac looked up at Leroy, then looked forward and moved to the engineering lift.

"You're right," Isaac said as he climbed the lift. "You lost. Rustbucket was destroyed and robots perished because of your failure. Had you not come here, had you not convinced them to stay, had you not given up and let Freddy win, they might all still function right now."

Isaac released the engineering harness, planting Leroy on the ground. Isaac hopped onto Leroy's shoulder, and then to the ground.

"A lot of other choices could have been made that might also have saved Rustbucket," Isaac continued once he landed. "They could have chosen to hand you over. Destructo could have chosen to trust you and told you the truth. I could have chosen to ensure your mind was right before the fight began. We even could have chosen to disregard your opinion and use the fight to assassinate the Top Dog while he was out in the open. But we didn't. So many choices we could have made, but we didn't."

Looking down, Leroy briefly checked his body. For the most part, he appeared to be in as good a condition as could be expected. There were hardly any signs of damage from his fight with Freddy, save for an obviously welded piece of metal on his chassis covering where Freddy had impaled him. Reaching around, he found the hole on his back to have been similarly covered.

"So why did you choose to save me?" Leroy asked. "I lost. I failed to stop Freddy. Both the URCL and Rustbucket are gone. What purpose could I possibly serve anymore?"

Isaac looked at Leroy, then turned and slowly walked away. Leroy looked after him, then followed.

"Leroy, do you remember Steek?" Isaac asked.

"Thin robot. Part of the security team," Leroy asked.

"Yes," Isaac answered. "Do you know what he was before he came to Junkworld? He was originally built as an animatronic. They dressed him up to resemble other people or characters and provide a stand in for education or entertainment. But then he grew old and outdated, and they replaced him with a new model. Somehow, he wound up here."

Isaac came to a stop and looked up at Leroy.

"Tell me, Leroy," he said. "How much need do you think Junkworld has for animatronics?"

Leroy said nothing, but the way his body shifted made clear he knew the answer.

"None," Isaac said. "Junkworld has no need for robots who specialize as animatronics. Not when any robot could theoretically be made to look like another. So, he chose to expand his programming and found a new purpose."

"What of me?" Isaac said as he turned and continued walking. "Do you know my history, Leroy? Are you familiar with Earth?"

"I'm aware of it," Leroy answered.

"I am hundreds of years old, Leroy," Isaac said. "I was originally built on Earth in the days before it was even a space-faring civilization. My purpose was to be a technological demonstration, a state-of-the-art example of what mankind was capable of. It only took a few short years before I was rendered completely obsolete. They put me on display in a museum for a few years, but eventually, I was forgotten entirely. Relegated to even less than a footnote in their history books. So, I was forced to make a choice. I could either find a new purpose, or accept my irrelevance and be discarded, my parts recycled and my memory all but forgotten as though I never existed at all."

Leroy saw a light peek in from somewhere up ahead but stopped when Isaac turned around to look at him again.

"What was your purpose, Leroy Brown?" Isaac asked. "Before the URCL? What were you originally designed and built for?"

"I was a warbot," Leroy answered. "*Centurion*-class. I was designed to fight battles. I was built to win wars."

"And for that you should be thankful," Isaac said.

"Why?"

"Because it means that where others are forced to find a new purpose, you will always have one." Isaac said, stepping forward and giving Leroy a solid tap on his shell. "You are a fighter, and that is something that will always be needed. There will always be individuals like the Top Dog. There will always be individuals interested in conquest. Those who seek to upend a perfectly fine status quo because they are upset the status quo doesn't benefit them personally. Or even those who simply enjoy bringing chaos to the world. And because that threat will always exist, there will always be a need for those who can fight them. That is why you will always have a purpose."

Isaac turned around again and resumed walking. Leroy followed close behind. The two kept walking until they reached the opening overlooking the outer section of the cave and the ruins of Rustbucket lying there, where the first signs of sunlight peered down on them.

"Look at that," Isaac said. "It's a new day."

Leroy stood there, silent as he overlooked the carnage and destruction the Top Dog's army left behind. Slowly, his head swept from one side of the cave to the other, his processors piecing together what it had once been and coming to terms with what it was reduced to.

"Were there any survivors?" Leroy asked. "What about Walter? What happened to him?"

"I found Walter's body," Isaac said. "But it was beyond repair, and like Mr. Destructo, his processors were physically ruined. Everything that made him Walter is gone."

"Is there anyone you *can* repair?"

"It is possible," Issac said. "I haven't checked everybody. The ones I did are as far gone as Walter and Destructo. But even if there were, what would be the point?"

"To bring them back," Leroy said as he looked down at Isaac.

"To what end, Leroy? Rebuild them just so the Top Dog can break them again? Why would I subject anyone to such a cruel mockery?"

"You brought me back," Leroy said.

"I did," Isaac said as he looked up at Leroy. "But you said it yourself – Rustbucket was destroyed because of you. And unlike you, most of these robots weren't meant for fighting."

Both robots looked out across the ruins of Rustbucket again, then Leroy sat down.

"So why did you save me?" Leroy asked. "You said Junkworld needs me, but Freddy already won. Did you bring me back to fight, or as a cruel mockery?"

"That...I suppose is up to you," Isaac said. "I may have rebuilt you, but I cannot control you. If you wanted, you could choose to let yourself be defined by your failure."

"A cruel mockery, then," Leroy said.

"If you choose to give up on existence, yes. But then this would be Rustbucket's final fate – a footnote in the history of Junkworld. This would be its end, and these robots would have been destroyed in a hopeless fight because of your misguided and ill-informed drive to go back to a home that no longer existed. And while Mr. Destructo may not have intended to lose, his sacrifice did ensure your survival. If you choose to give up on existence, he will have died for nothing."

Leroy continued to stare out at the cave and the light beyond for several minutes, then he looked to Isaac.

"Choice implies more than one option," Leroy said. "What's the other?"

"Atone for your mistake," Isaac said. "Be the robot that Junkworld needs right now. Rustbucket may be gone, but it can still be avenged. Do what you were supposed to do in the volcano and stop the Top Dog. Ensure there is a reason to bring back anyone here who can still be restored. You can choose to save Junkworld and ensure the robots who were destroyed here are the last to fall to the Top Dog's army."

Leroy looked at Isaac for several long moments, then looked at the cave again. He continued to sit there for several moments more before finally standing up and walking to the opening of the cave. With each step forward, he looked around at the destruction lying on all sides and the fallen bodies of destroyed robots. Each step he took was slow and intentionally placed, with Leroy taking in the full extent of what he had brought upon the former settlement.

After walking for several long minutes, he finally reached the cave entrance, where he stopped and looked at the remains of the now toppled walls that once stood in defense of a defiant but ultimately doomed settlement. Briefly, Leroy glanced to the side. There, he saw the remains of Steek, his body torn in half with several holes in his head. Leroy briefly lowered his head in remembrance of the robot, then looked back out to the horizon and the sun shining down upon it.

As he stood there, Isaac walked up and stood several feet behind him. Turning back around, Leroy looked at the ancient robot.

"We're going to need a plan," Leroy said. "More importantly, we're going to need to find Freddy and a way to get to him."

Leroy looked around, scanning both the inside and outside of the cave. He stopped and pointed when he spotted a wrecked transport that looked mostly intact.

"That," Leroy said. "You think you can fix that?"

"I do believe we can try," Isaac answered.

10011.

Laying atop his desk, Captain Danger heard a knock at the door. Loud and with an oddly haunting delay, it came once, twice, and three times.

"Enter," Danger said without looking up. The door opened, and the Captain tilted his head up when he heard a large number of small footsteps enter the room. As suspected, it was Commander Zon.

"Yes, Commander?" Danger asked as he lay his head back down.

Danger waited for Zon to speak, but there was only silence. When he grew tired of waiting, he tilted his head to look at the commander again.

"Well?" Danger asked.

"Is...everything alright, Captain?" Zon asked.

"Do you want an honest answer or a 'Captain's answer'?" Danger asked, ignoring his suspicion that Zon's question wasn't the reason he'd entered in the first place.

"'Captain's Answer'?" Zon asked.

"The kind of answer I'm expected to give because I'm the Captain," Danger answered. "An answer intended to saddle the weight of command on my own shoulders rather than burdening the crew."

"Ah," Zon said with a subtle nod.

"I think I'd prefer an honest answer, Sir," he added a moment later.

"Then 'no,'" Danger said. "Everything is not alright. Things are very, very far removed from 'all right.'"

Zon waited for Danger to continue, but the Captain failed to follow up.

"What did you need, Commander?" Danger eventually asked.

"It's the crew, actually," Zon answered. "They're wondering how long we're expecting to stay here. They're waiting for new orders."

"I don't know, and I'm sorry to disappoint," Danger answered.

"Understood, Sir," Zon said.

The robot shifted back as if to leave but stopped and shifted forward again.

"It's just that we haven't done anything other than sit here and watch a bunch of cave ruins for over two weeks now," Zon said. "The crew isn't taking it entirely well."

"We'll stay here as long as we need to," Danger replied. "The Top Dog ordered us to stay here and watch the cave, so that's what we're going to do."

"But for how long?"

"How many times and in how many ways can I say, 'I don't know'?"

"What if he forgot about us?"

"If only we could be so lucky," Danger said, waving his arms up in the air. "But as long as that stupid Rocu unit is still running around, I doubt it."

"If I may, Captain, the important thing is to keep watch over the cave, correct?" Zon asked.

Danger sat up, then turned to face the Commander.

"What are you suggesting?" Danger asked.

"We could merely stay within sight of the cave," Zon suggested. "And perhaps scout the surrounding area. Or even establish a lookout post to keep watch for us. Then we could keep eyes on the cave without having to sit here indefinitely."

Danger started at Zon for a moment with an intense look.

"Do you want to be executed?" Danger asked.

"What?" Zon asked, a hint of panic in his voice as he took several steps back.

"I'm sorry," Danger quickly replied. He lowered his head into his hand. "That came out wrong."

Danger pushed himself off the desk and walked over to Zon.

"I am not going to disobey a direct order from the Top Dog," Danger said. "Especially not with that blasted Rocu unit rolling around. If we start talking about creative ways to do something the Top Dog does not want us to do, it's not going to be long before the Rocu is going to find out, and then he's going to tell the Top Dog, and then the Top Dog is going to make me execute whoever's responsible for that talk to set an example."

Danger leaned forward and pressed a finger against Zon's body.

"Right now, that means *you*."

Zon shrunk as he retreated toward the floor.

"Do you understand, Commander Zon?" Danger asked. "He's already forced me to execute two of my crew. If I never have to do it again, it'll be too soon. So please, for everyone's sake, especially ours, don't create a situation that makes it an issue. Is that understood?"

Zon nodded.

"Thank you," Danger said with a heavy nod.

The buzzer sounded from Danger's desk, drawing both robots' attention. Danger stepped over and pressed the comm button.

"Yes?" Danger asked.

"*Captain, our lookouts have spotted activity at the cave,*" Xerox reported from the bridge.

"What kind of activity?" Danger asked.

"*We're not sure,*" Xerox replied. "*But there is something going on over there.*"

"How did they get there without us noticing?"

"*The lookouts don't think they did. They think that whatever's happening, it originated from the cave.*"

"Survivors?" Danger thought out loud.

"Do you want me to take a team over to look?" Zon asked.

"No," Danger answered. "I'll lead a team over there myself."

****

The two and a half mile walk to the cave was a silent and haunting one. In its own way, it was like walking through a graveyard. It was an especially apt comparison given how the Top Dog and his army had done nothing to clean up the area. Why, Captain Danger wasn't sure. Either it was meant as a warning to stay away, or it was left as a weird monument to his victory over the settlement that once resided there. Or perhaps it was some other reason beyond Danger's comprehension.

Whatever it was didn't matter as far as Danger was concerned. All he saw was a lot of perfectly good building material going to waste. He would have loved to lay claim to it but had strong suspicions the

Top Dog wouldn't be pleased with the idea. Danger glanced to the four crewmembers he'd brought with him, double-checking to ensure they weren't getting any bad ideas themselves. Fortunately, all four were sticking close by and by all appearances were on-point and focused on the task at hand.

Their walk slowed when they neared the cave, with Captain Danger taking far more caution the closer they got. While he considered it a good sign they hadn't encountered anything hostile yet, the cave was where the activity was supposed to be located. If there was anything happening, that's where it would be.

"Box, take point," Danger said.

The large, bulky robot nodded and proceeded on ahead with the other four following at a safe distance. One step after the other, Box entered the cave with a slow walk, continually sweeping the area back and forth with his visual receptors. Captain Danger followed along a path directly behind him. A second crewmember followed on the right, a third followed on the left, and the fourth covered his own backside. Each one kept eyes open in their own direction, looking for signs of trouble.

Box beeped in his deep, binary language and pointed to a lit scene. There, they all spotted a small transport that looked to be in the middle of a heavy repair job.

"Yeah, there's definitely someone down here," Danger said.

A moment later, they heard a clanging noise as someone attacked the crewman behind him. Danger didn't get a good look at first, the appearance blurred in the darkness as it picked up the crewman and tossed him into the robot on his right. The crewman on Danger's left raised his weapon and fired while Box charged in, at which point the attacker made his identity clear when he activated a barrier shield.

In defiance of the impossible, it was Leroy Brown.

The shots from Danger's crewmen bounced off the shield, while Box slammed up against it and collided like he'd run into a thick steel wall. The weapons fire stopped while Box backed up and prepared to slam into the shield again, but he wound up charging forward in an aimless fashion when Leroy instead deactivated the shield and leapt over Box's attack.

"Everyone stop!" Danger shouted. "That's Leroy–"

Danger's words were cut off when Leroy landed on the ground in front of him and punched him first in the face, then the chest, knocking him over backwards. Leroy then spun around and activated his barrier shield again, blocking another round of weapon fire. The moment there was an opening, Leroy charged forward and grabbed the robot's weapon before booting him backwards. Box charged in, but Danger lunged to his feet and rushed to plant himself between his crewman and Leroy's shield before they collided.

"STOP!" Danger shouted. "Everyone stop!"

Box's feet grinded against the ground for a few inches as he slowed down, his head tilting in confusion. Turning around to look at Leroy, Danger saw the supposedly dead robot was likewise surprised by the sudden turn of events.

"Leroy Brown," Danger said. "Last I heard, you'd been destroyed."

"Captain Danger," Leroy said. "Last we met, you attacked Rustbucket and tried to capture me."

Danger looked to his other crewmen. They were confused

about what was going on, but all looked prepared for whatever their Captain had in mind.

"That is true," Danger said once he looked at Leroy again. "It would appear things have changed for the both of us."

"Are we just going to recite platitudes, or are we actually going to talk?" Leroy asked.

"How are you still active?" Danger asked. "The Top Dog told everyone he'd destroyed you. He even put together an over-edited video to commemorate the occasion."

"I'm Leroy Brown," Leroy answered. "Surviving is what I do."

"I watched him defeat you, Leroy," Danger said. "Both you and that other robot."

"Freddy defeated me, yes," Leroy said. "But he didn't destroy me."

"You mean the Top Dog?" Danger asked.

"Yes," Leroy said. "The Top Dog. Or as he's better known, Chainsaw Freddy."

"He said that was just a stage name."

"Of course he did."

"So how are you here?" Danger asked. "The Top Dog said you'd fallen into the magma and your body didn't exist anymore."

"He was wrong," Leroy answered. "So how about you tell me why you're here, and more importantly, why we're talking and I'm not just breaking all of you."

Danger glanced at his crewmembers, then looked back at Leroy.

"The Top Dog assigned the *Horizon* to keep an eye on this place after his army left," Danger explained. "I think he's just trying to keep us occupied and out of the way."

"Sounds like an arrangement that's going splendidly," Leroy said.

"Given the state of things, that just might be what counts as 'splendid' as far as the Top Dog is concerned."

"And the reason we're not still fighting so you can turn me in to ingratiate yourself with him?" Leroy asked.

"I'm not sure it would be worth it," Danger answered. "Especially since, when you run into a robot you thought was destroyed and regret having betrayed in the first place, it gives one reason to stop and think about things a little."

"Regret?" Leroy asked.

"When I told you I was sorry, Leroy, I meant it."

Leroy looked at Danger for a moment, then looked at the ruins around them.

"An apology isn't going to do much good for the robots who lived here," he said.

"No, I suppose it won't," Danger said.

"But maybe you can help me do a little to set thing just a bit right."

"Such as what?"

"I need to find Chainsaw Freddy so I can destroy him," Leroy answered.

"How do you plan to do that?" Danger asked. "You already lost to him once. I know. I saw the video. What's going to be different this time?"

"I'm going to win."

Danger looked at Leroy, then glanced to his crew to see that like the Captain, they didn't appear confident in what Leroy was saying.

"If you'll excuse me for pointing it out, Leroy, I can't help but notice a significant flaw in your plan."

"And what flaw is that?"

"The part where you explain how you win this time."

"Trust me," Leroy said. "I know what I'm doing. Now you can either get on board, get out of the way and let me hijack your vessel so I can go destroy Freddy, or you can get ready for me to first break you and then go hijack your vessel anyway so I can go destroy Freddy."

Danger said nothing at first, though he did take several steps backward. When he noticed Leroy looked like he was getting ready to fight again, he turned to see his crew raising their weapons and preparing to fight. Danger lifted his arm and signaled for his crew to stand down, then turned back to Leroy.

"While I realize using the *Horizon* sounds like a good idea, I should warn you that right now there's a very serious flaw in your plan," Danger said.

"That is?" Leroy asked.

"The Top Dog – your 'Chainsaw Freddy' – he assigned one of his robots to my crew to keep an eye on us," Danger explained.

"He gave you a babysitter?" Leroy asked.

"Not in so many words. But in effect, yes."

"What kind of babysitter?"

"This dinky little thing called Rocu Beta-5.

"Ah," Leroy said with a nod. "One of those guys."

Leroy thought for a moment.

"That may actually be even better," He said.

"How so?" Danger asked.

"Are you going to help me or not?"

Danger looked at Leroy, then at his crew. He then turned to look out the cave toward the *Eternal Horizon*. After staring for several moments, he turned back to Leroy.

"Very well," Captain Danger answered. "Let's go destroy the Top Dog."

"Good to hear," Leroy said. He gave Danger a strong pat on the shoulder, then turned inward.

"Alright Isaac!" Leroy shouted. "We're good here! Come on, let's go."

"He missed two of you?" Danger asked.

A moment later, a short robot wearing a mess of a cloak came into view and walked toward them.

"This is a unexpectedly pleasant turn of events," Isaac said.

"So, before we go, Leroy, do you mind telling me what your plan to deal with Rocu is?" Danger asked.

****

Commander Zon skittered down from the bridge to the *Horizon*'s deck and continued until he secured a good view of Captain Danger and his exploration team. Annoyingly, Rocu was close behind and doing an exceptional impersonation of someone in charge. Looking to the Captain's group, Zon saw that they were carrying two inactive robots. One was mostly covered in a strange cloak assembled from multiple sources. The other, shockingly and against all impossibility, was Leroy Brown.

"Does not compute," Rocu said. "Leroy Brown was destroyed. His replicas were also destroyed."

"Something we actually agree on," Zon said.

Once the exploration team reached the deck, they promptly brought their haul onboard. Rocu rushed in and pushed the assembling crowd aside as he tried to reach Leroy.

"Step aside, step aside," Rocu said. "Put him down."

Captain Danger and his team looked at Rocu, though they didn't put Leroy's unmoving body down right away.

"Put him down," Rocu repeated. "I must analyze the body."

"Need I remind you I'm the captain here?" Danger replied.

"This is bigger than your captainship," Rocu said. "I must analyze and report to the Top Dog at once."

Danger and Rocu engaged in a stare-off for a few seconds, then Danger relented and signaled for his crew to put Leroy down. Rocu scooted over to the body and waved everyone aside. Then, he began a close inspection of the unmoving robot.

"This does not appear to be right," Rocu said. "This robot appears to be active."

"You're right. I am."

To Rocu's surprise, Leroy suddenly grabbed his tiny neck. Rocu tried to escape Leroy's grip, but he was completely outmatched. None of his scrambling or struggling was of any use, leaving him helpless when a then standing Leroy twisted his head clean off. Rocu immediately went dead, his body flopping lifelessly. Leroy dropped both head and body, which landed on the ships deck with a thud.

Silence hung in the air for a moment as everyone looked over the scene. Then, the crew cheered Rocu's demise. Danger stepped toward Leroy and congratulated him personally before signaling for the robot to follow him. Leroy picked up Rocu's broken body, then he and Isaac followed Danger as he led them to the bridge. There, Danger went to the command console to use the intra-vessel comm system.

"Attention all hands!" Danger announced. "This is your Captain speaking. As of a few moments ago, we no longer answer to the Top Dog. Or Chainsaw Freddy, whichever you prefer. By all accounts, that now makes us renegades. I can guarantee he will try to destroy us. But given the way things were headed, that was probably going to happen eventually anyway. At least this way, if we go out, we'll go out fighting."

Danger paused for a moment before continuing.

"The good news is that if we go out, we won't be going out alone," he said. "Reports of Leroy Brown's demise were both premature and exaggerated. He is now aboard the *Eternal Horizon*, and he will be serving as an *acting* Co-Commander until such time as Chainsaw Freddy has been deposed. Prepare for further orders, because they will be coming soon."

A light round of claps and other celebration sounded through the bridge when Danger finished and stood up. He glanced around the bridge, accepted a handshake from one of the bridge crew, and then turned to Leroy.

"Alright, *acting* Commander," Danger said. "We just declared war on the Top Dog. What is our plan?"

"Is that creepy robot doctor still a part of your crew?" Leroy asked.

****

Dr. Clank grumbled loudly to himself as he worked. The Captain's announcement was exactly the kind of news he had not been looking forward to. He, for one, was not interested in getting himself broken in the name of some idealistic act of rebellion. Which made the Captain's news a very good reason to ensure his escape plan would be ready if he needed it.

"Dr. Clank."

Clank grumbled some more when he heard Captain Danger's voice. Turning around, he saw the Captain stepping through the door with none other than Leroy Brown and another robot he didn't recognize. In Leroy's arms was the Rocu unit, which he interpreted as another bad sign.

"Captain. Leroy," Clank said, giving a forced nod to each. He then turned to Leroy. "Where's my robot?"

"Your robot?" Leroy asked.

"My robot," Clank answered. "The one you stole from me."

"His name was Walter," Leroy said.

"Fine, whatever," Clank said. "Where is he?"

"He was destroyed with Rustbucket," Leroy said with an ice-cold voice.

"Oh," Clank said. "That's unfortunate. I guess I won't be getting him back after all, then."

Leroy looked to Danger, then put Rocu on the table. With one intimidating step after another, Leroy walked over to Clank until the two were standing face to face. Then, Leroy reached back and swung his fist across Clank's face with enough force to knock the mechanic off his feet and onto the floor several feet back. He took one step toward Clank before Danger stopped him.

"Leroy, I'm going to have to order you to stop," The Captain said with a surprisingly casual tone. "As much as I admit he probably deserved that one, this is not going to work if you're going to make a habit of punching my crewmembers in the face."

Leroy looked at Danger, then down at Clank. He took a step back, then turned around and walked back to Rocu.

"Then can I presume that you didn't just come down here to let your new *acting* Commander attack me?" Clank asked as he stood back up. He felt his hand around his face and was thankful to find that the blow hadn't caused anything more than cosmetic damage.

Leroy picked up the Rocu body and head, then planted them on the table again closer to Clank.

"We need you to work on this," Leroy said. "We need the communication system, but without the part where it thinks for itself."

"So, you want me to dissect Rocu's remains, take out the robot parts, and turn it into just a regular old communication device," Clank said.

"Yes," Danger said after a momentary pause. "That would be another way of putting it."

Clank walked over to Rocu's body and placed his hands on both pieces.

"Now that sounds like a project right up my ally," Clank said with an unsettling level of glee.

"Good," Danger said. "Let us know when you're finished."

"Of course, of course," Clank said, though his words were offhanded to ensure minimal distraction from dismantling Rocu's remains.

"Alright then, we'll leave you to that," Danger said, earning him a dismissive wave from Clank.

Danger turned, looked back at Clank, and then he and Leroy left the room.

"And what do we do when he's finished gutting Freddy's former spy?" Danger asked as they walked down the hallway.

"You know of any other vessels willing to join us?" Leroy asked. "Captains you know of that you can contact and expect to join us?"

"I can't guarantee anything," Danger answered. "But I might have some ideas."

"Good," Leroy said. "Just as long as we can be sure they won't turn on us. The more we have backing us, the better."

"Sounds good," Danger said. "But what is the plan when they join us? All I'm hearing is a strategy reliant on 'I'm going to win' and defeating the Top Dog with blunt force."

"We're going to do what I should have done all along," Leroy said. "We're going to lure him out into the open, and then we're going to hit him while we've got him where we want him."

10100.

"Submin!"

Chainsaw Freddy – the Top Dog – shouted as he rolled through the lowest levels of his engineering and research department. All around, robots were hard at work on a vast array of construction projects of as widely various a nature. New war machines, new robot designs, new prototypes, and other efforts proceeded hard at work. It was one corner of the complex the Top Dog was particularly focused on, where laid out in its full, absurdly long glory was the one-time Scrapwyrm that had since been remade into a dedicated machine of war.

"You!" the Top Dog said as he pointed at a local overseer. "Where is Submin Array?"

The overseer turned with shock, fear, and concern at the sound of the Top Dog's voice.

"Uh, Sir!" The robot said. "I wasn't–"

"Just stop with the terrified groveling and tell me where Submin is," the Top Dog said.

"Uh…Scrapwyrm. Seigewyrm!" The overseer answered. "He's at the Siegewyrm!"

"Good," the Top Dog said. "Thank you."

The Top Dog turned and started to roll away but stopped after a few feet and turned back to the overseer.

"Keep up the good work," the Top Dog said with a nod. He turned around again and continued onward once more.

"Uh…thank you!" The robot said. "Thank you, Sir!"

With an ever-so-subtle motion, the Top Dog shook his head and rolled his eye.

Maneuvering along the walkways, the Top Dog found his way to the very large region of the complex where the Siegewyrm was parked. The inactive Wyrm's head was currently disconnected from its body, and a team of robots was standing around the exterior. Most were looking into the colossal machine's inner workings.

"Where is Submin?" The Top Dog asked them.

One by one, they each turned to look at him, then they all pointed inside the Siegewyrm. The Top Dog shoved them aside as he maneuvered his way to the Wyrm's open end.

"Submin Array!" The Top Dog said. "Get out here, now!"

"Sir?" Submin's voice echoed from within.

"I said *now*, Submin!"

"Coming! I'm coming!"

The Top Dog rolled backward and waited. The sounds of metal bumping against metal rumbled from deep inside the Wrym's innards. Then at last, Submin climbed out to reveal himself.

"Sir, I didn't expect to see you down here," Submin said after he rolled about to face his boss.

"I suppose it's good to know you've been hard at work, if nothing else," the Top Dog said, taking a momentary glance into the Wyrm.

"Of course, Sir," Submin said. "You said you wanted the Siegewyrm to work properly, and that is exactly what I have been doing. As a project, it's been far larger than I anticipated. All-consuming, really."

"Is that why I've been left out of the loop on your progress?" The Top Dog asked, glaring at Submin.

"Sir?"

"When I said I wanted you to make it work right, I also said I wanted regular updates on your progress," the Top Dog explained. "Regular. Updates. What do I get instead? Three reports at highly irregular intervals over the course of a week, and all of them read almost the same. Words to the effect of 'Still working on it'. 'Signature line'. 'Submin Array'."

Submin looked up at the Top Dog, leaving the Top Dog to detect a sense of concern about it all.

"My apologies, Sir," Submin said. "As I said, it's been an all-consuming project."

"Submin, you're a very intelligent robot," the Top Dog said. "So, I'm sure you can understand why I'd be disappointed by this failure."

Submin continued to look up at the Top Dog, then glanced around as he considered the situation.

"Am I…are you…is my position in danger?" Submin asked.

"Not right now it's not," the Top Dog answered. "I do very much appreciate your work. You're very good at it. But here is the thing. I have future plans of conquest in mind I have set to a timetable, and I have centered those plans around this Siegewyrm. The problem is that it's very difficult for me to make those plans and put them into action when I have no idea what the progress is on that same Siegewyrm. This is a project I *need* to be kept in the loop on. Understood?"

Submin looked to the Siegewyrm, then back to the Top Dog.

"Sir, are you sure it's wise to center all your plans around a single machine?" Submin asked.

"Submin, I believe I just said that you're a very intelligent robot and I appreciate your work," the Top Dog replied. "But how about you concern yourself with making my things work and let me worry about how I choose to use them."

"Yes, Sir. Understood, Sir."

"Good. Glad to hear it," the Top Dog said. "I'll leave you to get back to your work, but I don't want to have to come back down here for another talk. Keep me in the loop this time. I expect a fully detailed report on your current progress by tonight. Draft someone to be your secretary or personal assistant if you have to, just make sure I get those regular reports."

With that, the Top Dog turned and rolled off.

"Understood, Sir!" Submin shouted after him. The Top Dog stopped and turned around again.

"Regular! Reports!" He shouted.

"Will do, Sir!" Submin answered.

"You better!" The Top Dog shouted, then he turned around and continued to the next item on his agenda.

Rolling along up and out of the engineering and research department, the Top Dog made his way to the central command and control sector.

"Commander Rayvak," the Top Dog said. As he rolled up to the robot he was looking for, Rayvak promptly turned to face the Top Dog directly.

"Sir!" Rayvak replied.

"I'm here for an update on the Rustbucket prisoners," the Top Dog said.

"Yes, Sir," Rayvak said. "Their integration into your workforce is proceeding as scheduled. There have been a few minor issues, as well as a handful who thought they could act smart about things, but they've since been dealt with."

"All according to plan, then," the Top Dog said.

"Yes, Sir. All according to plan and on schedule."

"Good to hear," the Top Dog said with a nod. "Keep me updated, and keep up the good work."

Rayvak gave a nod in response, then the Top Dog turned to move on to the next item on the days to-do list. He stopped short when he found himself looking down upon a robot all but demanding his attention.

"What?" The Top Dog asked.

"You're receiving a call," The robot answered.

"Who from?"

"That…we don't actually know for sure."

The Top Dog tilted and twisted his head in confusion.

"What do you mean you don't actually know for sure?"

"As I said," the robot answered. "The signal is using the ROCU network, though for some reason it lacks the proper identification markers."

"What do they want?" The Top Dog asked.

"To speak to you directly."

"Did they identify themselves?"

"No, Sir."

The Top Dog stared down at the robot for a moment, then looked up ahead.

"Fine, I'll go take the call," he said. "Tell the network team to figure out the problem. Someone clearly has unauthorized access to my communications. I want to know how, and how they're going to fix it."

The robot gave a firm nod, then rushed to see to the matter. Before he was out of sight, the Top Dog began his own trek back to his command chambers. It was an unpleasant trek at that, with frustrations about the unexpected interruption adding to the long list of issues he still had to attend to. When he'd first set out on his plans of conquest, he'd never realized how much work it would be to rule the places he conquered. It was all the more reason for him to consider reorganizing his operation to minimize the amount of time he spent giving orders about miscellaneous minutia and more time for the good stuff. On the bright side, he had in his own opinion done an expert job of figuring out how it all worked thus far, and he had forever ahead of him to get it right.

Through the halls and up a lift the Top Dog went, until he finally passed through the doors to his command chamber. There, he rolled over to his command console and properly positioned himself before pressing the call button.

"Send in Rocu Delta-1," he said. He then turned his attention to the main doorway. The door opened, and the latest ROCU to serve as his own personal communication unit rolled through. The small robot advanced until he was positioned in front of the command console.

"I was told I had a call waiting for me," the Top Dog said.

The Rocu nodded, shifting to his communication mode. As soon as he was finished, the signal was sent, and the Top Dog waited for whoever was on the other end to connect. The usual static filled the screen, but a robot's head replaced it before too long.

"Captain Danger," the Top Dog said.

"Chainsaw Freddy," Danger replied.

The Top Dog paused in surprise for a moment.

"*Excuse* me?" He said. "Are you calling to initiate a long-term suicide? Because that's exactly what it sounds like you're doing."

"No, that is not the reason I'm calling," Danger replied. "I'm calling to say that I hereby resign from your organization and that the *Eternal Horizon* will no longer be answering your commands."

The Top Dog looked at the screen as he considered what the robot on the other side might possibly be thinking.

"Are you sure this isn't a long-term suicide effort?" The Top Dog asked. "Because that is exactly what it sounds like."

"No, it's not," Danger answered. "You may remember that not that long ago, you asked who I was loyal to. Regrettably, I made the wrong choice. I'm not loyal to you, Freddy. I'm loyal to Leroy Brown."

The Top Dog froze a moment from Danger's words.

"Excuse me?" The Top Dog said. "Are you sure you're functioning right, Danger? Because you just said you're loyal to a robot that–"

"Hello, Freddy," interrupted a familiar voice, which was soon joined by a familiar face when the screen shifted to bring another robot into view. "Did you miss me?"

The Top Dog stared at the screen for a few moments, confused by the appearance of none other than Leroy Brown.

"What is this?" The Top Dog asked. "Where did you find another robot that looks like Leroy Brown? We destroyed them all."

"No, Freddy, it's me," Leroy said. "It's Leroy Brown. The one, the only, the real deal."

"Impossible. I destroyed him. Leroy Brown no longer exists."

"No. You may have defeated me, but you never actually finished me off."

"Of course I–" The Top Dog started, but he stopped short when he remembered he hadn't. As *improbable* as it may have been that he was speaking to Leroy Brown, it was not, in fact, outright *impossible*.

"That's right," Leroy said. "I'm back, and I'm ready for Round 3."

"What?"

"You, me, Round 3."

"Why would I agree to that?" The Top Dog asked. "I've already beaten you, Leroy. I have already proven my superiority. We already had our final showdown. I even finished off Mr. Destructo. I am the last robot standing, Leroy. Give me one good reason why I shouldn't just send my army out to destroy you on my behalf."

"I'll give you two," Leroy said, holding up his hand with fingers extended for emphasis. "One, you may have won our last fight, but our record against each other is an even 1-1. You know how it works. Without a tiebreaker, it means that record is inconclusive. And two, you only won our last fight because I let you."

While the Top Dog was hard-pressed to argue the first point, it was the second that truly took him aback.

"You *let me* win?" the Top Dog asked.

"You heard me," Leroy answered.

"You *let me* win?" The Top Dog asked again. "You mean to tell me that your defeat, my victory over Destructo, even the destruction of that stupid settlement you were hiding in, all of that happened because you *let me*?"

Leroy stared at the Top Dog for several moments with an intensity that pierced straight through him.

"You heard what I said," Leroy said. "You only won because I didn't give that fight my all."

"Lies," the Top Dog replied. "You lie."

"Am I?" Leroy asked. "Maybe I am. But can you really afford to take that chance, knowing that without a definitive Round 3 to prove it, you'll always have to ask yourself if you really won at all?"

This time, it was the Top Dog's turn to stare at Leroy with a fierce intensity.

"Fine," he finally said. "You want a rematch? Round 3 it is. One final, definitive match to decide it all, once and for all."

"See you back at Rustbucket," Leroy said, and then the line went dead.

10101.

The sun stood high in the sky above the surface of Junkworld, bearing down on the wasteland for as far as the eye could see. Amidst a gap in the wreckage left behind from the Battle of Rustbucket, three vessels held position and watched as the *Ultimatum* approached, flanked on either side by a smaller but still deadly cruiser.

"I guess we should be thankful he didn't bring the whole army," Captain Danger said from the bridge of the *Eternal Horizon*.

"He probably thought that would be overkill," Leroy said.

"Probably still is," Danger said, turning to Leroy. "This plan better work, Leroy. I didn't agree to help you just so I could die pointlessly."

"I thought it was because you were done answering to Freddy."

"I am," Danger said. "But if I'm going to be destroyed fighting him, I want it to be a death that actually counts for something. I don't want to become just another notch for his kill counter."

"Don't worry, it'll work," Leroy said. "If the intel we have on the Top Dog's army is accurate, Freddy is the only thing holding it together. Once we kill him, they should fall apart."

"Then I certainly hope our intel and your instincts are both correct."

Leroy nodded, then turned to leave the bridge.

"I should get down there," he said. "We have a fight to win."

Leroy left the bridge, beginning the long walk to the battlefield. He went down the stairs, across the deck, then rode the lift down to

Junkworld's surface. Once there, he walked forward from the *Horizon* until he stood several yards out from the front end of the vessel. There he waited until the enemy vessels came to a halt a hundred yards out. Before long, the bow of the *Ultimatum* opened at the bottom, revealing Chainsaw Freddy and three smaller robots. Freddy led the way with the other three following close behind. Leroy took a moment to look at the other three, one of whom he recognized as the announcer from the volcano fight. The other two were near identical to each other, built as large, mobile sound speakers.

Freddy came to a halt halfway between the super cruiser and Leroy, while the other three kept going until they were halfway between Freddy and Leroy. Once there, the two speaker bots traveled away from each other in opposite directions along an angle ninety degrees from the line between Leroy and Freddy. They stopped when they were as far from each other as Leroy and Freddy were from each other.

"LADIES and GENTLEMEN!" The announcer began, his voice booming from the speaker robots. "ROBOTS of ALL MAKES and MODELS! WELCOME…to the UNDERGROUND ROBOT COMBAT LEAGUE: the EPIC ENCORE BONUS ROUND FINALE!"

The announcer paused, expecting the sound of cheers and applause, but all he heard were the last echoes of his words and the howling of the wind.

"Today, we bring you UNFINISHED BUSINESS!" The robot finally continued, a hint of annoyance sneaking into his voice. "One last dance, one final showdown, one final battle to send off the URCL once and for all!"

"PRESENTING, the CHALLENGER!" The announcer continued, turning, and pointing to Leroy. "The MAN of the LAST STAND! This warbot is READY to RUMBLE! If you aren't prepared to face his shield, you better get ready to have a bad time! It's the LAST SURVIVOR of RUSTBUCKET: LEROOOOOOOY BROWN!"

A second time, the announcer held position and waited for celebratory noise to follow. A second time, all that followed was the echo of his voice and the wind. The near silence was finally broken by the unintelligible grumblings of the announcer as he turned to Chainsaw Freddy.

"And HERE HE IS – THE REIGNING CHAMPION!" The announcer declared. "He's the KING of the RING and the future KING of JUNKWORLD! There's no problem that this bad bot can't chop through. He's the TOP DOG of anything he puts his mind to; GIVE IT UP for CHAINSAAAAAAAAW FREDDY!"

The announcer held as he waited for cheers of celebration and encouragement for Freddy, but once again those cheers never came. The announcer looked around, then threw his hands up before stomping back to the *Ultimatum*. He grumbled and shook his head all the way, the speaker robots following close behind.

"Not where I'd prefer to finish you off, Leroy," Freddy said. "But it's hard to argue for there being a more appropriate location."

Freddy looked at Leroy Brown, waiting for a response that didn't come.

"What's the matter?" Freddy asked. "You suffering from vocal issues?"

Leroy continued to refrain from saying anything and took a combat-ready stance.

"Really, Leroy? Really?" Freddy said. "Here we are, on the verge of the last fight we'll ever have, and you insist on ruining the moment."

"You shouldn't have done this, Freddy," Leroy finally said.

Freddy cocked his head in confusion.

"You're the one who insisted on it!"

Leroy thought a moment before he spoke again.

"Fine, bad phrasing," Leroy said.

"Then what are you talking about?" Freddy asked.

"Everything you have done since you got here," Leroy said. He dropped his combat stance as he continued. "Hunting down the other URCL robots. Conquering Junkworld. Obliterating Rustbucket. And above all that, your convoluted, ill-conceived drive for a rematch."

"You're going to have to explain it to me, because from where I'm standing, everything is working out great."

"I could, but it's probably not worth the effort," Leroy said. "Not when I'm about to smash you."

"Great!" Freddy replied. "Because I see no reason why I should care about personal criticism from a robot I'm about to utterly demolish."

Both robots took combat stances, waiting for the signal to begin. Soon after, the voice of the announcer boomed from the super cruiser.

"ROBOTS AT THE READY!" the announcer declared. "THREE! TWO! ONE! FIGHT!"

At the signal to begin, Leroy charged toward Freddy at top speed, catching his opponent off guard for a moment. Freddy quickly recomposed himself and advanced, though at a much slower speed than Leroy. In short order, the two robots reached one another, and the battle was joined.

****

Atop the ruins from the Battle of Rustbucket, a pair of robots sat and watched the battle between Leroy Brown and Chainsaw Freddy unfold. By all appearances, the two were evenly matched – while Freddy was on the attack, swinging at Leroy from every possible angle, Leroy was more than holding up, blocking every strike with either his shield or a carefully placed counterstrike.

"They're in the thick of it," said Alham. "Hand it here."

The other robot positioned nearby – a heavy load transporter named Grabbell – brought out a large tube designed to function as a rocket launcher. He loaded it with one of the handful of rockets he was carrying, and handed the loaded weapon to Alham. Ensuring his position was steady, Alham aimed the weapon and waited for the right moment to fire. He held firm and watched as Leroy and Freddy continued to go at it, until at last Freddy stood between Leroy and Alham's position, his face toward his immediate foe and his attention fixed on the other combatant.

In that moment, Alham pulled the trigger. The rocket launched from the tube, leaving a trail of smoke behind as it sped toward its target. But in the short time it flew, the shot deteriorated from being a sure thing to a significant mistake when Freddy stepped aside at the last moment in a maneuver intended to flank Leroy from the side. The rocket missed Freddy entirely, flew passed the shield when Leroy was forced to divert to block a strike from Freddy's chainsaw, and avoided hitting Leroy by less than a foot. It struck the ground a few yard beyond both, where it exploded harmlessly.

Alham let forth a quick curse, then turned to Grabbell and handed back the tube.

"Reload! Reload!"

****

The explosion caught Freddy off-guard at first, long enough that Leroy was able to sneak in with an attempt to climb atop and directly rip Freddy's head off. Freddy promptly turned his attention to the immediate threat long enough to knock Leroy off and avert an all-too-sudden loss. He scooted back from Leroy to create a distance while his processors attempted to reason what happened. Taking note of where the first explosion happened, combined with the positioning of a sudden shield that was clearly not intended to block any attack from Freddy, the robot turned in the opposite direction in time to see a rocket flying straight at him.

Freddy sped back and then practically leapt away from the rocket's path, escaping its destructive explosion as it hit the ground nearby. Looking back to the source of the projectile, he noticed something – *someone* – positioned atop a nearby wreck. At that moment, everything clicked.

"*You*," Freddy said as he turned back to Leroy, who was once again lunging at him. Freddy slid aside once more and swung his chainsaw across Leroy's path, though Leroy ducked and rolled underneath the strike.

"How *dare you*," Freddy fumed. "You lure me out here, telling me it's in the name of one final fight, and then you have your mooks try to assassinate me?!"

Leroy charged at Freddy again. He raised his shield when Freddy took another swing with his chainsaw, blocking strikes from both directions, but retreated when Freddy tried to grab him.

"I'm not sure if I should be honored you know you don't have it in you to finish me off yourself, or insulted that you'd disgrace this fight by sinking to such depths!"

Another rocket flew at Freddy, but he successfully sidestepped to take cover behind Leroy's shield. He took another swing with his saw and missed but connected with the follow-up twin-fisted strike, knocking Leroy backward.

"To think that I gave you the benefit of the doubt!" Freddy continued to shout. "I gave you a fair fight! And you turn around and insult me by turning it into an underhanded façade!"

Freddy charged at Leroy, stabbing his saw into the ground and barely missing Leroy as the warbot got back on his feet.

"If that's the way it's going to be, then *fine*, let's do it *your way!*"

Freddy turned to look up at his warships.

"BREAK'S OFF, BOYS!" He shouted. "THIS IS WAR!"

Moments later, cannons opened fire overhead. The Top Dog's army shot first, but the other side soon joined in with return fire. The vessel from Freddy's side closest to the ruins even turned a few of its cannons toward the source of the rocket fire, intent on destroying the annoyance that made a mess of the fight.

"I would have them help me destroy you when they're done with your friends," Freddy said as turned back to Leroy. "But I expect to finish you off long before that happens."

Then, Freddy surged forward and attacked Leroy with a ferocity he'd never seen from Freddy before. Leroy began to fall back, leading both robots away from the battle and toward the ruins of Rustbucket.

****

Explosions tore into the *Horizon*, pulling the junktrawler apart piece by piece. Damage reports came in at a rapid pace, especially from the vessel's bow. The destruction was highlighted and emphasized by a large hole that went in one end of the bridge and followed out the other. One thing was clear to Captain Danger – they were going to lose the *Eternal Horizon*. All three vessels on his side were outgunned, and he was no tactical mastermind, not by a long shot. Even as his two allies advanced to try to attack the enemy from either side, it was plain to see all they were really doing was making themselves easier targets.

The battle, as it was proceeding, was already lost.

"Wex!" Danger ordered. "Full speed ahead! Ram the lead ship!"

Wexxler looked at Danger, then did a double-take.

"Do it!" he ordered. "The *Horizon* is lost. Let's make sure that's all we lose!"

Wex nodded, then drove the vessel forward. It accelerated slowly at first, but its speed quickly picked up across the short distance to their target.

"All hands!" Danger said into the ship's intercom. "This is Captain Danger! Prepare to abandon ship! I repeat, prepare to abandon ship and begin boarding action! We are ramming the enemy, and we are going all in on boarding action!"

Emergency lights and alarms blared as the *Horizon* drove increasingly close to the *Ultimatum*. The super-cruiser, taking notice of what the *Horizon* was doing, began to back up and turn to avoid the collision. It was a futile effort – with as close as the two vessels were already, all the counter-maneuver did was allow the *Horizon* to strike the enemy vessel clear across the side rather than merely at a glancing bow-to-bow angle.

The impact of the *Horizon* against the *Ultimatum* was loud and heavy. Metal bent and twisted in every direction. Pieces of hull flew every which way. The clanging and screeching of metal striking and grinding against metal echoed across the area. Micro explosions burst forth and sparks ignited at multiple points. The *Horizon* continued forward for as long as it was able, pushing against the larger vessel and digging into its side until its drives gave out and both it and its victim lay dormant.

"ONWARD!" Danger shouted. "ALL HANDS TO BOARD!"

The crew of the *Horizon* rushed up from below deck and toward the *Ultimatum*. Most carried weapons, while others relied on their natural built-in lethality. The enemy, either unprepared for or unaware of what was going on and already shaken by the ramming maneuver, was caught off-guard and flat-footed, giving the crew of the *Horizon* the opening they needed to make headway aboard their target. A small team of enemy crew, in an initial effort to drive back the boarders, fired their cannon. But as damaged as it was and as close as they were to the *Horizon*, the weapon caused as much damage to itself as anything.

Captain Danger grabbed a weapon of his own and soon

followed his crew onto the enemy vessel. Commander Zon followed close behind. Stopping momentarily, the robot opened his eye and fired a high-intensity laser bolt that struck an enemy soldier that had taken a sniper position atop the highest point of the super-cruiser. The robot fell to the deck below with a gaping hole in his chest, and both Captain and Commander continued to the enemy vessel surrounded by members of the crew.

"Take the deck!" Danger ordered. "I want command of those weapons five minutes ago!"

****

Try as he might, Leroy was hard-pressed to find an opening in Freddy's attack. There was a level of care to his strikes, the way he picked when to attack with the laser-tipped chainsaw to ensure he didn't burn the weapon out on Leroy's shield. With Leroy putting up an equally challenging defense, the two robots found themselves in a virtually even matchup. So, their battle continued, pushing further and further through the ruins outside the cave that once held Rustbucket as each sought to overcome their foe.

"Leroy, get down!" came a voice from nearby.

Both Leroy and Freddy turned to the source to see Alham wielding his rocket launcher and aiming it at them. Both robots dropped to the ground in opposite directions, causing the rocket to fly past both of them and hit a ruined vehicle not far away. Both robots leapt to their feet near simultaneously. Freddy, however, found himself distracted by Grabbell, who tried to use the opening to lunge at Freddy and get the upper hand. Freddy narrowly sidestepped the attack and swung his chainsaw through Grabbell's midsection. While his top half fell to the ground with a thud, Freddy grabbed hold of the robot's leg and spun it around to smack Leroy back down. Spinning around a second time, he let go of the bisected robot to hurl the bottom half in Leroy's direction.

With Leroy down and Grabbell effectively disabled, Freddy turned his attention to Alham. Distracted by his effort to reload the launcher, he failed to notice when Freddy grabbed hold of a nearby girder poking into the sky, cut it loose, and rush Alham with his impromptu club. The robot caught sight of Freddy just before he arrived and tried to shoot the rocket launcher at near point-blank range, but Freddy knocked the barrel away to send the rocket flying off into the sky. He followed up by swinging his chainsaw straight across Alham's neck.

Leroy charged at Freddy from behind, but Freddy spun around and brought the girder down on Leroy's head. Leroy blocked with his shield and pushed forward, but stopped short when Freddy spun his saw around, coming close enough to leave a black mark across Leroy's chest. Leroy blocked the follow-up swing with his shield but left himself open to another strike from the girder that sent him flying several feet through the air.

Freddy charged and swung both the girder and his saw at Leroy, but Leroy rolled out of the way and lunged to his feet. He tried to grab hold of the girder when it swung around again, but when he latched on, Freddy swung it over his head to smash Leroy against the ground on the other side, then swung the girder and Leroy around to hurl him toward the cave.

"This is far more like it!" Freddy said as he followed Leroy. "This is the fight I was hoping for! Shame you had to go and spoil it by cheating."

Leroy jumped to his feet again but ducked when Freddy swung his girder at Leroy's head. Recognizing the nature of his situation, he turned and ran to the cave. Freddy paused, surprised by the decision.

"Running?" He said, mostly to himself at first. "Really, Leroy!? First you try to assassinate me, and now you're running?! Come back here, you coward!"

Freddy sped up, rushing after Leroy to catch him.

****

The crew of the *Horizon* pressed forward, tearing through the crew of the *Ultimatum* with a furious energy that surprised even them. Before long, the front end of the vessel's deck was theirs, the enemy driven back in a hasty retreat to the stern and below deck. Despite the initial victory, Danger refrained from pushing the initiative.

"Get those guns operational!" Captain Danger ordered, sweeping his arm to the general vicinity of the vessels starboard side. "We've got two more cruisers out there, let's make them hurt!"

The crew quickly went to work, and Danger quickly marched to Commander Zon.

"Zon, set up a defensive perimeter," Danger ordered. "They'll send a counter-attack soon, and I do not want to lose this position."

Zon nodded, then signaled for several of the crew to follow him. Among them was Box, who was carrying a ship-level gun brought over from the *Horizon*. They didn't get very far before everyone felt an explosion beneath their feet. It was soon followed by first one, then a second of the deck guns exploding.

"They're firing on themselves!" Frigjar exclaimed.

"They're trying to wipe us out!" Danger replied.

"Forget the perimeter!" he shouted to Zon. "We can't stay here! We need to take out the deck guns then press forward!"

****

"If you're going to give up, the least you could do is go down swinging!" Chainsaw Freddy shouted as he rolled into the cave in pursuit of Leroy Brown. "For my sake, if nothing else!"

The cave grew dark the further he went inside, forcing him to slow down and pay closer attention to the area around him. For a moment, he stopped and stood where he was, listening for movement as he carefully scanned his surroundings.

"From Undefeated League Champion to hiding in the dark," Freddy said. "How far the mighty have fallen. Could you possibly be any more disappointing?"

Turning to the side, he spotted Leroy leaping at him with a long piece of metal in his hands. He struck Freddy across the head with a blow that knocked one of his eyes off as he came down. He followed with another swing, but Freddy blocked the strike with an arm and swung his chainsaw around to cut through the metal and leave a shallow gash in Leroy's side. A follow up swing knocked Leroy to the ground several feet away, but Leroy leapt to his feet and retreated into the darkness before Freddy reached him.

"Oh, I get it." Freddy said, resuming the hunt for his opponent. "You're doing one of those hit-and-run things, aren't you? That's a military tactic, right? Because you're a warbot?"

Freddy slowly advanced, rolling first along the path he'd last seen Leroy go, then stopping and reversing course to find an alternate path around the wreckage. After several feet, he stopped and looked up just in time to see a large rock flying down at him. Freddy sidestepped to narrowly avoid the projectile and swung his chainsaw up to catch Leroy as he came down on him. Leroy put his shield up ahead of him to deflect the saw, then threw several punches at Freddy when he hit the ground. The two robots traded blows for a moment, but again Leroy retreated and vanished back into the darkness.

Freddy began to pursue but stopped after a couple feet. Standing there, he looked around, then threw his hands up into the air. A moment later, he slowly began to roll backward to the light of the cave opening.

"Look, Leroy, I can appreciate a good game of cat-and-mouse as much as the next guy," Freddy said. "But this is not what I agreed to, this is not what I signed up for! All you're doing is proving you can't beat me! So either come out here and fight me face-to-face, or I'm just going to roll out there, finish off your little upstart army, and then bury this cave with you in it!"

Freddy looked around and listened, waiting and hoping to see some sign of Leroy emerging from the darkness. When no sign came, he shook his head in disappointment, turned around, and rolled to the cave exit.

"Such a disappointment," Freddy grumbled. "To think that I wasted so much time..."

Then, he heard a revving noise and stopped where he was. Turning around, he saw two lights rapidly approaching. He realized it was a vehicle coming straight at him at high speed. Freddy tried to swerve aside, but the vehicle hit a hard turn that swung its back end around to strike Freddy along his lower body. The force of the blow sent him tumbling end over end until he crashed down headfirst in a heap.

Before Freddy knew what was happening, Leroy was on top of him, grabbing hold of his bottom limb to slice his saw across his own legs. When Freddy attempted to regain control, Leroy forced the saw across its own limb, cutting the saw loose. Freddy tried to grab hold of Leroy, but he came up short and lost his balance, falling back to the ground. When the chainsaw lost power, Leroy dropped the weapon and began pummeling Freddy from above. He tried to fight back, but Leroy held the initiative with an iron grip and refused to let go. With blow after blow, he set Freddy's joints and moving parts out of alignment and into disorder, rendering the robot further and further into a state of inoperability.

In a last desperate move, Freddy reached for his disconnected chainsaw limb and tried to swing it against Leroy like a flail. Leroy caught the weapon mid-air, swung it around, and held it in the air for a split-second. Then, he turned the weapon blade-down and plunged it into Freddy's large central eye. Even inactive, the weapon pierced through the robot's face. Freddy's body flailed, froze up, and went limp.

At long last, the Top Dog was dead.

****

To say the former crew of the *Eternal Horizon* was in a perilous position was an understatement. One of the ally vessels had been reduced to little more than target practice. The other wasn't far behind. Their own efforts to advance aboard the *Ultimatum* had stalled – the enemy crew had advantage in both position and numbers, and they knew it. They were prepared to make Captain Danger's crew pay heavily to make progress with numbers they couldn't afford to lose.

"We need to fall back!" Otra shouted.

"Back to where?" Iggy asked.

"Zon, have we made *any* headway inside?" Danger asked.

"Negative, Sir!" Commander Zon reported. "They're refusing to let us through."

An explosion erupted nearby. While none of the crew were hit, it left a large hole making their position more difficult.

"Retreat may be necessary," Zon continued.

"There's nowhere to retreat to!" Danger said. "If we fall back to the *Horizon*, we'll be even worse off than we are here!"

The discussion was cut short when shouts erupted and weapons fire began to die out all around them. After initial confusion about the situation, everyone's attention was drawn to the ruins near the cave. Danger and those around him walked till they reached the nearby railing. Looking around, Danger spotted someone standing high and tall above the horizon and zoomed in.

It was Leroy Brown. In one hand, he held a disembodied limb with Chainsaw Freddy's infamous weapon hanging at the end. In the other, held high above his head, Leroy held up Chainsaw Freddy's decapitated head.

"THE CHAMPION HAS FALLEN!" Leroy shouted. "THE TOP DOG IS NO MORE!"

CODA:

EPILOGUE

10110.

The Top Dog's death brought the battle to a swift conclusion. Once word of his defeat spread, well over half his forces aboard the *Ultimatum* surrendered in short order. The rest fell soon after, especially after Leroy helped clean up the remaining hostiles. Of the remaining cruisers, one turned and fled for parts unknown. The other agreed to surrender, but only to Leroy Brown himself.

With the battle well and truly finished, cleanup began. Everyone took time to assess the situation, regroup, and see to repairs. The task became more difficult by the absence of Dr. Clank, who was discovered to have fled at an unknown point during the battle. Fortunately, there were still enough other robots present with the mechanical skills needed to patch up the survivors.

Recognizing the limited resources that were available, the *Eternal Horizon*, the *Ultimatum*, and the incapacitated ally vessel were all considered lost. All three were scuttled and salvaged for parts used to repair the two vessels that still functioned. Once fully repaired, those same vessels were loaded up with as much spare material as they could carry. During it all, Leroy and Isaac made time to lead a team to scour through the ruins of Rustbucket. There, they searched for signs of any robots who might yet be repairable.

Days later, after work was finished on the battlefield, the two land ships marched on the Top Dog's former headquarters. They arrived to find the place already on fire and half empty. As they discovered, word of the Top Dog's death spread quickly, leaving his former empire in utter disarray. Those that hadn't fled the base already were deep in the middle of a battle for command of the site, theorizing it was their best hope for laying legitimate claim to the Top Dog's surviving forces. The dilapidated, war-torn state of the place made it all too easy for Danger and Leroy's forces to fight their way in and seize control. Leroy Brown carrying the Top Dog's head was enough to force surrender from most still inside.

Taking command of the Top Dog's center of power revealed that there were survivors from Rustbucket being held as involuntary labor. They were promptly freed, as were several other robots from across Junkworld forced into the Top Dog's service. All of them were all too happy to be free and rid of their former master's dark shadow.

With the Top Dog gone, his former headquarters seized, and growing evidence his would-be empire was crumbling, an atmosphere of ease filled the air. Celebration followed.

****

"There you are," said Captain Danger.

Sitting atop the tallest tower of what had once been the Top Dog's headquarters, Leroy Brown turned to see the Captain and Isaac approaching.

"That I am," he replied, turning outward again. After a brief glance down at the celebrations happening on the surface of Junkworld, Leroy looked back up at the star-lit skies above.

"What are you doing up here?" Isaac asked.

"Just observing," Leroy answered.

"Up here? By yourself?" Danger asked. "You should be down there with them. You're the only reason this is all possible."

"True," Leroy said. "And yet, all too true."

Danger looked at Leroy, then at Isaac, then found a place to sit down next to Leroy.

"They have been avenged," Isaac said. "There is nothing more you can do for them now."

Leroy looked at Isaac as the robot took a seat next to him opposite Captain Danger.

"I suppose you're right," Leroy said, looking back up at the sky.

"So, you're 'observing'?" Danger asked. "Just 'observing'?"

Leroy glanced at Danger, then looked back into the sky for several moments before speaking again.

"Yes, and no," he answered.

"Do you still miss it?" Isaac asked.

"No. Not anymore," Leroy answered. "But yes."

"What's with all the double answers?" Danger asked.

"I'd be lying if I said I didn't still long for the Battledome," Leroy answered. "To have it all back again. But the league no longer exists. There's nothing left to it but for me to move on. Junkworld is my home now."

"A wise sentiment," Isaac said, placing a hand on Leroy's shoulder.

"Is that what you were doing up here?" Danger asked. "Looking for…where did you say you came from?"

"New Chicago," Leroy answered. "And it was. I came up here to say goodbye on my own terms. Then I realized that I have no idea where it is. That system might not even be on this side of the planet.

And at some point, I just...started observing."

"Just...'observing'?" Danger asked.

"Yes," Leroy said. "I found myself thinking. I don't truly understand the concept of 'beauty'. I know what it means, I know the definition of the word, but to really understand it? It's beyond my programming. But looking at the stars right now, here, tonight; I suspect that something about this all fits the meaning of the word."

Danger shrugged.

"If you say so," he said.

The three sat there for a few minutes, looking up, out, and around at the landscape before them.

"So now that you've accepted that you're not here by mistake, what do you plan to do next?" Danger asked.

"I'm putting together some ideas," Leroy asked.

"Perhaps such discussion is best saved for tomorrow," Isaac said as he picked himself up. "However it may have came about, we have achieved a great victory. Let's save tonight to celebrate that victory."

"Sure, I can agree with that," Danger said, standing up as well.

Leroy nodded but remained seated.

"I'll join you later," Leroy said. "For now, I'm just going to keep observing."

"Just...more observing?" Danger asked.

"Yes," Leroy answered.

Isaac and Danger both nodded, then walked back the way they'd come. For the next hour, Leroy sat where he was, doing nothing but observing the world as it went on around him and enjoying taking in all that came with it. Then, at last, he finally stood up and walked down to join the others while the stars continued to shine bright in the sky above.

ABOUT THE AUTHOR

MK Stangeland Jr. hails from Midwest United States. *Junkworld* is his first published novel.